D0299391

Also by Luca D'Andrea in English translation

The Mountain
Sanctuary

LUCA D'ANDREA

THE WANDERER

Translated from the Italian by
Katherine Gregor

MACLEHOSE PRESS
QUERCUS · LONDON

First published in the Italian language as
Il Respiro del sangue
by Einaudi Editore, Turin, 2019
First published in Great Britain in 2022 by MacLehose Press

This paperback edition published in 2022 by
MacLehose Press
an imprint of Quercus Editions Ltd
Carmelite House
50 Victoria Embankment
London EC4Y 0DZ

An Hachette UK Company

A CIP catalogue record for this book is available
from the British Library

ISBN (MMP) 978 1 52940 790 7
ISBN (Ebook) 978 1 52940 791 4

10 9 8 7 6 5 4 3 2 1

Designed and typeset in Minion by CC Book Production
Printed and bound in Great Britain by Clays Ltd, Elcograf S.p.A.

MIX
Paper from
responsible sources
FSC® C104740
www.fsc.org

Papers used by MacLehose Press are from well-managed forests
and other responsible sources.

to Alessandra,
who is the way home

One

1.

"Don't believe everything they say, you big baby. It's the first step that's the hardest. After that it's a piece of cake."

Freddy turned and gave him an irritated look that meant something like *Stop staring at me, or we'll be here all day.*

Then, after a lazy flick of the tail, the St Bernard lifted his leg again and focused on what he had been trying to do before being interrupted – turning the side of the road into a miniature Jackson Pollock.

2.

If anyone had remarked on how sad it was to have a 110-kilogram St Bernard as your only friend, Tony – formally Antonio Carcano, also labelled "Sophie Kinsella in lederhosen" (a description dripping with that succulent brand of venom the literary world reserves for scribblers blessed with success) – would have been very surprised. Him – sad? Why should he be?

No, the real issue was that, for some time now, the corner of his brain in charge of keeping him awake at night had been constantly repeating the words Dr Hubner had uttered during the most recent check-up. "Get used to the idea that this big puppy is now of a ripe old age, and prepare yourself for the event that . . ."

Damned charlatan. Freddy was not old. Freddy was ten years old, and Tony had read that some St Bernards reached the age of eleven and even twelve.

Of course, the little furball that would start trembling so badly when there was a thunderstorm that the only way to soothe it was to sing "Another One Bites the Dust" was a distant memory. And, for that matter, Freddy was no longer the nimble animal who would jump on his bed at dawn to remind him of his duties, either (now he just panted in his face with an accusatory look, waiting for him to wake up), but . . . to go as far as saying that he had one foot in the grave? No way.

Freddy was fine. Absolutely fine. He had just *slowed down* a little, because of the intense heat.

And at that very moment, as though to allay Tony's fears, a jet spurted out from under the large dog's back leg. A timid little squirt, not the vigorous fountain of a few years ago, but still a healthy pee which allowed Tony to draw breath and become aware of the insistent buzzing disturbing the silence of the countryside. A motorcycle. Nothing out of the ordinary. Some Valentino Rossi wannabe or other occasionally mistook this maze of narrow roads amid the apple orchards for a race track, but since Tony belonged to the school of thought that you could never be too careful, he put Freddy on the lead and moved as close as possible to the kerb. Caution is the mother of routine. And routine is at the root of a long, prosperous life.

By the time it had travelled a few metres through the mugginess of that June Sunday morning, the buzzing had turned into the roar of a muddy white Yamaha Enduro that downshifted, tilted to the side and, tracing a black strip on the asphalt, halted right next to Tony and Freddy, making them quickly step back a little further.

The young woman driving the Enduro wore shorts that revealed slender long legs and a bright-red vest with a star, but it was not her outfit Tony found alarming, to the point that he shielded the St Bernard behind him. It was the flick knife. In his experience, people who felt the need to carry around that kind of gear rarely harboured good intentions.

The knife was peering out of the back pocket of the two-wheel fanatic as she performed a nimble twirl, got off the Yamaha, removed her helmet, turned, and without a word shot him a look brimming with hatred.

Long, curly hair of that very blonde shade of blonde. Slender build. Pale eyes. Delicate, almost cat-like features that made her look like a singer of that syrupy-voiced, heartbroken-but-sexy kind that was trendy in the nineties, a pop star whose name Tony suddenly (and with a touch of panic) felt it was important, *essential* even, to remember.

In vain.

For a few extended seconds, the young woman did not move so much as a muscle and just stood there, arms crossed, staring at him so furiously that he actually wondered how such a minute body could contain all that rage and not explode.

Alarming, Tony thought, looking at her. Perhaps even *dangerous*. Which was absurd, because, with or without a knife, the young woman barely weighed fifty kilos, and if she tried to attack Tony he would easily disarm her and make her harmless. Besides, why should she attack him, anyway?

The answer came when the stranger slipped a small canvas rucksack off her shoulders, took out an envelope and handed it to Tony. His hands felt suddenly cold as he took it.

The envelope contained a photograph that brought to light a number of things Tony had gone to great lengths to bury. First of all, a taste. The taste of mud in the spring. The taste of the place where the photo had been taken twenty years earlier: a village with geraniums at the windows, enclosed in a valley in north-east Tyrol. Kreuzwirt. Just a glance, and it all became clear to him. And panic swept over him.

March 22, 1999, 10 a.m. In the left-hand side of the picture, a cara- biniere was frozen just as a "What the fuck do you think you're doing, you arsehole?" was popping out of his mouth. In the centre, on all fours and covered in mud, was Tony. A twenty-year-old Tony looking straight at the lens, *smiling*, next to a third subject in the tableau: a sheet from which a hand, a face and a mane of blonde curls emerged.

A sheet that barely covered the dead body of a young woman of just twenty: Erika. Erika Knapp. Or, as everyone called her in Kreuzwirt, Spooky Erika.

Erika Knapp, who looked like Fiona Apple, the broken-hearted-but-sexy singer whose name suddenly surfaced in Tony's memory with such impetus it nearly made his head burst. Erika Knapp, known as Spooky Erika, who on the night of March 21, 1999, left behind an orphaned child with an unusual name: Sibylle.

And, twenty years after her mother's death, Sybille Knapp – the young woman on the Yamaha, the young woman with the flick knife in her shorts and the loud vest who, like Erika before her, bore a resemblance to a curly, blonde version of that now outmoded pop star – flushed and, unable to restrain herself any longer, barked a simple question.

"Why were you *laughing*?"

Tony was startled. He wanted to explain, to tell her what had happened. Instead, all he could do was flinch again as the young woman drew nearer, looked him in the eye, shook her mane of blonde curls and slapped him right across the face, making his nose bleed.

"You're a . . . a *bastard*."

Then, disgusted, she turned away, retraced her steps, put the helmet on and jumped back in the saddle. She gave the engine a rev that made Freddy whimper, and the Yamaha vanished in a cloud of dust. The roar became a buzzing once again, then the buzzing died away.

Tony stood motionless, shuddering, and watched the bleeding easing off as it dripped to the ground, listening to the silence of the countryside until Freddy, restless and perhaps a little scared, nuzzled him.

Tony calmed him with a pat on his massive, wrinkled head, folded the photograph (on the back of which a female hand had written an address – in Kreuzwirt, naturally – and a phone number), put it into the pocket of his jeans and wiped his face like a child, with saliva and a tissue. Once he had finished, he walked away, ignoring the St Bernard's worried glances.

Half an hour later, he reached the district where he was born and grew up, which Bolzano's residents – some affectionately, others not so much – called "Shanghai". Back home, he filled Freddy's bowl with fresh water, threw his dirty clothes on the floor and jumped in the shower.

Once he emerged, he holed up in his study, switched on the computer and searched for the song that had made Fiona Apple famous back in the day: "Criminal". As soon as the bass guitar and drums started marking the rhythm, Tony felt the onset of nausea, but he was not overwhelmed by it. He did not allow himself to be. He wanted to discover, to know who had given Sibylle that damned picture and why. He used the music and his nausea to recall faces, circumstances, words. The click-clack of his keyboard, the smell of stale coffee and Jim Beam.

Sole delle Alpi.

How long had this adventure of sorts lasted? A month? Two? The newspaper had closed down in 2001 and there was a temping agency in its stead. The only member of staff Tony had (despite himself) got on with back then was that oversized braggart called Michele Milani, the paper's photographer. And although that damned snapshot had been taken by Milani, Tony ruled him out of his list of suspects. He had attended his funeral in 2008. He had placed a bottle of bourbon next to his headstone, certain that the loquacious bastard would have appreciated the gesture.

But then who had given Sybille the photograph? A nasty piece of work, Tony thought. Someone so resentful and shameless as to keep it for two decades without—

Giò.

Giovanna Innocenzi. High cheekbones, square bob and a fondness for black clothes. An arrogant sneer during even the worst tragedies. Giò, the queen of crime news. Giò, the queen of gossip. Or, as Michele Milani had rechristened her, Giò, the grand duchess of the kingdom of bullshit.

Giò, who . . .

The St Bernard put his massive head on his thighs.

"I agree, Freddy: it's a really bad idea."

Two

1.

It was five in the afternoon, and by the time Sybille had finished her shift the thermometer hanging on the door of the Black Hat was showing twenty-nine degrees. Aunt Helga always said that the hottest summer had been in '81, but Sib had trouble believing it. She could almost feel the heat of the asphalt through the soles of her shoes.

Still, if the temperature had risen that high in Kreuzwirt, at an altitude of 1,200 metres, then in Bolzano, perched at the bottom of a valley that was not even 500 metres above sea level, Tony was bound to be swimming in a putrid stock of mugginess and sweat.

Small consolation, as well as brief. The journalist in black had revealed that Carcano's books sold well ("the world is full of frustrated housewives to fleece"), so Tony most likely had air conditioning – that *worked*, unlike the unit Oskar would get around to fixing at some point. Or the non-existent one in Erika's house, where Sib lived.

Tony . . .

Sibylle could not get the expression in his eyes when she had slapped him out of her mind. Astonishment? Guilt? She was almost certain it was fear. But of what? Of the arsehole slasher she kept in plain sight in her back pocket, because that was the area the Black Hat creeps aimed for when she was in the vicinity? Perhaps. That was what the arsehole slasher was for.

Except that Tony had not given her the impression that he was a wimp.

Rather, he seemed like one of those rubber-coated gadgets that look like toys at first sight but actually conceal metal innards. As though the scruffy jeans, cheap T-shirt and dog on a lead were just a screen on which to project a film so pedestrian that it was suspect. A wall masking a ditch.

But to shield himself from what?

Sibylle did not know, and after the scene in the apple orchard she probably never would. And this, in addition to the heat, and what had been happening to her since Perkman's funeral – the anonymous envelope, the nights spent tossing and turning under her sheets and all the rest – made her feel on edge.

Because Sib had not left Kreuzwirt to schlep a hundred kilometres of twisting, turning roads just to wallop (and a nice hard wallop it had been, she had to admit) a guy who made a living selling sentimental doorstops. Seeing how much petrol the Yamaha guzzled down, it would not have been worth it. No, Sibylle had wasted time and petrol so she could actually speak to Tony.

Shake hands, introduce herself, show him the picture of Erika by the lake, and ask him about it.

Listen to his answer.

But when did Sib ever manage to stick to a plan? Never – that was the point. Because she was impulsive. Because at the most inappropriate moments the side of her that Aunt Helga had christened Sibby Longstocking would rear its head, and whenever Sibby Longstocking stuck her oar in everything went pear-shaped. You could bet on it.

Sibby Longstocking never held her tongue and was always sticking her nose in business best stayed clear of. And that morning, when she had found herself in front of the man who, twenty years earlier, had laughed next to Erika's body, Sibby Longstocking had the brilliant idea of slapping him, irretrievably sabotaging one of the most promising chances she had ever had to discover what happened to Erika on the night of March 21, 1999.

Just remembering it made Sibylle furious. With Sibby Longstocking and with herself. With the whole world. And Erika. *Especially* with Erika.

Erika ruins your life. Erika brings trouble. "Erika's coming to get you," as the Kreuzwirt children would say when they did not know she was listening. Sib had grown up with that bullshit. *In spite of* that bullshit.

"Shit!" she said out loud.

And not because putting on the biker jumpsuit she usually wore when she wanted (or needed) to rock out with her Yamaha down dirt roads and paths for a while had been like plunging into a bath of boiling water, but because, until the day of Friedrich Perkman's funeral, Sibylle had been stupid enough to believe everything she had been told: unlucky Erika, gentle-hearted Erika.

On June 8, while her fellow townspeople and the crowned heads of the Autonome Provinz were paying their final respects to Friedrich Perkman, somebody (Sibylle still did not know who, and if she was clever she would stop wondering) had left a photograph in her letterbox.

Not the Polaroid the journalist in black had given her – the one with Erika under the sheet and Tony smiling. The *other* one. The impossible one.

The one with the hummingbird smile.

The photo that said: *Did you really believe it? Remove the word "sui-cide". Replace it with "murder". See how that sounds.*

From that day forward, Sib had stopped sleeping and started asking questions. Discreetly. Although she suspected not discreetly enough. Judging by some of the looks she thought she got, at least. But maybe it was just paranoia. Another gift from Erika: Sibylle was growing paranoid. Because the picture of Erika, the lake and the hummingbird smile, the picture she had not yet had the courage to show to a soul (not even Aunt Helga) had opened her eyes.

Something about Erika's death did not add up. And the deeper Sib dug, the more connections, contradictions and coincidences emerged to obsess her and persuade her more and more that she had not gone mad. Not at all.

Erika had not committed suicide.

Erika had been murdered.

Once again: "*Shit.*"

Sibylle put on the helmet and stepped on the gas. The Yamaha roared.

A few heads turned towards her from behind the windows of the dance hall. Sib only failed to show them the middle finger because she had already darted away. She needed air. To race. Just that. Speed had the power to clear her head. And adrenaline to calm her down.

Sibby Longstocking never shut up, never managed to stick to a plan of any kind and was a disaster when dealing with writers and St Bernards, but she could ride the Yamaha like the very devil.

She left Kreuzwirt, turned off the asphalt road and slipped onto the narrow dirt tracks between the trees, the ones which, before the sawmill went bankrupt, had carried the woodcutters in their jeeps, and which only a lunatic would have considered mapping. Left the stench of peat bog behind her and plunged deep into the forest, going even faster, dodging branches, taking flight whenever the bumps on the track allowed it, ignoring rocks, downshifting and *smiling*.

It was working.

It always worked.

It worked again that afternoon, until something large, red and nasty cut her off.

Three

1.

Finding Giò had been a piece of cake – she was listed in the directory. But getting on a bicycle in the thirty-nine degrees in which the city was floating ("And it doesn't look like it's about to drop!" Signora Marchetti, his neighbour, had chirped in the strange tone halfway between triumph and ferocity that some elderly people use for bad news) and reaching her front door had represented a Herculean task.

Ringing the bell, accepting a coffee and enduring barbs about writers who sold detritus they passed off as caviar had been excruciating.

Getting immortalised by signing a copy of *A Kiss at the End of Days*, his latest novel, and imagining the comments on the gossip website (Giò called it "alternative information" and he had to put up with that, too) that had given Giò a new lease of life after she was let go as editor-in-chief of *Sole delle Alpi*'s crime section, had proved such a gruelling test to his nervous system that, once the meeting was over, the scorching outside air had seemed as fresh and rejuvenating as a spring breeze.

In summary: *Sole delle Alpi* no longer existed, Michele Milani was dead and buried and Fiona Apple had vanished from radio schedules, but Bloody Giò was still exactly as he remembered her. Worse than ever, perhaps. And to think that some people had the nerve to call *him* a misanthrope.

Still, it had not been a waste of time.

Pedalling down the streets, deserted because of the heat, bathing in sweat, thinking about what Giò had revealed between drops of poison, Tony reached the conclusion that, whether he liked it or not, there was only one thing to do: go to Kreuzwirt. In person. He owed it to Erika. And Sibylle. And to himself.

Unfortunately, he realised, there was only one *correct* way to return to that place.

And so, less than half an hour later, both dog and owner were standing in the car park under the Eurospar supermarket in Via Resia, Freddy slobbering on the concrete that stank of damp and sewage, Tony looking askance at the rolling shutter of the garage, thinking he was about to break the oath he had faithfully kept for twelve years. The St Bernard gave him an impatient tap with his paw and Tony smiled.

Pinocchio had the Talking Cricket, he thought, wiping the sweat from his forehead, and I have a fat St Bernard. It could be worse. Peter Pan got lumbered with Tinker Bell.

Tony pushed the key into the lock and gave the door a tug. The hinges squeaked, the shutter vibrated and a few specks of rust drifted down to the ground. Freddy sniffed them and vanished into the darkness, which smelled of mould, dust and engine oil.

The light switch was still where Tony remembered it, to his left. The strip lights flickered. Happy, Freddy wagged his tail. He liked cars, while Tony preferred bicycles. Still, even he had to admit that this car was quite a sight. Not just any Mustang, but a bottle-green Fastback like the one Steve McQueen drove in *Bullitt*. A 428 engine with 335 horsepower. Faithful in every detail except one: there were no CD players in 1968. "Sacrilege!" the Californian engineer from whom Tony had ordered it had protested on the phone. An insult. Why ruin such a jewel? An astronomical bonus had silenced his objections.

Tony sat behind the wheel, wondering (partly in hope) if the years the Mustang had spent down there had turned it into an expensive ornament.

But the engine started at the first attempt, and Tony realised that there would be no easy way out of this.

If you cannot prevent contact, then go with the fall. That was what Lucky Willy had told Sib when she had persuaded him to teach her to drive. If you have to fall, then do it well.

Sibylle let go of the handlebars, abandoned the motorbike to its fate, let herself go and prepared to become a spring. That was the trick. Fly and roll. In that order.

Springs bounce from side to side, collide with walls, and if you throw them from a plane they survive. Springs don't absorb the shock because springs are clever. They draw energy from the collision and use it. Act like a spring and you'll survive.

But remember one thing: this little trick works only if you're not about to slam into a brick wall at the speed of light. In that case, springlike or not, get ready to meet your ancestors. So best not to, don't you think?

Sib was not heading for a brick wall or going (too) fast, so she followed Lucky Willy's instructions. Fly and roll.

Only, Lucky Willy had not told her it would hurt. Like hell.

While the Enduro went crashing against the trunk of a fir with a spatter of metal, plastic and bark, Sibylle saw the world beyond the visor of her helmet become a green-and-black kaleidoscope, felt a sharp pain in her hip and arm, and an even sharper pain in her shoulder. She closed her eyes, opening them again to find the world had settled into a screen of fir branches and sky.

Almost immediately afterwards, the fir branches and the sky were hidden by something Sib was unable to make out except in fragments. Bloodshot eyes. Gappy front teeth. A dimple on the chin. The arsehole from the red pickup, she figured.

Hunched over her, the guy kept repeating, "You alive? You OK? You alive? You OK?"

Sib ignored him.

She could move her head, which was good news. What about the rest? She tried her feet and legs. They were still there. Her arms also responded to her commands.

Hooray for Lucky Willy.

The guy would not stop yapping. Sibylle raised her hand to make him shut up.

"I'm alive," she grumbled. "I'm OK. Let me catch my breath, will you?"

She forced herself to sit up, removed her helmet and unzipped her biker suit. She breathed in air that smelled of pine, then stood up. A huge effort, with an unpredictable outcome.

"Sure you don't want a doctor?"

"I'm . . ."

A lie.

Sib leaned forward, her hands on her thighs and hair over her face, mouth wide open. Another thing Lucky Willy had forgotten to tell her. The panic, the shock. There was not a single cell in her body that was not quaking.

Breathe in, breathe out. Repeat. And once more.

Breathe in, breathe out. Repeat.

Gradually, the trembling stopped.

"My motorbike," she said, wheezing, still unable to raise her head. "Is it in bad shape?"

She heard the guy walk around the pickup. He let out a low whistle.

"I know someone in Brixen. I can call him. A mechanic. He's very—"

"Is it a write-off?"

The sound of a lighter, the stench of a cigarette. No reply.

Sibylle worked up the courage to see for herself. She leaned on the bonnet of the pickup so as not to lose her balance. She was walking as though she had only learned to do it a couple of days ago.

The Yamaha was a wreck. Sib approached the carcass of the motorcycle. All that saving. All that work. She shook her head and sniffed. She hated crying. Especially when someone was watching.

Sibby Longstocking rushed to her help.

She pushed back her tears and started kicking what was left of the Enduro.

"Fuck! Fuck! Fuck!" She turned on the guy who had cut her off. "Do you realise you could have killed me? Where were you looking? What—?"

Suddenly, the details Sib had made out only in fragments, like the gap between the front teeth, the monotonous voice, the wide forehead and the broad shoulders, turned into a single, coherent picture. Sibylle's hand quickly reached around to the back pocket of the biker suit.

"Keep away from me, OK?"

Her hand grabbed at nothing.

She'd lost the arsehole slasher.

3.

Freddy was slobbering with his mouth open, happily mauling the air coming in through the window. Tony kept his eyes on the road, the speedometer hovering just below the limit. He was remembering a game he and his dad would play on Sundays after dinner, when his father was not in a foul mood or doing a shift at the steelworks.

This is how it went: Tony would spread the road map out on the table while his father closed his eyes (*don't cheat*, Papà), lit an MS and waited for his son to say the name of a locality, however tiny, as long as it was within the provincial boundaries. Then, tracing invisible lines with his free hand, his father would tell him how to get there.

He never made a mistake.

Kreuzwirt? Easy-peasy. It's a hundred – a hundred and twenty kilometres away. Only let's not take the A22 because motorways are for tourists or people in a rush. Bolzano, northbound. Take the SS49, past Brixen and Vahrn. Shortly afterwards, come off the SS12 and take the SS49, which becomes the SP40 and then the SP97 until Bruneck, where it swerves and becomes a three-digit SS, the SS621 that leads you to Sand in Taufers, with its nice castle perched over the village. Keep going east and get ready to get off the SS621 and take the SS621-K.

The K is an alternative route that takes you straight to the ninth and smallest community district in Alto Adige (in the stifling present, Tony listed the other eight: Bolzano, Burggrafenamt, Überetsch-Unterland, Salten-Schlern, Eisacktal, Pustertal, Vinschgau, Wipptal – funny how some things remained etched in your mind), *and it's not easy to spot, so keep your eyes open.*

The K alternative. Don't forget. At this stage, once you can smell the peat bog, the Tote Mose . . .

Tote Mose. Dead Moses. But, after what happened to Erika, some joker had mangled its name. From Tote Mose to Tote Möse.

Dead pussy.

Tony sighed.

. . . here you are in Kreuzwirt. Only, tell me something. What the hell are you going there for? It's the only village in the whole of Alto Adige without a church. Actually, it's the only one in the whole of Italy not to have one. Besides, don't you know it's full of bloody Krauts and arseholes in general?

Under the signpost marking the entrance to the administrative territory of the town of Kreuzwirt, somebody had glued a sticker that said:

SÜDTIROL IST NICHT ITALIEN

Alto Adige is not Italy.

Tony would have gladly done without it.

4.

The man extinguished his cigarette, crumpled it with his calloused fingertips and threw it far away.

"Fancy a lift home, honey?"

"Fuck off."

The man who had just narrowly missed dispatching her to the Otherworld was not just a random stranger. His name was Rudi Brugger, and Sibylle had seen him countless times at the Black Hat. Rudi, the custodian of Kroth Villa. Toad Villa. The Perkman villa.

Though "custodian" didn't really cover what Rudi did for the Perkman family. Sure, he trimmed hedges, repaired gutters and placed deterrents to stop foxes from crossing the boundaries of the property. But, above all, Rudi solved *problems*. That was what Lucky Willy had once revealed to her.

Keep away from him. He can be a good laugh when he wants to be, but as soon as Karin Perkman snaps her fingers . . .

Not that the Perkmans had that many problems. Nobody in Kreuzwirt would ever speak badly of them, let alone do anything to cross them. The Perkmans had saved the town when the sawmill closed down. They gave work to anyone who came knocking at their door and shielded the valley from rowdy waves of tourists. Good people, everyone said. Generous.

The Perkmans. Who, as soon as Sib began asking questions about Erika's death, had sent Rudi.

Sibylle prepared to fight.

Rudi winked at her. A "you and I understand each other, honey" kind of wink.

Sibylle set herself to dart away.

Without dropping his odious little smile, Rudi walked heavily back to the pickup, sat behind the wheel, reversed back onto the dirt road and vanished in the direction of the town.

Mission accomplished. Message delivered.

Sibylle had just discovered that she was a problem for the Perkman family. At the expense of her Yamaha. She collapsed on the ground and allowed herself a scream.

Just one, but a very, very long one.

Four

1.

When the sharp peaks of the Rieserferner Group began to conceal the sun, as the gradually cooling air came alive with exciting sounds (buzzing, whistling, mewing, croaking, rustling and all kinds of calling), Freddy saw the young female human (young and very frightened, judging by the scent of her sweat) who had sent their routine belly up that morning.

He watched Tony approach the wreck the young woman was dragging and try to take it off her, noticing also how she angrily pushed him away.

Then, just when the St Bernard thought it would be nice to at least *try* to catch one of the exquisite bats that were starting to circle not far away from his nose, Sibylle opened her front door, Tony followed her in, and Freddy was forced to go after him.

The two humans began to talk, although Freddy wouldn't hear much of their conversation, because he was fast asleep within ten minutes.

Five

1.

Erika had come back. As though she'd had second thoughts.

On the evening of the Maturaball, Erika had said goodbye, kissed her little girl on the forehead, left, then come back. Come back and knocked on the front door, even though she had the bunch of keys in her diamanté clutch bag.

It was this detail that would fill Aunt Helga with remorse. If only she had realised. If only she had sensed it. But how could she have?

The clutch bag had been a gift from Oskar. Inside it, Erika had found two fifty-thousand-lire notes and a message: *We are proud of you!* Moved, she had wiped away a few tears and hugged Oskar, practically crushing him.

But Erika had not tried to return the money, because she knew she needed it. Sibylle was a darling, but, naughty or nice, children cost a great deal.

Just like the dress for the Maturaball that Helga had insisted on paying for out of her own pocket.

Up until the very last minute, Erika could not make up her mind between red and black. In the end, she had gone for red, and Aunt Helga agreed. It was a provocative, daring, sexy dress. In other words, it suited her to perfection. And even though on the evening of the 21st, while her aunt was helping her do her hair, Erika had done nothing but complain about it making her look like a surfboard (leading Aunt Helga to point out that, though her mother had certainly not had a dairy up front, it had not prevented half of Kreuzwirt's young men from courting her), Helga knew that Erika was excited about the dress. And about the Maturaball. And life. Things were improving, or so she thought.

After all, Erika had come back. She had waited for Helga to get up from the sofa, place the baby in the cradle and open the door. Then – and this, too, would torment Aunt Helga for years, in her waking moments as well as in her dreams, when she would relive that terrible moment – Erika had smiled and given her a caress.

"I forgot to tell you how much I love you."

"I love you, too. Are you sure you're not cold?"

"No, I'm fine like this."

And Aunt Helga had closed the door.

2.

Instead of walking out of their driveway, turning right and going down to the Black Hat to meet Karin, Betta and Gabriel as arranged, Erika had turned left. Towards the forest. Wearing pumps which, by the time she had left the carriageway and slipped down a path, were all splattered with mud.

One of them, the left one to be precise, would be found the following day by a volunteer, about a kilometre from the lake, immersed in a puddle more or less at the spot where the forest gave way to the peat bog. Erika had lost it and hadn't bothered looking for it. And why should she?

It would be no use where she was going.

The lake might have had a name on the map but for Kreuzwirt residents it was simply "the lake". In late March, its waters were usually coated with ice. But the winter of 1999 had been oddly mild. The Föhn had blown relentlessly throughout January and February, preventing the snow from settling. It was around fifteen degrees at that time of the evening. Way above average. That was why Erika left the house with just a thin cardigan over her shoulders and nothing heavier. That was why there was no ice to stop her from doing what she did.

Erika stepped into the water. It reached up to her ankles. Then her calves. Then her knees. Few people in Kreuzwirt went swimming in the lake. Not just because of the foxes that infested the area, or the insects, or the peat bog with its less-than-appealing smell, but because everybody knew that the lake was deep and dangerous. Those who had gone in, perhaps to cool off in the summer heat, spoke of a sudden drop about a metre from the shore. Beyond that point it was like falling into a well. Erika went past it.

The cold water did the rest.

3.

When, at 4 a.m. on March 22, while taking one of the frequent strolls imposed on him by his insomnia, Dr Horst saw her floating face down, he knew immediately that he had found a dead body. Even so, he pulled off his jacket and rushed into the water. A heroic act, everyone said.

With some difficulty, since in 1999 he was fifty-two years old and not exactly fit, the doctor brought Erika back to shore, checked her pulse just to be certain, then used his mobile to call the carabinieri.

The nearest barracks were in Sand in Taufers, about thirty kilometres away. The carabinieri took an age to arrive, but it did not occur to Horst even for a second to leave Erika alone in the peat bog.

The possibility that his wet clothes could consign him to a quick death from hypothermia did not cross his mind. He stayed by the water's edge, pacing up and down, teeth chattering, his arms tight against his chest, looking at the young woman's face, her hair spread over the mud, wondering why the hell a girl like her – why . . .?

The carabinieri reached him half an hour later, equipped with torches and questions.

Although the Maturaball had officially ended at 1 a.m. with "Love Hurts" by Nazareth, which had allowed the couples to snog without any embarrassment in the drizzle that had started to fall over Kreuzwirt at that very moment, there were still many young people out and about when the beacons on the jeeps lit up the town's main street.

Word quickly got around. Spooky Erika was dead.

4.

"Then the reporters arrived."

Sib looked at him with her focused large blue eyes, tapped on the picture of him smiling next to Erika's body and crossed her arms.

It was his turn to speak now.

Tony sighed. He had got the Mustang out for this, so why beat about the bush?

"1999 was the year of the forklift."

Six

1.

One of Tony's father's colleagues was retiring in December, and Giuseppe Carcano was not one to miss such a golden opportunity. Shaking hands here and buying drinks there, he extracted a promise that, if his son were able to drive a forklift by Christmas, the position would be his.

"It's a real job with real wages," he told Tony. "All you have to do is enrol in the course, learn to drive one of those old bangers and you'll have food on your table for the rest of your life."

Tony tried to object. "They're saying the steelworks are going to close down. They're saying they can't keep up with China and India."

Many families in the area had lost their income overnight. China and India were producing three times the amount of steel at half the price. As a result, the streets of the Shanghai district were suddenly filled with ghosts.

And the bars with zombies.

"Fuck that," his father snarled, upset. "You know what they pay workers over there? Fucking globalisation. I'm telling you, it's a con. But the steelworks aren't going to close. It's just a phase. You know when the Indians and the Chinese will start producing the same quality steel as us? When Krauts stop tossing *their* crap into our district."

In other words, never, as far as Giuseppe Carcano was concerned. Still, instead of launching full-on into one of his rants, he smiled. "Look, you're very lucky. You won't even have to go anywhere near the furnace. Dump your gig at the paper. I'm offering you a real job. A man's job."

A *gig*.

It was not yet a month since Tony had walked through the door of the editorial office of *Sole delle Alpi*, introduced himself and said he wanted to learn the trade. Become a journalist. Tony was not sure why he had done it. Maybe so he could change the world. Or maybe to piss his father off. Or both.

His first article was about the Kurtatsch cherry festival. A hundred and fifty words. He had paid the bus fare there out of his own pocket. His second covered the chess tournament in Oberau, the district on the other side of the river Eisack from Shanghai. Tony had cycled there. Two hundred words and the honour of a credit. Well, actually just his initials, "A. C.", but his mother was so pleased she cut out the piece and put it in her wallet so she could always have it with her.

As for his father . . .

"If you really believe this is your future," he said, "then go ahead. Starting today I want you to pay your mother one third of the rent. How much do they pay you, Tonino?"

Hit and sunk. Nobody at *Sole delle Alpi* had ever mentioned payment.

Tony did not even have a name among the editorial staff. Except for . . .

Seven

1.

"Hey, newbie!"

March 22, 1999, 8 a.m.

Milani had a broad smile on his face as he announced, "There's a body in Kreuzwirt. Shall we go?"

"What about Giò?"

Milani lit a cigarette. "She's not picking up. It's your big chance . . ."

Milani's car was a mess. Papers, empty bottles and cans, pages from newspapers, receipts, porn magazines and ash – ash everywhere.

"All we know for now is that her name was Erika. Maybe a suicide. But if you're lucky it was murder. How old are you?"

"Twenty next May."

"You know what would be a real kick-start to your career? Murdered and raped. In that order. A fucking necrophiliac. Now that's what you need to bump up circulation. Ideally a serial killer. People drool over serial killers. And terrorists. Same thing, anyway, but without the imagination, don't you think? Back in '88 you were a little runt who didn't know shit, but I was around. *Ein Tirol*. I loved the bastards. Bombs, flyers, anonymous phone calls, police trying to be reassuring while politicians were shitting themselves, and vice versa. The riots. Our sales spiked like never before. And bear in mind that *Sole* was founded in '54."

Tony was nine years old in '88 but, despite what the photographer

Milani apparently thought, he remembered quite a bit. The helicopters, the police vans, the swastika painted on the school gate that made the teacher cry. The drug addicts. His father's clenched fists. His mother's red eyes. For Tony, Shanghai would always be that. A district where fathers always walked around with clenched fists and mothers always had red eyes.

"Shouldn't Giò write the piece?"

Milani, who was easing the Citroën between two carabinieri cars, braked abruptly.

"Can you write your name without making a mistake? As far as I'm concerned, that's all you need to knock an article together. Or are you chickening out?"

"Giò's—"

"Wake up, newbie," Milani said while grabbing lenses and crammed bags from the back seat. "You know why Giò always manages to beat the competition?"

"Because she's good?"

Milani gave him a menacing look. "Or because she's screwing someone, maybe a magistrate, maybe a very married, very influential magistrate who gives her a lead in exchange for a quick fuck. You've clearly got a lot to learn."

They advanced into the forest. Then into the peat bog. Soon, Tony was splattered in mud up to his knees. In the pocket of his jeans, he had the Moleskine he had bought himself to look sharp. He took it out, worried it might get wet, and discovered he had left his pen at home.

"Look, isn't that wonderful?"

The lake was glistening in the crisp air of that March morning, but it was not the lake the photographer was referring to. From the top of the small hill where they were standing, Milani and Tony could see the carabinieri talking among themselves and, in particular, the sheet from under which hair was spilling out.

It was the first time Tony had seen a dead body.

"Raped and murdered. Shall we bet a beer on it?"

"I don't drink. And I don't gamble," Tony replied. "Why do you say raped and murdered?"

"I swear I'll make a man of you sooner or later. Did you see the banner as we drove through the town? Maturaball. Do you know what a Maturaball is?"

Tony knew, though he'd never had anything to do with one. No Italian ever attended a Maturaball. And it was not the usual issue of *bloody Krauts*, who called Italians "shitty *Walscher*" and everyone else "manure".

The Maturaball was a party to celebrate graduation, but only in German schools (in Alto Adige, schools were strictly divided into Italian and German ones – how could they keep the fields in the province nice and glowing green without a sustainable and constant source of excrement?).

Except that the Maturaball took place *before* the final exams, something no sane Italian would ever dream of. It would be like appearing before Professore Tamanini (Tony's nightmare teacher) for the written maths test after breaking a hundred mirrors or testing a ski track while carrying a litter of black cats.

No, thanks.

"Sex and alcohol. That's what a Maturaball is about. Maybe the little tart agrees to slink away with a boyfriend, he cops a feel but she's not ready, so – are you taking notes?"

Tony looked around. "Doesn't look like an ideal place for slinking away, does it?"

"And how would you know what goes on in the minds of those fucking Krauts?" Milani put the bags down on the ground and sneered. "You've got a lot to learn and that's what I'm here for. Ready? Do you know what a real journalist with balls to spare would do with a shrinking violet like you? One of those real journalists with integrity who aren't afraid to get their hands dirty?"

The photographer gave Tony such a powerful shove that he flew down the hill. By the end of his involuntary run, caked in mud from top to toe, the revolting taste of peat bog in his mouth, Tony was well past the carabinieri cordon. Next to the sheet. Face to face with the body. Eye to eye. And he realised that it was not a body.

It was a *young woman*. A . . . sad young woman. Frightened. Calm. Terrified. Radiant. Upset. Carefree. Happy. In love. Angry.

Alive.

Tony heard Milani's voice calling him. Dazed and bewildered by what he had read in the young woman's eyes (*Erika, her name is Erika, it's not a body, it's a young woman called Erika who, until a few hours ago, was like me, breathing, dreaming, alive*), he turned towards him. And when the photographer framed him with his Nikon and shouted "Smile!" at him – just as a carabiniere was saying, "What the fuck do you think you're doing, you arsehole?" – Tony *smiled*.

2.

Because when someone hands you an envelope, you take it. And when someone tells you to smile, you . . .

Eight

1.

The one Sib had called "Erika's house" was on the fringes of Kreuzwirt. To reach it you had to drive across the town and follow a gravel path. There were blackberry bushes all around it, which Freddy had immediately liked.

It was also the only house in Kreuzwirt with no geraniums at the windows. Maybe Sibylle didn't have green fingers. Or maybe she didn't have time. Or couldn't care less about geraniums. After all, at least blackberries are edible.

The interior was furnished plainly. And it was a dreadful mess – an artistic kind of mess, as Tony would have described it. Books, magazines and DVDs stacked up all over the place. But no *Vanity Fair* or *Elle* for Sib. Only journals about mechanics.

A Black Sabbath poster, with Jimmy Page sneering at Les Paul. Just a few photographs. Sibylle as a child. Sibylle as a teenager. Not a single one of Erika.

Sib invited him to sit down on a wobbly armchair, in an open plan room with the kitchen in the corner. A clock shaped like a cat was beating time. The cat was called Felix, and had the same expression as Jimmy Page.

Tony cleared his throat. "Now if you don't mind," he said, "rewind and give me a summary of the previous episodes."

"How I found you? How I found the picture?"

"Two questions and a single answer: Giò. The only person who could have given you both the photo and a lead on where and when to find me without—"

"Witnesses?" Sibylle said, pointing at his nose and immediately regretting it.

"Distractions," he said, correcting her, with a half-smile. "Hardly an impossible task. I've always been a creature of habit."

"Walking Freddy. The same streets, the same time, like a Swiss watch. Giò used the expression 'dead boring.'" Sibylle crossed her legs. "At this point, I imagine it's easy to work out how I got to Giò."

"You imagine correctly. You dug up the old papers. The only one that went beyond a polite mention was *Sole delle Alpi*. Two articles signed 'A. C.' The first, three thousand words, the second, two thousand. Since you didn't know who the mysterious 'A. C.' was, you looked for the crime editor at the time, Giovanna Innocenzi, and Giò isn't exactly what you'd describe as a lover of anonymity. It took me less than a minute to track her down."

"And three hours for her to get to the point. Your books. Your success. Sarcasm, sarcasm, sarcasm. And the nickname she pinned on you back in March '99," Sibylle said, absent-mindedly massaging her sore shoulder. "Explain *that* to me."

Tony leaned against the back of the armchair and clenched his fists. When he noticed Sib staring at them, he forced himself to relax, with an embarrassed grimace.

"'The Recommended One.' In the days following Erika's death, Giò stopped calling me 'newbie' and started calling me that instead. She did it again today, you know? Like some kind of comradely joke."

Sib did not reply, but it did not escape her notice that his fists were clenched again.

"And twenty years later," Tony said gloomily, "I find out that back in '99 *Sole*'s principal advertiser applied pressure to make sure it was me and not Giò who pursued the story."

"And *Sole*'s principal advertiser," Sibylle said, hoping her voice betrayed no emotion, "was Friedrich Perkman."

Tony rubbed his hands on his jeans. They had finally reached the present. Now came the hard part. The two plus two that had prompted him to disinter the Mustang.

"Tell me the truth, Sibylle—"

"Sib. It's just Sib."

"Sib. You don't believe Erika committed suicide."

For someone who made a living from writing, these six words had been really hard to get out.

"Not exactly," Sibylle said. "I know for certain that Erika didn't commit suicide."

Felix the Cat struck nine-thirty. A moth was frantically circling around the ceiling lamp.

"How can you be so sure?"

"Why did the newbie suddenly become 'The Recommended One'? What was the connection between 'A. C.' and the Perkmans? Let's put our cards on the table."

"Nothing! Nothing *whatsoever*," Tony said, red in the face. "I didn't even know the Perkman family existed at the time. I was just a boy. And frankly, even now—"

Sib snapped her fingers and smiled.

A smile that took Tony by surprise.

"Anger."

"What do you mean?"

"Your expression when I slapped you. I've been thinking about it all day. It wasn't fear. It was anger. But not towards me. You've got too much of it for that, and it's too deeply rooted. There's more, isn't there? And somehow it has something to do with Erika."

Tony indicated the cardboard box next to Sibylle. "What have you got there?"

"The 8th of June."

Nine

1.

On June 8, while Kreuzwirt was filling with the BMWs and Mercedes of South Tyrol's bigwigs, Sibylle had allowed herself a lie-in, since Oskar had decided to keep the Black Hat closed as a sign of mourning.

When she left home, meaning to go for a ride on her Yamaha, she saw the letter. The envelope was sealed. No sender. A shy admirer, perhaps?

If only.

Sibylle knew she was quite attractive. The ogling, handsy maniacs at the Black Hat had not taught her anything she did not already know. Except that no sooner had she opened up a little with the young men who passed the First Glance Exam (and subsequent Pillock Test) – cute enough to arouse her interest and not so stupid that she would refuse to go to bed with them for the sake of a little exercise – than they would scurry away. *I'm not ready for you yet. It's me, I . . . Surely you can see that.* Sib had heard it all.

The problem was that Sibylle was a complicated girl in a part of the world that loved order. The young men who courted her were simple. They wanted a girl who would marry them in the Church of Sand in Taufers and commit to churning out two or three brats in succession and spending the rest of her life cooking, ironing and making sure she was ready and willing on Saturday nights. Really not the kind of future Sib had in mind.

Sure enough, the envelope contained no passionate declaration of love, but a black-and-white photograph. An *impossible* photograph. Erika lying by the lake, wearing her Maturaball dress, her hair caked in mud, her face turned towards the dawn.

And a symbol traced next to her body.

2.

Tony turned white.

"What's that doodle?"

"Evidence that Erika was killed."

It wasn't there.

The symbol drawn in the mud right next to Erika's body wasn't there in 1999. He hadn't seen it when Milani had flung him head first down the hill, and nobody had mentioned it during the police briefings.

Therefore . . .

Sibylle pre-empted his objection.

"It's not a photomontage. I had it analysed by a nerd in Bruneck. He thought it was a still from a film. The camera film is from the period. The light suggests it was shot a few minutes after dawn. It's authentic." Sib drew a breath and began rummaging through the box. "Spooky Erika could read the future. Did you know that?"

Tony recalled that the Spooky Erika business had surfaced very quickly in '99, but little else had come to light. A daydreamer. Few friends. An extra boost, Milani had remarked with bitterness, for the suicide theory. No murder. No post-mortem rape. *Say goodbye to your scoop, newbie.*

Sibylle showed him a deck of tarot cards. "These were Erika's. Do you know how they work?"

"Why? *Do* they work?"

"Everyone has a different way of laying them out. Some people arrange them in a circle or a triangle, others in groups of three or four. Everyone has their own system. This is how Erika did it."

Sib began to arrange the tarots on the coffee table. Two parallel vertical lines of three cards each, very close to each other. She added two more at the base, creating a kind of arrowhead. Then two more higher up, so as to form . . .

"It looks like a serpent's head."

"Erika used to call it 'the hummingbird smile'. Can you picture it?"

The pattern of cards on the coffee table was identical to the symbol drawn in the mud next to Erika's body.

Fuck.

"Now look at the photo carefully," Sibylle said. "See the serial number? The one I found in the letterbox was the first one taken at the scene of Erika's death. The others are here." A thin file bearing the stamp of the Bolzano court. "I got it from the public prosecutor's office. It has the statements of the carabinieri, the photographs taken that morning and the autopsy report on Erika. Notice anything strange?"

It stood out like a clown at a funeral. The serial numbers of the pictures in the file went from seven to fifty. Moreover, the light in these images wasn't the same as in the missing photographs, as though they had been taken later in the morning. Erika's body was positioned differently and, just as Tony remembered, there was no symbol next to her.

"I think the hummingbird smile would have led to questions, but since someone made it disappear, everything was straightforward. On the 21st, Erika killed herself by drowning in the lake. On the 22nd, the autopsy was carried out, and confirmed death by drowning. Suicide. On the 23rd, the body was cremated. Look at the signature of the doctor appointed by the court to write the report."

The handwriting was untidy but legible. Doctor Josef Horst. The man who had discovered Erika's body at 4 a.m. on March 22, 1999.

Tony wiped his forehead with his hand. He was sweating.

"So, in your opinion, Horst kills Erika and draws the symbol in the mud, but when the carabinieri arrive he regrets it, wipes it out without them noticing, and somehow makes the pictures they had already taken disappear. Then he falsifies the autopsy. It doesn't add up."

"No, it doesn't. I think Horst found Erika's body and didn't see the hummingbird smile at first. Understandably. It was night-time. It was dark. He was upset. He noticed it only at dawn, when the carabinieri had already taken pictures one to six. That's when he erased it. Then   "

"He silenced the carabinieri?" Tony said. "Made the pictures disappear? Don't you think it's a bit . . . far-fetched?"

Sib studied Tony's expression.

Perplexed, frightened. Incredulous.

Sibby Longstocking took control.

"Do you know who persuaded Aunt Helga to have Erika cremated? Horst. No body, no chance of a second autopsy. And guess what happened to the first carabinieri to reach Horst by the lake? They're dead. One from a stroke in 2003, and the other in a car accident in 2010. The daughter of the one who died from a stroke now works for the Perkmans. His colleague was about to be dismissed from the carabinieri in '99, because he'd beaten up a street vendor. But guess who saved him from ending up on the street? Friedrich Perkman. Who was buried the same day somebody put this picture in my letterbox. Fuck, Tony, *bischt Blint*?"

No, Tony was not blind.

Just as it did not escape his notice that Freddy's muzzle had turned almost entirely white, it was quite clear to him that very little about Erika's death made sense. Except for the decision to assign the story to a newbie. Unpleasant as she may or may not be, Giò was an experienced journalist. She would certainly not have got herself shafted like a small-time newbie.

Come to think of it, did he remember the last words he had exchanged with Milani?

Yes, he did. The taste of Jim Beam and the starless sky and . . .
Fuck.

Milani had dragged him around the valley, accompanying him to police press conferences. He had been with him even during interviews. Not to mention the fact that it had been Milani who persuaded him to go with him to Kreuzwirt. Michele Milani: the lead the Perkmans had put around his neck.

Tony suddenly felt sick.

Murder.

The word floated in the air in all its horror. If Sibylle was right, if Erika had been murdered, if Horst and Perkman had buried the enquiry, then somehow he had been an accomplice. Tony rubbed his eyelids. Millions of coloured little lights and a gloomy certainty.

He could tell Sibylle hadn't finished yet.

"What else have you discovered?"

"What everybody here in Kreuzwirt knows. That since March 21, 1999, Friedrich Perkman's son, Martin Perkman, the brother of Karin Perkman, who among other things was one of Erika's best friends, has not been seen in town."

"Disappeared?"

"Locked up. In Krotn Villa."

"Toad Villa?" Tony translated, thinking he had misunderstood.

"What do you know about the Perkman family?"

"That they have loads of money."

"It's a little more complicated than that."

Ten

1.

Friedrich Perkman was born in 1950. At the age of eighteen, he persuaded his family, farmers for generations, to entrust him with their savings and allow him to make the odd investment. It paid off. At the age of twenty, orphaned by an avalanche, he acquired a 50 per cent stake in the Kreuzwirt sawmill and started to buy up land all around it: after discovering that the landslide that had killed his parents had been caused by negligence, he swore that nobody else in Kreuzwirt would ever die like that. From his viewpoint, buying land was the most practical way of ensuring this.

From '70 to '72, his revenue increased, but in '73 the sawmill was forced to cut back on production, leaving him practically bankrupt. Friedrich took that as a challenge. If the old markets were dying, new ones would be emerging. He succeeded with the help of Dr Horst, who appeared in Kreuzwirt that same year.

Horst was born in a small town in the canton of Bern, but lived and practised in Geneva. That was where they met. On one of his business trips, Friedrich was forced to call a doctor because he had a nasty flu. That day, a friendship was born that would last a lifetime.

In 1973, when Horst arrived in Kreuzwirt, he was riddled with debt, a widower with a one-year-old son, Michl, and a stack of brilliant ideas but no means to put them into practice. Horst had studied at the University of Geneva, which was cutting-edge back then, and there he had seen the potential for electronic calculators. All he needed was someone like Friedrich, someone who could operate in the world of business. Horst was the nitro and Perkman the glycerine. Once they got together, the sky was the limit.

Horst's death in 2006 was a severe blow to Friedrich. Their friendship had been a pillar of his life. They shared everything: ambitions, food, even a house, Krotn Villa, Toad Villa, which had been erected in '74 on the site of the Perkman family *maso* and grew in cubic capacity in tandem with Friedrich's ever-expanding fortune.

The barn where his ancestors had raised emaciated cows became an elegant additional wing, and the vegetable garden was turned into a greenhouse for rare plants. Two new storeys were added to the main body of the house, as well as a guest annex and a turret that overlooked the peat bog. The ivy-covered walls marking the perimeter came next, with their marble toads flanking the gate, and finally, in 1994, Perkman added the mausoleum in which he would bury his wife and where, fifteen years later he, too, would be interred.

If, in '73, sharing Krotn Villa with Horst had been a necessity dictated by financial constraints, in time it had become a habit that endured even when, in 1978, Friedrich fell in love with Christine Talfer.

When she and Friedrich were married, Horst was best man and Michl was the ring bearer. Even after the wedding, Horst continued to live in the villa – Christine insisted, because she enjoyed taking care of Michl. She loved children and wanted to have some of her own. In 1980, the couple had twins. Martin and Karin.

2.

Sibylle stood up and went to get a bottle of orange juice. She poured some for Tony and herself. She took a packet of aspirin from a cabinet and swallowed a tablet, knowing it would have no effect but hoping for the best.

"How's your shoulder?"

"I told you, it was just a fall."

"Not just any fall. That bike's a write-off."

"The bike, but not me."

Sib returned to her seat and handed Tony a Polaroid of three girls and a young man with their arms around one another. "This was taken a few days before the Maturaball in '99. Do you recognise her?"

First on the left was Erika. Next to her stood an attractive girl with two long, dark braids and bright-blue eyes; then another blonde girl, frowning, with a piercing gaze; and lastly the only male in the group, who wore thick glasses and looked self-conscious.

Sib pointed at the blonde girl with the intense expression. "Karin Perkman."

"Is that Martin?"

"No, that's Gabriel," Sibylle explained. "There are no pictures of Martin."

"Not even school photos? When everyone poses with the teacher at the end of the academic year?"

"That was strictly forbidden. When Martin and his sister were three years old there was a fire at Krotn Villa. A short circuit. Karin wasn't hurt, but Martin was disfigured and lost the use of his left eye. That was in 1983. Martin hadn't been all there since then. He became 'aggressive'."

Tony raised an eyebrow. "What do you mean?"

"Martin and Karin attended the local primary school. Perkman wanted his children to be a part of the community, because Kreuzwirt meant everything to him. Remember his obsession with land? Nowadays, the whole valley belongs to the Perkmans. The peat bog, the woods – everything. Have you seen any tourists around? You know what Friedrich did when people started to get the idea that tourism could be a good business opportunity for us here, too? He hired a bus and showed them the true cost of tourism. Rubbish, concrete, trees felled and increasingly shrinking pastures."

"But from an economic point of view—"

"Kreuzwirt is one of the wealthiest places in Alto Adige. Perkman knew how to take care of his fellow residents. For example, the sawmill closed once and for all in 1975, but Perkman managed to reallocate all the workers, including those who'd already lost their jobs in '73. And that's not all. He also turned the sawmill into a civic centre. It wasn't just the villa that grew along with Perkman but the whole of Kreuzwirt. If you ever needed anything, all you had to do was knock on his door."

"As Horst did."

"And he wasn't the only one, trust me. And Karin carries on this tradition. Every five years we elect a mayor, but everybody knows it's the Perkmans who are in charge. Kreuzwirt is short of nothing, except poor people and tourists. Clean air and geraniums at the windows all around. Anyway . . ." Sibylle moistened her lips with a sip of orange juice and carried on. "In 1988, Martin attacked a girl in his class. Betta, the girl with the braids. He was taken out of school and educated at home by Dr Horst, Perkman and Lehrerin Rosa, the Kreuzwirt primary-school teacher, who from then on went to the villa twice a week. I've searched the school archives and found only one document with just a few lines that refer to an unspecified 'incident'. Nothing else."

Tony could see the logic in that. "Martin and Betta were minors in '88, so it's understandable."

"You don't understand. In Kreuzwirt everybody knows everything. They know that Oskar's girlfriend, the one he was supposed to marry, jilted him because he drank too much at the time. They know that Signora Grünberger has used psychotropic drugs ever since she lost her husband, though she goes all the way to Brixen to buy them because she's embarrassed. Everybody knows everything."

"Except what happened to Erika in '99 or to Betta in '88, right?"

Sib nodded. She took another Polaroid out of the box.

"1996. This is the school roof. The kids would secretly go and sunbathe there. You just have to go up the fire escape at the back. These are Karin and—"

"Is this a scar?"

Sib smiled a Sibby Longstocking smile.

The scar, at least fifteen centimetres long, was just below Betta's navel.

"Maybe this doesn't date back to '88," Tony said. "It might have nothing to do with Martin. You can't be certain."

"That's possible." Sib's expression implied the exact opposite. "From 1988 to 1999, Martin was seen only rarely. Usually in the car with his father. Or else in the woods or the peat bog with Karin, Horst or Michl. Never on his own or in town. Then, in 1999, around the night of March 21, 1999, to be precise, Martin disappears altogether, swallowed by Toad Villa. No-one has seen him since." Sib leaned over towards Tony. "Not once."

"Do you think Martin Perkman could have killed Erika? That Horst discovered the body and that he and Perkman buried the whole affair? And that subsequently, in order to conceal the scandal or to –" Tony searched for the right words – "because they loved him, they decided to shut him away in Toad Villa for ever?"

"It's worse than that." For the first time since she had begun to talk, Sibylle hesitated. "There's the business of the curse and the ghost. After Erika's death, somebody started to draw the hummingbird smile on the walls in Kreuzwirt. Erika became a kind of local bogey man. 'Erika's coming to get you.' That kind of thing."

"Very amusing . . ." Tony muttered, frowning.

"The fact is, it started within a few hours of Erika's death. Nobody knows who it was. What we do know is that all the kids in that Polaroid have somehow been cursed by Erika's death." Sib's voice dropped down to a whisper. "I've always thought of it as nonsense, but now I'm beginning to believe that the curse and the ghost are real."

The young woman bit her lip, trying to gauge the effect of her words on Tony, but he just kept staring at the four young people in the picture.

So she continued. "After Erika's death, Karin became colder, more distant, sullen. They say it's because Friedrich forced her to work at the family firm, but . . ." Sib indicated the shy boy in the Polaroid. "Gabriel. The son of Signor Plank, Kreuzwirt council's only employee. Aunt Helga told me that Gabriel was so distressed by Erika's death that he didn't even go to her funeral. Within a year, his father applied for a transfer and he left with him. He hasn't set foot back in town since. Then there's Betta, Miss Top-of-the-Class with a great future before her. Except that she didn't take the curse into account. Look."

Sib took a newspaper article from the box. The headline said it all: CAMPER DROWNED.

"July 11, 2005. Betta drowns in a stream less than a kilometre away from the lake where Erika died. It gives you the chills, doesn't it?"

Tony glanced at the newspaper clipping. "It says here that Betta was drunk, lost her balance, hit her head, fainted and landed face down in the stream. I can't see anything mysterious in that. You say Karin changed? The Perkmans have great responsibilities and responsibilities change people. Gabriel hasn't been seen in town? Too many bad memories. That's understandable."

"Yes, but guess who established Betta's cause of death? Again, Horst. Another coincidence? It's possible. But . . ."

For a moment, Tony thought she would be unable to complete her sentence. Her eyes were puffy. She was tired, drained. Frightened.

"You must understand," Sibylle murmured, "that ever since I started asking questions, Kreuzwirt has fallen *silent*. Do you know what the chances are, of a town like this having nothing to say about such a strange series of events?"

"The same," Tony whispered, "as the chances of a magnate like Perkman insisting on a newbie covering the death of Spooky Erika."

Or else, he thought, looking at Freddy snoring peacefully under the window, the same chance someone from Shanghai has of writing a string of bestsellers.

Tony got up and opened the window. Kreuzwirt was pitch-black. There were more stars than in Bolzano and the air was cool and pleasant. Even so, Tony was bathed in sweat. He stared at the outline of his Mustang. After a long pause, he turned to face Sybille. "What's the next move?"

Eleven

1.

Back in Bolzano, after saying goodnight to Freddy, Tony tried to sleep. He needed it. However, every time he closed his eyes, his mind would drift to the headstone of the little girl without a head.

Via Virus.

Legend had it, the former proprietor of the Via Virus house had made a pact with the devil: to live for a thousand years in exchange for the head of a little girl, his daughter. Except that no sooner had it been severed from the body – even before the blood could be wiped from the axe – than the head began to speak. *We will always be together, Papà.* And if you had the guts to go past the stone dogs (which, they said, would snarl) and the tombstone of the headless girl (who, they swore, changed names every day) and knock ten times at the door of the bewitched house, you, too, would hear her. *And if you don't believe it, you're nothing but a poofter.*

In the summer of 1990, Tony was eleven years old and had only a vague idea of what a poofter was, but he was the only one of the group to go past two canine statues – which hadn't so much as whimpered. He walked up the gravel alley and saw the tombstone. It was worn by time and he was unable to read the inscription. Maybe it wasn't even a tombstone. And so he walked up to the door and knocked. No girl. No ghost. Peeved, he tried the handle. The door was open, and Tony went in.

There were heavy curtains at the windows and pictures with elaborate frames. A well-to-do house, as his mother would have said. The frames were alright, but the paintings were dreadful. They looked like exercises in geometry. No axe, no severed head.

At this point Tony was facing a problem. If he told people about his endeavour, nobody would believe him unless – and here he was struck by a sudden flash of inspiration – he had evidence. But there was only valuable stuff here, and he was no thief. Did the rich really possess nothing worth less than the gold necklace his mother would show off only at weddings and Christmas?

He was about to leave empty-handed when he smelled something, and the smell led him to a kitchen furnished in Tyrolean style. Timber-clad walls, a crucifix, impeccably polished glass and enamel and, on a table, freshly baked biscuits.

Tony was already picturing munching them while calling the friends waiting for him outside cowards (coward *poofters*), when an old man appeared out of nowhere. Dishevelled white hair, the wild expression of one who has cut his own daughter's head off and is now ready to do the same to a snotty-nosed kid from Shanghai (and what would his ghost say, once he had been decapitated? *I am an idiot and I deserve this?*). They stood staring at each other, frozen, like gunslingers in a Sergio Leone film, until the old man roused himself with a kind of violent spasm, pursed his lips, swelled his cheeks, jutted his chin forward, and the silence of the Via Virus house was broken by the explosion of an ungainly fart, like the protracted cawing of a crow, followed by a (hysterical) laugh on the part of Tony, who grabbed a biscuit and bolted like a bat out of hell.

Unfortunately, once he was safe he discovered that his friends had already made off, and so the crumbling biscuit in his hand was worthless. Nobody would believe him. Life was crap. Even worse, there was nothing of interest whatsoever to be found in Via Virus. No statues of snarling dogs. No ghosts. No bloodied axes. No mysteries. Nothing but an old man who spent his time baking biscuits and breaking wind.

It was such a sad thought that he forgot to get rid of the evidence of his misdeed, so when his mother asked for an explanation and Tony was forced to tell the truth, he was welcomed into the adult world.

Ghosts did not exist, pacts with the devil did not exist, but monsters did. Because a former SS officer nobody had the courage to put on trial and send to prison was living in the Via Virus house. An old man with dishevelled white hair who was trying to cheat death by giving himself artistic airs.

In other words, if you look into the abyss, the abyss looks up at you. But if you are born in Shanghai, not only will the abyss cast down its eyes (the least it can do) but you will always find something you can munch on between its jaws.

Nietzsche was just born in the wrong district. And Tony spent a sleepless night.

Twelve

1.

At dawn, he made himself coffee, said hello to Freddy, fed him, watered him and took him for the usual walk. And it was while the St Bernard was Pollocking here and there, that Tony realised why his mind had made him relive the Via Virus adventure.

Putting aside curses, "Erika's coming to get you", sinister deaths and the whole folklore Sibylle seemed to believe in or wanted to believe in (just as he had wanted to believe in the headless little girl), there was just one *concrete* thing left as a point of departure for anyone trying to shed light on Erika's death.

The symbol. The hummingbird smile. The discordant note. Not so much who might have drawn it or erased it, but the symbol per se. Erika used it as a pattern for laying out her tarots – but why? Had she invented it or found it somewhere? What did it mean? Strange that Sib had not thought about it. She was a bright girl. Clever. Brave. And definitely . . .

His leg still raised, his tongue unrolled and dripping, Freddy was staring at him with what looked like the smug smile of someone who knows a thing or two.

"Attractive, yes," Tony said. "You're right. You're worse than Polianna. Consider yourself in disgrace."

Bolzano is a city of avid readers. Every district has its own library, and there are many bookshops scattered around: Italian, German and multilingual. Tony would hang around pretty much all of them, but had a soft spot for one in particular.

It had an odd name, Carnival, and was hard to get to from Shanghai since it was located in the old town, but the shelves were bursting with true gems, and Chiara, the tattooed bookseller, always had the power to make him smile.

Freddy, on the other hand, liked Carnival because Chiara always had a supply of his favourite brand of treats. But Tony was a man of his word, so Freddy had stayed at home, though under the air conditioning unit, with Polianna brushing his coat. He never did manage to be strict with the St Bernard.

Much to his surprise, Tony discovered that Carnival stocked a large number of books about tarot and related subjects.

Chiara, the head-banging bookseller, explained that the New Age section was the most popular among their customers. Without it, the bookshop would have closed down years ago.

That was the upside.

"The downside is I've had to learn about all this crap. Did you know that amber cures hangovers?"

"Have you tried it?"

"It doesn't work," she said, looking forlorn. "And did you know that jade attracts wealth?"

"No, but . . ." Tony drew the hummingbird smile on a sheet of paper. "Does this symbol ring any bells?"

"*Nada*. If you like I can ask around among the lunatics that buy these books. Spread the word." Her eyes lit up. "Is it for a new novel?"

3.

A few minutes later, with two bags full of books slung in the boot of the Mustang and a little ahead of schedule, Tony decided to take a nap in the car park outside the Aurora, an old people's home where, according to Sibylle, Lehrerin Rosa, the teacher who had tutored Martin Perkman from 1988 to 1999, was living.

He nearly cried out when Sib tapped on the window of the Mustang. He had been dreaming about the headless little girl.

Thirteen

1.

Tony hated that smell. Camphor, disinfectant . . . And lily-of-the-valley. They sprayed it everywhere. Lily-of-the-valley or essence of rose. As though there was nothing else.

He had only just come in and already could not wait to get out.

"Lehrerin Rosa, you have a visitor," the carer said, opening one of the many doors in the nursing home.

It took some nerve to call Aurora a place where people went to die, Tony thought as he closed the door discreetly behind him.

Lehrerin Rosa, a gaunt woman, removed her reading glasses and put them down on the magazine she was leafing through, pen in hand: crosswords. She indicated the chairs.

"You're exactly like your mother, my child. Do you know that?"

The nurse had told them that the patient had more bad days than good. And that they had picked the right time to visit.

"Do you recognise me? Do you know who I am?"

Lehrerin Rosa gave Sibylle a beaming smile. "You're Sibylle, Erika's daughter. Your mother was beautiful, but you . . . you're even more so. And you clearly have guts. You're here to talk about her, aren't you?"

Lehrerin Rosa spoke a perfect German, so even Tony could follow easily enough.

Sibylle moved the chair closer to the bed.

"Yes. I'm trying to find out who she really was."

"Do you know the villa?"

"Of course. Everyone does."

"The children were delightful. So was your mother. Always with her tarot cards. Karin was the only one concerned with homework. That girl was serious, just like her father. But very cheerful, don't get me wrong. They would all get together in the villa library. Around that oval table. And they'd start giggling at the slightest thing. Erika, Betta, Karin and that stand-offish little boy . . ."

"Gabriel?" Sibylle suggested.

"Gabriel, yes. In the evenings, when Dr Horst allowed it, they would go up to the turret. There's a telescope up there. Horst was an amateur astronomer. They would look at the stars. I'd go with them, too, sometimes. It was the only time Gabriel would relax. He said he wanted to be an astronaut when he grew up."

"What about Martin?"

Lehrerin Rosa's gaze drifted past Sibylle. "My Martin . . . my little mole."

"Because of his eye?"

"That's so cruel – no!" the Lehrerin said. "Because of his favourite book, the one he was always asking me to read to him. At least one chapter a day, or there'd be such a fuss. *The Wind in the Willows*. Have you ever read it?"

"A children's classic," Tony said in his slightly broken German. "Kenneth Grahame."

"Mole was Martin's favourite character."

Sibylle ran her fingers through her curls. "Lehrerin Rosa, do you know why Martin was taken out of school in '88?"

"He only gave her a fright, but you know what children are like – a tiny cut and they cry for hours on end. Betta's parents threatened to report him, but Friedrich made them see sense. Martin was a good little mole, with his blind eye that always watered whenever he tried to read. He loved to read, except that . . ." The old teacher's face hardened. "I know what they say in town. Lies."

"What do they say in town, Lehrerin Rosa?" Tony asked.

She looked at him as though she had only just noticed his presence.

"That he was retarded. Martin was big and tall, with a burnt face. They called him a *monster*, but he'd never have hurt a fly. He and Betta were always laughing. He would pick her up and she'd laugh and laugh. Even after the accident. It was just a little flare-up, you see? Nothing more. Martin would sometimes get angry. But only when provoked. Betta was not the goody two shoes she appeared to be, and she could be spiteful. Besides, a scar like that never killed anyone."

She adjusted her sheet and smoothed out the creases. She seemed angry.

Sib tried to calm her. "Everyone in town told me that there was never a better teacher than you."

Lehrerin Rosa smiled, pleased. "Is that what they say?"

"Trust me, you've left wonderful memories in town. Since you knew him so well . . . in your opinion, what was wrong with Martin?"

"Nothing," the woman said abruptly. "Martin was paying for other people's prejudices. Stop speaking badly of him, like that dreadful, dreadful Dr Horst used to. Martin wasn't unkind, and he definitely was not as stupid as that charlatan always claimed. I once gave him a test without telling Friedrich, and he turned out to be even cleverer than Karin."

She sighed.

"He had some difficulties . . . that I can't deny. And his disability didn't help him make friends. They said it was he who broke into Kreuzwirt houses to steal ladies' underwear. That's just silly. Martin was a good boy. You don't believe me? The day of the eclipse, in '99 – August 11 – fell on my birthday. I had a splitting headache, so instead of standing in the square, watching the sun disappear, I went back home. And what do I see as soon as I close the door? A huge shape that scares the hell out of me. I switch on the light, and guess who it is?"

"Martin?" Tony ventured.

"My little mole. With a beautiful bunch of flowers," Lehrerin Rosa said, giving the mattress a pat. "That rascal had remembered my birthday!"

"Did he often do that? I mean, bring you flowers on your birthday?"

"At least until I ended up here. It's too far even for him. Does a child like that deserve to be tied to a chair like Signor Perkman and Dr Horst used to do? I don't think so. No child deserves to be treated like that. Dr Horst, alright, but what about Signor Perkman? If only his wife had been in better health. She wasn't well, and I didn't have the heart to tell her what they were doing to my little mole. My poor Martin."

"Was Martin free to leave the villa?" Sibylle said.

"He wasn't allowed to, Friedrich would have been angry, but every now and then ... every now and then he managed to slip away. My little mole was shrewd. Later, after Signora Perkman died, Friedrich cut down on the staff and there was less surveillance."

"But Horst—" Tony tailed off.

Lehrerin Rosa was not there with them. Her mind was following different paths, in a distant time.

"Friedrich, Karin and Martin lived in the villa. Sometimes, Peter – Signor Brugger – who was a widower, would bring his young son Rudi along when there was no school. Peter built the greenhouse, you know? Signora Perkman loved that greenhouse. It helped her endure the pain of her illness. It had been Friedrich's idea, but Peter built it. Lilies, roses ... It was stunning. After Signora Perkman died, it was abandoned; the gardener had been let go, so Friedrich gave Peter the job of custodian. And since he didn't want people around anymore, he bought him a house in Kreuzwirt."

The Lehrerin reached out to her bedside table, picked up a glass of water and moistened her throat.

"Friedrich took care of Kreuzwirt's people. He had many flaws, but he helped everybody." She looked at Sibylle again. Through Sibylle. Immersed in the past.

"Then there were Dr Horst and his son, that handsome boy, who's also a doctor now. He always had a bit of a temper on him. Markus

Horst. No, not Markus. *Michl.* The girls fancied Michl, and his father would tell him off. He said they distracted him from his studies. Karin certainly fancied him. In any case, the villa was almost deserted by now, so Martin grabbed every opportunity he could to take a walk in the woods." Lehrerin Rosa gently touched Sibylle's blonde curls. "And perhaps to meet Erika. Erika was the only one who truly accepted him."

"As fellow oddballs, they had something in common."

Lehrerin Rosa burst out laughing.

"That was just what your mother used to say. Do you know that Erika had a talent for imitating animal cries? She would often do it for Martin. He would laugh and laugh and . . ." She broke off and pumped her fist into the air. "Martin would never, ever hurt your mother. That's what you're thinking, aren't you? Because you wouldn't be here otherwise. Everybody's forgotten all about me now. Everybody except Gabriel. He came to see me. Years ago. With that long hair, looking like . . . oh, don't remind me."

"Did Gabriel ever ask you about Martin?" Tony said. "Or about Erika?"

Lehrerin Rosa laughed uproariously. "Gabriel only mentioned Erika. But what he was really interested in was the ghost. The ghost and the Perkman library. I hope the kids have stopped playing those horrible tricks. 'Erika's coming to get you.' Writing on the walls. Rude, rude. Have they stopped?"

Sib shrugged. "Not quite."

"Then tell them that there was already a Kreuzwirt ghost, even before she died," the Lehrerin said. "Even though they didn't call it that at the time."

Sib glanced at Tony. "What did they call it?"

"'The pervert,'" the woman replied, sniffing. "What else should they have called him? A pig who breaks into women's homes to do God knows what."

"Why did Gabriel want to know about the library?"

"It was very large. There were all kinds of books. At least four different encyclopaedias, because Friedrich was a man who wanted to know everything, and then there was the section that was always locked. With all the old, very valuable books. But I never saw it. I told Gabriel the same as I'm telling you now. Except that now I'm a little—"

"One last thing, Lehrerin. Look at this symbol. Have you ever come across it?"

The woman put on her glasses to examine the sheet of paper Tony was holding out to her.

"It's the hummingbird smile. That girl had such an imagination! Erika would use it to read cards and . . . This is what she would do."

Lehrerin Rosa picked up the crossword magazine and, without a word, ripped out a handful of pages and began to tear them into small pieces. The hummingbird smile appeared on her bedsheet.

"She . . ."

All of a sudden, her eyes went blank. With what looked like a super-human effort, she reached out to stroke Sibylle's hair. "Why did such a young and beautiful girl kill herself? Erika's death changed everything. Friedrich sacked me and I wasn't able to see my little mole again, except in secret. Gabriel . . . When he came to see me, years later . . . he was talking like a drug addict. And what about Betta? She died. Drunk. Even her body stank of alcohol, that's what Wolfie said, after he found her in 2005, or was it 2007?"

"It was 2005," Sibylle said.

"Time plays strange tricks, my darling, really strange. Things that happened a long time ago seem so recent . . . unlike things that only just happened . . . I can still hear those children laughing and . . ." Lehrerin Rosa wiped away her tears with the back of her hand, covered in veins and dark freckles. "Why did she do it? Why would a mother kill herself?"

She rested her head on the pillow and turned away, staring out of the window.

Sibylle got up. "Thank you."

The woman did not reply. Tony noticed her magazine lying open on the bed. The squares of the puzzle she had started all contained the same letters. One down. River that divides Florence in two.

Rosa.

Seven across. A much-loved Italian president.

Rosaros.

Twelve down. Capital of the United States.

Rosarosaro.

Fourteen

1.

Chiara, the bookseller, had kept her promise, and Tony's inbox was crammed with emails. At least half were from aspiring writers asking him to take a look at their creations. The balance consisted of various consultancy offers: fortune telling, personalised horoscopes, readings from coffee dregs. Everyone wanted to meet him, everyone claimed to be the custodian of some secret or other, but no-one appeared able to provide the answer he sought. Tony deleted them and once again immersed himself in A Guide to the Arcane, a manual so annoying it eventually gave him a headache.

2.

You could not call them tarots. God help you if you did. You would sound like a neophyte. The only thing worse than a neophyte was the kind of person who calls them cards. Wretches.

The ones Tony had before him were called "Arcana". A word that sounded much better than "tarots", he had to admit. According to the manual Tony was consulting, the Arcana were divided into "Major Arcana" and "Minor Arcana".

According to H. West, the editor of the headache-inducing volume, the Arcana had a long and mysterious history. Who had invented them?

When? Was it the Egyptians, who had extracted the knowledge from aliens? Or the Babylonians, who spent their days toying with demons and divinities?

Huffing and puffing, Tony had quickly scanned the introductory chapter. He had no use for Hermes Trismegistus or the Book of Thoth (written on gold slabs!). He just wanted to learn more about the subject. In practice.

That's if you could use the word "practice" in this context.

"Tony, what's that smell?"

It was Polianna, on the other side of the door to his study.

"Incense."

"Have you started smoking again?"

Tony had quit eleven years ago, but ever since Polianna had unearthed a pack of Camels in one of the crates that dated back to the move ("I'll get rid of them tomorrow," he'd assured her on the spot. "I promise, cross my heart"), she wouldn't stop harassing him.

"No."

He gave no explanation, and luckily Polianna – sixty-one years old, housekeeper, first-class cook, the first reader of his manuscripts and steely guardian of his morality – went back to her chores. And Tony to the cards. No! The Arcana.

Like most psychics, Erika had preferred to use the Major Arcana, leaving out the Minor. They were more powerful, according to the guide.

However, as Tony gathered while trying to make sense of page after page of dense, pompous prose, interpreting them was not as easy as he had thought at first glance.

First of all, the Arcana did not have a constant value. And Tony could understand that. In the Shanghai of his teenage years, a punch did not always mean a punch. There were punches given in friendship, even if they left you with a phenomenal bruise, and there were those that, although no more than taps, represented an order to decamp in haste. If you still could, that is.

Therefore, the Magician, the first card in the deck, did not necessarily mean *the principle* or *presence of spirit*. If upside down, the Magician meant *lack of security* or *distrust*. So far so good.

However, the meaning of every Arcana changed depending on the Arcana next to it. And this was a real mess. The right way up, the Magician next to the Sun meant *imminent happiness*. Upside down, well . . . he had not got that far yet. Given that there were twenty-two Major Arcana, there were too many combinations for his memory to store them all.

Tony opened the windows. The smell of incense was making him queasy.

H. West's fault. The expert said that to make tarots work better you had to *energise* them by burning incense in their honour. And since Tony had always been something of a swot, he had followed the advice. But enough was enough . . .

"Tony?"

"Yes, Polianna?"

"There's blood on this T-shirt."

What an idiot, Tony thought. He had forgotten about it. Sibylle's slap. He opened the door.

"A little nosebleed."

"It's because you never leave the house."

"I *was* out of the house when—"

"It's because you don't drink enough."

"I drink plenty, Polianna. At least—"

Polianna did not let him finish. "Have you been to the doctor?"

"I'm fine."

"And what's all that stuff?"

Tony followed her gaze.

His desk had been turned into a kind of altar. The candle. The incense.

The Arcana.

"It's for a new book."

"You do know all that stuff is a con, don't you?"

"Of course. As a matter of fact, the book—"

"Tony, are you writing a horror story?"

He did not reply.

"You're like a child, Antonio Carcano. You don't know anything, but you want to play with grown-up things. Do you know what that stuff's for? Who *needs* it? The devil. He's always on the lookout for new souls. And when he finds a fool like you he makes them believe that they can read the future with those things. Or speak to the dead. But—"

"It's just a book, OK?"

Polianna looked at him grimly for a few seconds. Then she went back to being her usual self.

"Dinner is in the fridge. You just have to warm it up. And this big baby needs to stretch his legs."

Tony went up to her and gave her a kiss on the cheek. "See you tomorrow."

"Remember to drink."

He loved this woman to bits.

Fifteen

1.

Schüttelbrot and speck at that time of morning were not Tony's idea of breakfast. However, he had followed Sibylle's example so as not to give an unfavourable impression. He had even smiled and praised the quality of the speck. In any case, Tony never joked with someone who owned this many weapons.

There was an abundance of them here, in this house surrounded by trees and a freshly painted fence, a couple of kilometres from Kreuzwirt. Shotguns in particular. Some were museum pieces, like the muzzle-loader above the fireplace, others were more modern, enclosed in a rack protected by impact-resistant glass.

Besides this arsenal, the walls of the room were adorned with stag heads of various sizes, a stuffed capercaillie, a couple of marmots, even a funny-looking *Vulpendingen*, as well as a lot of foxes. Tony counted fifteen. The old man must really hate the wretched creatures.

"Have you ever been hunting, Mr Writer?"

"Only for trouble, Signor Egger. My father once took me to the fairground – they had one of those games where you win a Teddy bear or something like that if you manage to hit a balloon. In my case, a wonderful remote-controlled car. I'm afraid I've still got it."

The old man chuckled. "Those things are designed to – how do you say in Italian?"

"Swindle you?"

"That's right, to swindle you."

Sibylle put a large glass brimming with iced tea on a table that had seen better days. "I'd like to thank you for seeing us out of the blue like this, Signor Egger."

"Wolfie, please. That's what your mother used to call me, poor girl, and my Margherita, too. Did they tell you – she was very fond of Erika?"

"Aunt Helga always said that Signora Margherita was a very special woman."

"*Genau.* She had a good heart. Like your mother. I was very upset when I heard what she'd done. Everybody liked Erika."

"And Betta?"

Wolfie's eyes narrowed. "Are you here because of her?"

"Partly."

The old man rose from the armchair, went to the window and adjusted the curtains slightly.

"I was the one who found her, but you already knew that."

"In 2005?"

Wolfie sat down again and crossed his legs. If it had not been for his mountain boots and his weather-beaten face, he would have looked like a retired teacher. "There was a small tent. A lot of bottles inside and nearby. I was doing my usual rounds. It was the damned bottles I noticed first. The bottles and the tent. It was yellow and it was open. I found some grass inside. Don't make that face, Sibylle, you know exactly what kind of grass I mean."

"That wasn't reported in the paper."

"And why would those nosy parkers have written about that, my girl?"

"Fair enough."

Wolfie took a crumpled cigarette from the pocket of his green-and-blue checked shirt and lit it with a microscopic lighter.

"Betta was no longer the good girl she had once been. I'm sorry to spell it out, but it's the truth. If you want lies, as my poor Margherita used to say, the nearest church is in Sand in Taufers. But Betta had a

brilliant idea. 'Sleeping-bag tourism', she called it. She set up an agency."
The old man gestured towards the speck. "Don't you like it?"

Sib and Tony each helped themselves to a slice. Freddy implored
both, but all he got was a pat. Speck was *verboten* for dogs like him.

"People would pay to scamper around with a guide," Wolfie continued, pleased, "shitting among the brambles and eating burnt food
by an open fire. Not in Kreuzwirt. Thanks to God and the Perkmans,
there were no tourists in the valley. It was a good idea. With all this
call-of-nature stuff, people are willing to spend heaps of money on an
experience. To get up close and personal with the mountains. Isn't that
what you young people call it?"

He was looking at Tony.

"Some do."

"Betta drank. A little too much. That's why she dropped out of university. She was the first person in her family to get a place, but she pulled
out after a couple of semesters. Or terms – I'm not sure how it works.
Margherita used to say that I had a degree in bullshit and caked dung."

A phlegmy laugh.

"How did Betta die?"

"How do you think, young man? She was drunk. She slipped. She
banged her head and kaput."

Wolfie stubbed out his cigarette. Tony immediately showed him the
paper on which he had drawn the hummingbird smile.

"Did you see this anywhere when you found her?"

"The hummingbird smile? Why would I—?"

"So you know about it?"

"Everybody knew about it. Besides, I told you, Margherita was fond
of Erika. And she knew that all children do is eat and shit. At least back
in my days shitting was free but now, with disposable nappies, even that
costs money. So she'd get her cards read for a few lire. Just to help her
out. You should have seen the two of them. I enjoyed hearing Margherita
laughing like that. She said Erika really could read the future." Wolfie
drummed on the armrest with his fingers. "Except that she didn't predict

the cancer. Who knows? Maybe if she had, Margherita would still be alive and I wouldn't be wasting my days shooting foxes. And . . ."

With the air of a man who has suddenly remembered something extremely important, Wolfie nodded at Freddy, squatting at Tony's feet. "He's got a lead, hasn't he?"

"Of course."

"Then make sure you always keep him on it here in the valley. Foxes."

"Since when do foxes attack dogs?"

"Rabies. Kreuzwirt is the only area in the whole of Alto Adige where it's endemic. Even if you put bait with the vaccine out for foxes and bats – because it's bats that transmit the disease – it's no use. Whatever we do, it persists. Have you ever seen an animal with rabies?"

"No."

"It's not a pretty sight. And I wouldn't ever want to be in the same room as a rabid St Bernard."

"Freddy wouldn't hurt a fly."

"Rabies does strange things to animals. If they get sick you have to put them down. Unfortunately you can't do that to people. You have to try to treat them. No, I'm not being cynical. The treatment is no fun. It hurts and few survive. But some do. Not many, but some. Lucky for you, Sibylle."

"I've never been bitten by a fox," Sib said. "I least I can't remember—"

"I meant your mother."

"Erika?"

"Your mother was . . . a little odd when she was a child. But it wasn't her fault," he quickly added. "Your grandmother, Helene, she wasn't quite right in the head. Helga's told you, hasn't she?"

Aunt Helga had confided that her sister suffered from a terrible illness that left her incapable of taking care of herself or her daughter. The town simply said her grandmother was mad as a hatter. In any case, Sibylle knew, yes.

Wolfie lit his umpteenth cigarette. "When she was a child, Erika liked roaming in the woods on her own. I guess it was better than staying at home. I'd often see her on my rounds. A beautiful little blonde girl who could spend hours talking to a robin or a weasel."

"Talking?"

Wolfie smiled. "Twittering. Or whistling at weasels. Or at kites. She said she could speak to the animals and that the animals answered her. Like some kind of fairy, you know? Except that animals are animals, not toys . . ."

Sixteen

1.

The little girl was crouching among the roots of the pine tree in the forest. She had left the house because her mother had started breaking plates. "It's much more practical this way," she had said cheerfully, and Erika had realised it was time to go.

She was crying. Her wound was still stinging but that was not why she was crying. And she was not crying because that morning she had got out of bed with a splitting headache that made her teeth chatter, or because they would have to eat straight from the saucepans that evening. Erika was crying because she was thirsty.

Terribly thirsty.

Only she could not drink. Whenever she tried to bring water to her lips she would be hit with overwhelming nausea.

Moreover, she was sorry about Signora Fox. She had always been nice to her. And yet, two weeks earlier, Signora Fox had bitten her.

Erika was crying more over that than the thirst. She had not seen Signora Fox since then and she wanted to apologise to her. Animals were good. They only bit or threatened you if you had done something to them.

Never the other way round.

"Sweetie?"

Wolfie. Usually, it was a pleasure to come across the gamekeeper. He was funny and he always gave her some special bubblegum. The kind that fizzed on your tongue.

"What's wrong?"

"Mamma's not well."

Wolfie lit a cigarette. Whenever Wolfie smoked it meant he felt like talking. But Erika just wanted to be alone.

"What about you?"

"I think I've got a touch of flu."

"Can I see that cut on your arm?"

"It's nothing."

"But you don't mind if I have a look, do you?"

Erika showed him Signora Fox's teeth marks. Wolfie turned pale. He cleared his throat and threw the cigarette on the ground. This alarmed Erika.

Wolfie never left a cigarette half smoked, let alone abandoned a lit butt in the forest. He would extinguish it with the sole of his boot, then put it back into his shirt pocket.

"Have you got a headache, sweetie?"

"Yes, a bit."

"Have you been bitten by a fox?"

Erika did not reply.

Wolfie slipped the shotgun off his shoulder and crouched in front of her.

"You can tell me."

"It was my fault." Erika struggled to hold back her tears. "Don't shoot Signora Fox, Wolfie. She's not nasty."

"I won't, I promise. Only tell me, when did she bite you? Yesterday?"

"Two weeks ago."

Wolfie took the flask and shook it. The sound of the water made the little girl shudder.

"It's very warm today, isn't it?" the gamekeeper said. "The heat makes me thirsty. Are you thirsty, Erika?"

Wolfie let some water trickle out of the flask. Crystal clear. Cool. Erika's eyes rolled back.

"She got upset. Spasms. Tried to scratch me. She looked possessed. I hid the flask and straight away she calmed down. I heaved her over my shoulder and ran to the town and from there took her by jeep to Brixen. To the hospital. If only Helene had paid more attention, or Erika had said sooner that she'd been bitten by a fox. Only she—"

"Spooky Erika had got it into her head that it was her fault," Sib commented sharply.

"This was back in 1992. She was a little girl. Living alone with an unhinged mother. You wouldn't say that if you'd seen what she had to go through. The Milwaukee protocol. Do you know what that is?"

Tony and Sibylle shook their heads.

"It's a cocktail of medicines. When I got to Emergency, the doctors didn't know which way to turn. No-one had been admitted with such advanced rabies for decades. And it's not hard to see why."

"If I'd been bitten by a rabid fox," Tony said, "I wouldn't wait two weeks before going to hospital."

"In that case the vaccine would be sufficient. Three doses. It hurts but it saves your life. The Milwaukee protocol is *nasty*. The doctor said there was a one per cent chance Erika would be saved. Margherita burst into tears. And so did I . . ."

"And Helene?" Sib said.

"Helene never went to visit her daughter. Never. The doctors called social services and social services rushed to your grandmother's. They found her trying to set the curtains on fire. She ended up in a psychiatric hospital, where she died a couple of years later. Social services had already entrusted Erika to your aunt Helga."

"I know."

"That day, when the doctors admitted Erika, I prayed – and so did Margherita, who never went to Mass and always had a peculiar rapport with Him up there. One per cent, Sibylle. There was a ninety-nine per cent chance that you'd never be born. But Erika was strong. And so was Helga. 'The town spinster,' she said to me when the court entrusted Erika to her care, 'who winds up with a daughter without the pleasure of labour.' Helga was as hard as nails. I've seen her cry only twice. The first time was when the doctors told her that Erika was out of danger. The second time was when they brought her back home in '98."

Tony was confused. "1998? Erika spent six years in hospital?"

Sibylle glared at Wolfie with so much hatred that, for a moment, Tony almost thought she was going to jump at his throat.

"Erika ran away from home in 1998," Sib said. "She came back home pregnant. She never said who the father was. And she came back *of her own accord*. She wasn't *brought* back home. That's what they always told me."

"Things aren't always the way they're told, Sibylle. You're an adult now. You should know that."

"Who?"

Wolfie bowed his head.

"Who found her? Where?"

Wolfie got up and opened the front door. "I'm not the one you should be asking, sweetie. And you — keep that St Bernard on the lead. There's no Milwaukee protocol for animals."

Seventeen

1.

"Why didn't you tell me?"

And why the hell did no-one mention it back in '99?

Ignoring his question, Sib growled, "Can't you make this piece of junk go any faster?"

Only speed could calm her down, and Sibylle did not want Aunt Helga to see her like this. Angry – no, furious, actually. She was likely to say something she would later regret. But the writer had a heavy arse and the Mustang would not go beyond forty kilometres an hour.

"Answer the question," he said.

Sibylle bit her lip. "I thought you knew. I didn't think it was important."

"Your mother vanishes a year before she dies and you don't think it's important?"

"The 1968 Mustang has a 300-horsepower engine. Horse – not tortoise – power," Sibylle yelled. "Eight cylinders, and you're barely using half."

Tony understood what she was getting at, but said nothing. And did not accelerate.

Wolfie must have reached out for his phone the moment Tony and Sib had left. By the time they reached Aunt Helga's house, with its regulation red geraniums at the windows and its small, well-cared-for perimeter of lawn, she was expecting them. There was a man with her Tony had never seen before. Tall, shaved head, a gold hoop at his ear that made him look like a pirate.

Sibylle got out of the Mustang even before Tony had time to bring it to a complete halt.

"We have to talk. Now."

She went into the house without another word, followed by Aunt Helga, a big woman with curly hair.

The guy who looked like a pirate waited for Tony to approach and shook hands with him. "Oskar."

"Tony."

The owner of the Black Hat was about ten years older than Tony and, judging by his biceps, could have floored him with one hand tied behind his back if he had wanted to.

Or tried to, at least, Tony thought. There was an instant of tension between the two men.

Then Oskar stood aside. By the time Tony reached the kitchen of the house where both Erika and her daughter had grown up (childhood drawings by both were hanging on the walls), Sibylle had already started assailing her aunt with questions.

"Speak to your aunt with respect," Oskar boomed behind Tony.

"You've done nothing but lie to me. Both of you," Sibylle said. "For years."

"Is this what you've been telling your boyfriend? That we're liars?"

Boyfriend. Classic.

Tony tried not to rise to this. "If you had something to say to me you would have said it outside. Far from the eyes of the ladies, if you see what I mean. You don't really want to act the tough guy, you're just wasting time. So shut up."

Hearing him speak like this, Sibylle stared at him.

Oskar turned to the young woman. "In actual fact, I'm the one who owes you an explanation. But first I want you to know something."

"Spare me the bullshit about how you did it for my own good, OK?" Freddy whimpered.

As Oskar began his account, Aunt Helga filled a bowl with water and put it down in front of the St Bernard. Nothing for Tony. Again, classic.

Eighteen

1.

The air was crisp, filled with the scent of pine needles. And beer. Especially beer. More subtle but still pungent, the stench of exhaust fumes. And, in the background, the smell of urine.

Oskar parked his white Volkswagen Golf, leaving the hazard lights on. There was no need, since the car park was practically empty, but he did it to remind himself that he was there just for the time it would take to grab a burger and a beer.

He stretched his back and headed for the kiosk, the kind you can find on the side of any motorway. A *brattaro*, as they call it in Alto Adige. The word had a banal but logical etymology. What does a *brattaro* do? He cooks *brat*wurst, hamburgers and all that's bad for your health. And drowns it in gallons of Forst. Hence the word.

Oskar sat by the counter, even though the heat from the hotplate was almost unbearable. He ordered a hamburger and fries with ketchup and Tabasco.

He was halfway through his burger when he heard a familiar voice. Oskar was normally one to mind his own business, and the *brattari* of this land were, at every latitude, oases of peace and love where everybody had the sacrosanct right to mind his own business. Except that it was Erika's voice.

And Erika had run away from home months earlier. Five months, give or take. And neither Helga nor the police had managed to find her.

Some people in Kreuzwirt claimed she had killed herself. But Oskar didn't think so. He had known Erika since she was this high, and he was fond of her – fond enough to give her a part-time job at the Black Hat. He knew that she would never do anything like that. She champed at the bit, that was true. Like everybody her age. They said they wanted to leave, they made great plans, but in the end these big plans came up against reality. Life was good in Kreuzwirt. Big plans were for city kids, not for them.

Oskar left the burger on his plastic plate, wiped his hands and approached the dark-blue Panda. A young woman was leaning over, talking to someone inside.

"Erika?"

The young woman turned, surprised. The Panda took off and disappeared.

"Oskar, what are you doing here?"

She seemed tired.

There were dark rings under her eyes and she looked like she hadn't had a decent meal in several days. Oskar fought the impulse to hug her.

Were those bruises on her arms?

"Your aunt is worried."

Erika bowed her head.

"And so am I," he continued.

Erika did not reply.

"They've been looking for you in the crevices. With dogs."

"I'm not dead."

"You could have written."

"What for?"

"Are you ready to come home?"

"I'm not feeling very well," Erika said.

Only then did Oskar hug her. He took her to Aunt Helga, and Aunt Helga called the carabinieri. The following morning, Erika woke up vomiting. Aunt Helga immediately knew why.

Let's hope the child is healthy.

That's what she told Oskar on the phone, as she asked him to give them a lift to the hospital. The bruises were nothing. Erika was slightly dehydrated. Other than that, she was perfectly healthy.

And, yes, Spooky Erika was pregnant.

Nineteen

1.

"Which *brattaro*?" Sibylle said. "The one on the 621? On the K?"

"It was different back then."

A nasty smile appeared on the young woman's face. "Was my mother a whore?"

Oskar crossed his brawny arms. Aunt Helga kept fiddling with her apron. Sib slammed her fist on the table.

"Was she a junkie? Or both?"

"Please, Sibylle," Tony said. "Calm down."

She turned to him, index finger raised. "Don't you dare. Don't you bloody dare."

"You're not like her," Tony replied calmly. "What would you have done in their shoes?"

"I would have told the truth."

"The truth," Aunt Helga said, "is that no-one has any way of knowing. That place . . . Were there any prostitutes there? Yes. Were there drug dealers? Everybody knows that. But are we absolutely sure that Erika prostituted herself? She never said anything."

Sibylle gave a huff of contempt. "And you never asked. Isn't this how things in Kreuzwirt work?"

"She had money on her when she left," Oskar said. "Not much, but enough to manage for some time. She was only away for five months."

"One hundred and sixty-three days," Aunt Helga said. "I can't tell you what we went through."

"Try."

"Or what?" Oskar said impatiently. "You'll also run away from home? Go off with this . . ."

Walscher.

". . . guy," Oskar concluded.

Sib was like a river bursting its banks. "Was she doing it already before she ran away? Was she prostituting herself? Were the tarots just a front? The money – where did she get it?"

"Her waitress wages. Tips from the Black Hat. She read cards. People would—"

"Give her handouts?"

"You're being unfair," Oskar said. "Everybody liked Erika."

"Do you mind if I start to doubt that?"

"Did we lie to you?" Aunt Helga said. "Yes. For your sake. For Erika's. And I'd do it again a thousand times over. As God is my witness. That's what Erika would have wanted. You have no idea how much she loved you. She would have done anything to protect you."

"Do you have any idea how much I hate that bitch?"

Aunt Helga turned pale. It was as though Sib had slapped her. Even Oskar seemed to feel the blow.

"She was your *mother*," Helga said, outraged.

"I don't have a mother," Sib replied. "I've never had one. I have lies. A heap of lies. A mountain of steaming manure. Erika was loved by everybody? Everyone liked her? That old tune. And yet Erika ran away from home. Erika killed herself. Or is that also a lie?"

"What do you mean?" Oskar said.

"I mean that people who are loved don't kill themselves. They don't run away. And they don't go around begging."

Helga exploded. "I forbid you to say these things in front of me. Erika never begged anyone. People wanted her to read their tarots. I hated those damned things. But it was the only thing that unhinged sister of mine had managed to teach her, and Erika never left home without them. Do you know what it was like bringing her up? When they first entrusted her to me, Erika would sleep on the floor. She'd take the blankets and huddle under the bed. Make a nest, like an animal. It took me months to persuade her to use the mattress. She'd keep the window open even in the winter. And then at school . . . She'd . . ." Helga seemed suddenly deflated. "She didn't have many friends. It was hard to get close to her."

"I've already heard that, Aunt Helga. Spooky Erika. Erika's coming to get you."

"Nonsense. Nothing but nonsense."

"I was born amid what you call nonsense."

"It's just people being malicious."

"Malicious? In a place as welcoming as Kreuzwirt? Really?"

Oskar put a hand on Sibylle's shoulder. "You have questions. I can understand that. It's only fair. But the truth is that Erika took the answers with her when she decided to commit suicide."

Sibylle moved aside and stood up. "She did not commit suicide. She was murdered."

Helga crossed herself.

Sibylle bowed her head, so that her hair concealed her face. She was not crying, though.

Tony could see her expression. This young woman was pure determination. He would never have been able to bear this kind of pressure at the age of twenty. He tried putting himself in her shoes and shuddered. He would have lost his mind, while Sib was not only holding it together but calm enough to force the other two to walk through a minefield. Neither Aunt Helga nor Oskar realised it, but Sibylle was grilling them.

Oskar burst into a laugh as fake as it was uproarious. "That's utter nonsense."

"And who would have killed her?" Aunt Helga said. "Is this what you've got into your head? Sweet Jesus . . . Everybody—"

"Loved Erika. Yes. Of course. Even the ones who draw the humming-bird smile on the walls? And mess around with the ghost?"

"It's just their way of dealing with it," Oskar said. "Childish. Horrible. But it's just a way of coping with the trauma. People laugh so they don't cry."

"People," Tony replied, correcting him, "laugh at what frightens them."

"Bullshit."

Sibylle stared at Oskar. "Do you really believe what you're saying?"

"Erika's suicide changed many things. It's still an open wound."

"Like Betta?"

Oskar glared at her. "And like Gabriel. You do know about him, too, don't you?"

"I've heard how he ended up," Sibylle lied.

Tony made a mental note never to play poker with her.

"He was a brittle boy. He started keeping bad company. Last time I saw him—"

"Oskar—"

"No, Helga, Sibylle will find out for herself sooner or later. We told you that Gabriel didn't show at your mother's funeral. That wasn't a lie. But I did see him at Betta's, in 2005."

"So it's not true that Gabriel never set foot in Kreuzwirt again."

"He stood apart. Long hair, beard. Dark rings under his eyes. Full of ticks. He kept looking around, as though he was paranoid."

"Or a junkie."

"That's right."

"Betta's dead. Gabriel's a drug addict. Karin—"

"Karin had a business to run. She had to grow up fast."

"And what about Martin?"

"Leave Martin out of it. That poor boy."

"He also fell off the grid."

"He's *sick*."

Sib changed the subject. "2005. Betta's funeral. Gabriel."

Oskar shook his head. "I went up to him. I wanted to say hello, to ask about his parents. But as soon as he noticed me, he drove off in his van. I haven't seen him since."

Bang, Tony thought. Oskar had just stepped into a heap of shit.

He stared into his eyes. "What van?"

"I can't remember."

"Drug addicts don't have vans. Drug addicts *work for somebody* who has a van. Tell us about that van, Oskar. What colour was it? Did it have anything written on it? Like, for example, 'Carcano Plumbers' or 'Tony's Shit-Shovellers'?"

"Drop it. All of you, drop it."

"And why is that? If there really isn't anything to discover—"

"There's nothing whatsoever—"

"About Erika? Why prevent Sibylle from having a chat with one of her friends?"

Helga intervened. "Have you tried talking to Karin?"

"The van," Sib said to Oskar. "Tell us about the van."

Twenty

1.

Tony tried not to dwell on what he was about to do. It was eleven o'clock at night the day after what he had started to call "the Tuesday I made friends in Kreuzwirt": the look Oskar had given him as they parted was worth including in the encyclopaedia under "We'll meet again, sooner or later".

But that was yesterday.

Right now, Tony was being eaten alive by mosquitoes, past worrying, and there was nothing he could do except check his watch and wait.

It was called free will: something nasty was about to happen because he would make it happen. And he would do it because those were the rules.

That was why he had left Freddy in Bolzano.

Aunt Helga's final words to Sibylle had been, "You're chasing after ghosts, my girl." Tony had been thinking about them ever since. Flannery O'Connor, an author Tony adored, once wrote that "ghosts can be very fierce and instructive". A description that fit what Sibylle was going through like a glove. There was a chance her mother's ghost could destroy her life.

Tony had seen it happen before. His father had been a man tormented by ghosts. The ghost of the poverty he had fled when he emigrated to Alto Adige had made him even more wretched. The ghost of the xenophobia that had welcomed him had turned him into the worst possible xenophobe. And then there was the scariest ghost of all. Violence.

Was this the instructive ferocity Flannery O'Connor had written about? he wondered, sipping his by now lukewarm beer. Perhaps. Or perhaps not. What on earth did he know about what went through the mind of a great writer? He was just Sophie Kinsella in—

"Tony? Carcano? *Midnight and a Kiss*?" Tony looked up from his glass. He smiled.

2.

Baldini Industrial Laundries: the pale-blue logo on the side of the white Fiat Ducato that Gabriel had driven to Betta's funeral enjoyed, at least in certain circles, something of a reputation.

That morning, while Sibylle was working her shift at the bar, Tony had paid a call to the headquarters in Merano, in a large hangar on the motorway to Sinigo.

Signor Baldini, a man of sixty or so, with a pair of hockey-player shoulders that were barely contained by his striped shirt, had welcomed him with a handshake, complimented him on the Mustang, and invited him into his office.

"I gather you're looking for Gabriel Plank?"

"I understand he was working for you in 2005."

"Why are you looking for him?"

"It's a private matter," Tony said, having prepared on the way.

"Is it about money?"

"An uncle of his is dying. And he's very fond of the boy."

"I'm sorry. That he's ill, I mean. But is he honestly fond of that piece of shit?" Baldini said, incredulous.

"He never married and he has no children of his own. He often looked after Gabriel as a child. Then they lost touch. I'm a friend of the family. He's a good man and he'd like to have a chance to say goodbye to him. You know how it is."

"He may be disappointed. Gabriel isn't a child anymore. At least not *that* child."

"Where can I find him?"

Baldini swivelled in his chair, turning to face the only window in the office.

The courtyard outside was fraught with vans toing and froing and staff pushing jam-packed trolleys. Even though the building was sound-proofed, you could clearly hear the humming of the gigantic machinery at the heart of it.

A chimney emblazoned with the company logo was spewing white smoke into a cobalt-blue sky.

"In hell, for all I care. And don't tell me I'm not an understanding person, Signor Carcano. He used to steal. Gabriel's job was to collect and return bedding and various things from hotels belonging to the company's clients. This is in 2003, 2004. In 2004, he gets caught red-handed going through a guest's drawers. He begs me not to fire him, says he's going through a bad patch, and since it was a first offence, I sort it out for him. But I'm not stupid, right?"

"Once makes you a thief," Tony said, "but twice makes me a fool."

Baldini gave an abrupt nod. "Exactly. Anyway, no more hotels. Too much temptation. I move him to hospitals and restaurants. What can he possibly steal from a hospital? Catheters and antibiotics? Seriously. And from a restaurant? Plates? Cutlery?"

"And yet he starts up again . . ."

"If only. One fine day it turns out this thieving drug addict and a mate of his have been using *my* vans for *their* deliveries, if you see what I mean. The kind of stuff that could land them in prison for a long time. And me along with them."

"So Gabriel was a thief, a drug addict and a dealer?"

"He was also violent. He'd beat anybody up over a trifle. His nerves would snap."

"So you fired him. When was that? 2005?"

"In November. He laid his hands on me." Signor Baldini gave a little smile. "Or let's say he tried to."

Tony scratched his chin. "I know I'm taking up a lot of your time, but I made a promise, I have to find Gabriel."

Baldini sniffed and drummed on the desk with his squat fingers.

"Don't try and take me for a ride, Carcano. You're a terrible actor, if you don't mind my saying. I know who you are. It's not Plank you want. He's small fry. You want the other one, the one with the cowboy hat. His mate. You're with the police, aren't you?"

"Is he still dealing?"

Baldini's expression darkened. "I don't want to talk about this."

"But you know where I can find him."

Baldini massaged his gums with his index finger and studied him.

"You'd have my gratitude. And not just mine," Tony said.

When Baldini supplied the information, Tony was dumbfounded. Road 621. Route K. Gabriel's cowboy friend was the owner of the hamburger and fries stall where Oskar had found Erika in '98. What a small world, Tony thought on his way back to Bolzano, and Alto Adige even more so.

Except that he did not believe in coincidences. The shy boy in the Polaroid was becoming more interesting and sinister. He had to be tracked down. The problem was that drug-dealer cowboys tend not to give out information easily. At least not willingly. That was the rule, right?

3.

Concealed in the thicket, Sibylle felt like an idiot. For the millionth time.

When Tony had called to tell her about the guy from the laundry, she said she was ready to knock Gabriel's mate's teeth out. *Immediately.*

"Let me deal with this," Tony had begged. "Let's wait till there's no-one around, I'll tell him I'm an old friend of Gabriel's, hand him a couple of banknotes, maybe buy something that's not on the menu to persuade him I'm not a policeman – in other words, reassure him.

Then I'll ask him a few questions. I pay my bills by making up stories. It won't be hard for me to come up with a convincing yarn. Meanwhile, you'll be there to watch my back."

That was when something very strange had happened. Sibby Longstocking had followed his advice.

Except that Sibby Longstocking, holding her phone, a whole host of mosquitoes staking out her red blood cells, had caught a crab.

Tony's plan had flaws in it. *Tony* was flawed.

Watching his back meant crouching among pine needles, with the smell of exhaust fumes (and something even less pleasant) in her nostrils, ready to call the carabinieri just in case . . .

"It won't happen. I know how to deal with these people. It was a long time ago and I'm certainly not going to ask him how he supplements his income, alright? Better safe than sorry, though. You can never be too careful. Trust me, I'm from Shanghai."

"And what's that supposed to mean?" she had asked, confused.

Tony had given her a disarming smile. But he had not replied.

Now, however, the more Sibylle thought about it, the more convinced she grew that behind the sweet words, reassurances and smiles, Tony had concealed a Mr Macho fib. And this was raising Sibby Longstocking's blood pressure.

She detested Mr Machos.

That was the first important check in the Pillock Test to which Sibylle subjected the men who managed to pass the First Glance Exam. An examination which, Sib had to admit, Tony would have passed without too much difficulty. He reminded her of the leading actor in one of her favourite films, playing the part of an ex-hitman whose dog gets killed by some crazy Russians – a dog that also happens to be the last thing he has left to remind him of the love of his life. End result: he goes and murders them all. One memorable line from the film went, "I once saw him kill three men in a bar with a pencil. With a fucking pencil!"

Sibylle loved the romantic subtext, Sibby Longstocking the bangs and the explosions. To be honest, Keanu Reeves was sexier than Tony. But still

When Sibby Longstocking saw what was going on at Tony's table, she felt the irrepressible urge to use the sweaty phone she was clasping in her fist to call him and tell him to go to hell. What was he doing?

Flirting in front of everyone while she was being bled dry by mosquitoes?

4.

The Czech Republic, she said. The most striking thing about her was her smile. Halfway between astonished and shy. And though her clothes were anything but shy (Polianna would have said the woman might as well not have bothered getting dressed at all ...), she did look truly astonished.

After all, what were the odds of coming across your favourite writer at a *brattaro* along the 621-K? About the same, Tony thought – no less astounded than her – as finding an admirer here, complete with a book in her handbag. Her name was Irina, she was twenty-four, and Tony did not believe for a second what she said about being a tourist there by chance, because it was all too obvious what she did for a living.

Tony had always considered his best work to be *Two*, which had propelled him to the top of the bestseller lists overnight, but Irina's favourite was *Midnight and a Kiss*, the one she now asked him to autograph.

"You know, it helped me a lot," she said.

"Helped?"

"With my Italian."

Tony burst out laughing.

"And I don't agree with what they say. Sophie Kinsella is different. Cheeky. You can say cheeky, can't you?"

"A lot of my colleagues would envy your mastery of the language."

Irina blushed, pleased with the compliment. "You're not like that.

There's always a kind of wistfulness at the end of your books. A gentle sadness. Am I making sense?"

"And I've never worn a pair of lederhosen, at that."

The young woman laughed, throwing her head back, then lightly touched his hand. A couple of seconds too long. Luckily, after that caress (because it had not been a chance contact, not at all), Irina put the book back into her bag, planted a kiss a few centimetres from his cheek, and headed to the *brattaro* car park on those stilts she wore in lieu of heels.

Out of the corner of his eye, Tony watched her approach a grey Nissan that had flashed its lights at her, bend down, talk to someone, laugh, walk around the car and get in.

But not before wriggling her fingers at him.

The Nissan vanished.

What a *shitty* world.

Tony gulped the rest of his beer and waited for the hands of his watch to get a move on. Sixty seconds are too long for a minute, he thought.

Twenty-One

1.

Hannes Berger had not felt like the stallion he once was for a while. He had only two things left from those days: large memory gaps and the cowboy hat he had purchased at a George McAnthony concert, a memento from when the business had not yet gobbled him up and drugs were an extra ingredient to enhance the flavour of the main course – life – and not the other way round.

After three overdoses and a great deal of trouble with the police, Hannes had made a clean break with the stuff. Or almost. He sold it, because money is money, but only indulged in the occasional sniff himself now, whenever he picked up one of the prostitutes who used his kiosk as a meeting point. Hannes was no longer the stallion of once upon a time. At most, he was a mule. Full of aches and pains and in need of a holiday.

Just like the guy at the back, slumped on the table, his head in his arms and a glass in his hand. Only his second. How can you get so drunk on just two beers?

Hannes turned off the lights. "Hey, you, genius!"

The guy did not stir.

Hannes untied the apron from around his waist and threw it at the kitchen sink. Grumbling, he approached and, propping himself up with his right hand on the greasy tabletop, leaned towards the man and shook him with his left. Roughly. "Wake up, genius."

The genius was not in the least drunk. The genius was not asleep. The genius gave him a flavour of something the ex-stallion with the cowboy hat knew well but, unlike certain substances, did not miss in the least.

The hand placed on the table became a blinding explosion of pain.

2.

Shanghai rules: if you can't beat them, beat it. If you can't skedaddle, strike first and strike hard. Hurt them and make them understand you're not afraid of getting hurt.

In this particular case, use the beer glass to smash his hand. Hands are what turned ape into man. They allow man to grab things, build tools, bend matter, split the atom and have fun watching the result. They can do this because they are sensitive and efficient. In other words, they have a myriad nerve endings. Strike the hand. Strike hard. Strike first. And do not stop. Because if you stop, you are done for. Those were the rules.

The cowboy went crashing to the ground.

Tony did not give him time to breathe. Or scream. He grabbed him by the collar, saw his eyes turn glassy and slapped him with an open hand. "Who's the one sleeping, genius?"

He hit him again. And a third time.

"Gabriel Plank. Does the name ring any bells?"

"No. Who the fuck are you?"

Four.

"Don't you dare lie to me."

Five.

"My hand," the cowboy protested. "You've broken it."

"Concentrate on what I could do to your face."

"You're—"

Tony was about to strike him yet again, but stopped and huffed. A corollary to the rules: people are scared of crazy folk. Act crazy.

"Fuck it, come on. Don't make me sweat. It's too hot."

Tony dragged the cowboy to the kiosk. He administered a couple of kicks to his ribs, flung the kitchen door open and began to rummage around. It did not take him long to locate the stuff. A reasonable stash. Heroin, cocaine, grass. Coloured pills.

"I also used to work in a place like this, you know?" he said, pouring beer into a glass. "A bar, not a *brattaro*, but it wasn't all that different. My father didn't want to pay for my studies, so I did what I could. I enjoyed being a barman. I made excellent cocktails. Everybody said so."

The cowboy was trying to stand up.

Tony poured some of the stuff hidden behind the propane tank into the glass of beer. Powders and tablets. All together. He stirred the mixture with his finger, which he then wiped on his jeans.

"Fancy drinking to my health?"

Hannes stumbled and fell. "You're crazy, you're—"

Tony knocked him back down with a kick. He bent over him, holding the beer, ready to pour it into his mouth. "Gabriel Plank. Or you get to drink the lot."

"We were friends. Partners."

"Skip the part I already know. You used the industrial laundry vans to sell shit to kids."

"Put that crap away and I'll tell you everything, OK?"

"Talk."

"Gabriel was just a client to start with. He wanted sleeping pills. He said he suffered from nightmares. So I'd sell them to him. Back then it was easy to obtain that stuff. Pharmacists didn't make a fuss."

"When are we talking about here?"

"They'd already knocked down those fucking towers. But only just."

"So how did he go from regular customer to business partner?"

"He was clever. And he needed more stuff."

"Pills or heroin?"

"He'd moved on to pills to keep him awake. Amphetamines. Except that he was short of cash."

"Show me an addict who isn't."

"Except that he had a job. He somehow managed to juggle the shit I sold him and the laundry. And he had that van. At the time I knew a lot of people and I could have made heaps of money with that van."

"And they say Italians have no entrepreneurial spirit."

"The business continued to grow. Even after his boss caught him stealing." Despite the pain in his hand and the fear, the cowboy laughed. "That loudmouth moved Gabriel from hotels to hospitals and restaurants. Hospitals. Any idea how many people need a helping hand for their night shifts?"

"You tell me."

"My back is killing me and my hand hurts like hell."

"Move even one muscle and I'll show you what happens when I really lose my temper."

The cowboy raised his hand. It wasn't a hand anymore. Tony fought back his nausea.

Later.

Not now.

"Gabriel kept taking the stuff and you offloaded him? I heard he turned violent."

"Not with me. No more than anyone else. But he was becoming—"

"Unstable?"

"Totally out of his mind. You know, paranoid. And the more he took the worse he got. He became obsessed with tattoos and some kind of voodoo crap. Started saying some strange shit. Ethereal worlds and ethereal people."

"What does that mean?"

"How the fuck should I know? He said some places were more ethereal than others. That if you scratched the surface you'd find . . . I don't know. A crock of gold?" Hannes snapped, forgetting his pain for a moment. "He was crazy. Crazy and wasted, do you understand?"

Tony put the untouched glass on the ground. Still clutching the cowboy's throat with his right hand, he took a piece of paper from the back pocket of his jeans.

"Does this symbol mean anything to you?"

Hanner's eyes opened wide. "He had it tattooed on his chest. He called it the something smile. The bat smile. I can't remember. I was wasted, too, back then."

"The hummingbird smile. Why were you scared of Gabriel? Go on. Tell me. Did he beat you up? Did he go around armed?"

"You don't understand."

"I'm a fast learner."

"Once ... Gabriel and I went off to get hammered. Somewhere in the woods. I can't remember where. We'd been smoking. I could hardly stand up. There was a stream – that I do remember. And a lot of trees. Gabriel and I started to partake. LSD. And when the hallucinations started, the bastard gets up, carves that damned thing on a tree trunk and tells me a friend of his was killed right there, where we were tripping."

"By who?"

"By a ghost."

3.

When Sibylle saw Tony slam the beer glass on the hand of the guy with the cowboy hat, all she could do was stifle a cry and keep still. Frozen. At this distance, she couldn't make out what they were saying, but she had a clear view of Tony's face.

She remembered what she herself had thought the first time she saw him, that Sunday morning, amid the apple orchards. *One of those rubber-coated gadgets that look like toys at first sight but actually conceal metal innards.*

She was not wrong.

Tony dragged the man, who kept screaming with pain, through the dust, and Sibylle suddenly understood. She had been working at the Black Hat since she was legally allowed to – in other words, since her sixteenth birthday. She knew all about randy males. What she was witnessing was not Mr Macho-style aggression.

Tony was not showing off like a rutting stag, nor was he savouring the taste of blood, like some nutters she knew.

She realised Tony had not confined her to the bushes, phone in hand, so she could call for help. She *was* the help. The one in control of the situation. If she said stop, he would obey. So the real question was: *how far will you allow him to go?* As far as it will take to make the cowboy spit it all out. Even if it means sending him to hospital. He's just an arsehole who deals in shit.

However, the moment it looked like Tony was about to maul the cowboy's face, Sibylle decided that it was time to intervene.

But there was no rush.

4.

"What year was it?" Tony shouted.

"2005. Autumn."

"Is that when you ditched him? Did he tell you he killed her, so you shat your pants? Is that it? Did you argue? Did he run off?"

"No. That happened in 2007. He never said he killed anyone. Are you crazy?"

"Tell me what he said, then. In 2005. Exactly."

"We were stoned. I can't remember it word for word. Just that he said a female friend of his had died there. That she'd been murdered. By a ghost."

Tony shook him by the shoulders. "Did the name Erika ever come up? Erika Knapp?"

"Yes. He kept talking about her. That's why Leah dumped him. You're—"

"Who's Leah?"

"Skinny bird with no tits. Like your friend."

"Is everything OK here?" Sib said.

"If you don't mind, we're nearly done."

"There's still time before the carriage turns back into a pumpkin," Sib replied. "Who's Leah?"

"Leah was an addict. Gabriel used to make fun of her, he said Leah meant 'cow' in Hebrew. They were a couple back then. Then she got fed up and left him."

"Any idea where they are now?"

"Gabriel? Leah? I don't know. I swear, I—"

Tony let go of him.

He wiped his hands on the cowboy's shirt and slapped him again. He stood up.

"One final question. Answer me and you'll live a long and happy life and never see my face again."

Hannes spat out a wad of phlegm and blood.

"Erika . . ."

"Leah was jealous of her."

"Erika was dead."

"I know that and you know that and they knew it, too. But that cow was jealous of a dead woman. Can you believe that?"

Without turning his back on Hannes, Tony went to the mobile kitchen. "Erika," he said. "Do you remember her hanging around here in '98?"

"That's exactly what Gabriel kept asking me."

"And what did you say?"

"No."

Tony crouched by the electric ring. "What else did Gabriel say about Erika?"

"What are you doing?"

"Erika. Gabriel. Speak."

"He said that she was an ethereal person in an ethereal world. Something like that. I don't know what it meant. He said she died in a lake. That everybody said she'd killed herself but that it wasn't true. He said she'd been murdered."

"By who?"

"Sometimes he said Erika was killed by a ghost. Other times it was more like she *was* the ghost."

"The ghost?" Tony said, still fumbling around. "The same one that, according to Gabriel, killed Betta? The girl in the stream?"

"And then, once, he mentioned the Wanderer."

Sibylle frowned. "Who's the Wanderer?"

"Gabriel only mentioned him once. Shortly before he disappeared. He said it in a way that . . ." The cowboy shuddered.

"Without any explanation?"

"None."

"And you weren't curious?"

The dealer opened his eyes wide. "I was scared. Fuck. The way he said it, the stuff he talked about. That tattoo. He kept picking at it. With his fingernails. With razor blades. He cut it. He was . . ."

There was a hiss, followed by a smell the cowboy knew very well.

Tony smiled. "Can you smell gas?"

Twenty-Two

1.

The Mustang didn't get very far. Just a couple of bends and Tony pulled over, drenched in sweat, his hands visibly shaking.

"Sib, do you fancy driving?"

They swapped sides and continued. Kreuzwirt was asleep. Neither of them spoke. Neither of them looked up when the Mustang drove past Toad Villa. The light was on in the turret overlooking the peat bog. Someone was watching over the town.

When they reached Erika's house, Sib turned off the engine and got out, as did Tony.

"You're an arsehole," she said.

"I know."

"You could have warned me."

"True"

"Mr Macho."

"Is that really what you think of me?"

"I think you look like someone who's about to throw up. Mr Macho never throws up."

"No, he doesn't."

"And I think there's a lot you haven't told me. About yourself."

"And that makes me Mr Macho?"

"Mr Unknown, rather."

Tony slid into the driver's seat, wiped the sweat from his forehead.

He closed the door and rolled down the window. "Do you want to give up, Sib?"

"No."

Tony started the engine and put the car into reverse.

"Tony?" she called out. "This whole thing is one big mess, isn't it?"

For the first time since they had left the cowboy's kiosk, Tony looked into her eyes, and Sib could see the infinite sadness in his.

"Ghosts can be very fierce and instructive," he murmured. "Are you learning anything?"

Sib moved away from the car, waved and went to her front door. Tony waited for her to close it, reversed and drove out of the alley.

Erika, he thought.

The hummingbird smile. Up there, the Perkmans were watching everything. Aunt Helga, Oskar and their well-intended lies. Gabriel and the tattoo. Gabriel and Betta. Betta and Erika. Erika and Betta and Gabriel and Karin. Martin the mole. And Erika again. The symbol.

Tony stopped dead in the middle of nowhere. He barely had time to open the door.

Twenty-Three

1.

The alarm clock said 10 a.m. Freddy was not there to contaminate the air with his smelly breath, and somebody had stuffed Tony's head into one of Baldini's industrial washing machines. His phone was flashing. Too many new things all at once.

"Freddy?"

Tony strained to recognise his own voice.

He groped for the box of aspirin he kept on his bedside table. No water. He put a couple of tablets in his mouth and started to chew them. They tasted revolting.

"Freddy? Boy?"

Tony flung his legs out of bed and sat up. He felt dizzy. And had a vision.

In this vision, he was waking up, somehow managing not to fall, and was going to the only place Freddy could possibly be hiding so late in the morning. The balcony. Whining, begging for somebody to take him out. Because when you need to go then you need to go. Except that in the vision Tony found the St Bernard lying in his kennel. Dead. *Prepare yourself for the event that . . .*

"Freddy? Boy?"

He stood up without stumbling. The balcony was empty, the house silent.

Prepare yourself for the event that . . .

"No, no, no . . ."

The kennel was empty. Polianna had left a note stuck to the roof.

Since you were up till the small hours, I'm taking Freddy
for his walk, then going shopping. There are croissants on
the kitchen table.

Polianna

PS – M. called the landline.
Twice. Sounded upset.

2.

Twice on the landline and seven times on the mobile. Was there an impending nuclear disaster?

After a strong dose of coffee, a croissant and an ice-cold shower, Tony finally felt ready to face Polianna's *Post Scriptum*. Tony adored M., alias Mauro Giuliani, the agent who looked after his contracts around the world. In particular, he adored the elegant and never over-the-top way in which Giuliani managed to bleed publishing houses dry without losing any of his panache.

When he picked up the phone, he noticed that among the sea of emails from esoteric "experts" which, just to be conscientious, Tony quickly skimmed through (a woman assured him she could predict the future by reading your pupils, a Russian who wrote prose worthy of Tolstoy was asking for a tête-à-tête, a lunatic who claimed to be the reincarnation of Saint John the Baptist had had a vision concerning him and, finally, one of the aspiring writers who had not received any reply was showering him with insults), there was one from Mauro.

The subject line consisted of three simple exclamation marks. The message itself was just a link to *Giò's Pearls*, the "alternative information" website that had brought prestige to the former queen of crime news. Two hundred thousand views a day, was her proud boast. As if that was supposed to mean anything to Tony.

Tony's face was centre stage. Cut and pasted next to that of a young girl in a miniskirt. Very pretty, wearing tight leggings.

Irina.

Whoever had taken the picture was clearly very skilled. Irina and Tony seemed to be sharing the kind of kiss that would not have looked out of place on the cover of one of his novels. There were other photos, too: Tony sitting down, staring into space, his beer in full view. Irina and Tony talking. Irina touching his hand. Irina getting up from the table. Tony walking past the Nissan, hands in his pockets, as though searching for his keys. Irina leaning towards the Nissan. Irina getting into the Nissan.

Imagination running amok.

"Milani would be proud of you, Giò."

The headline, in very large letters, left no doubt as to who had inspired this article:

THE WRITER'S HIDDEN VICES

Does the bestselling **romance** novelist enjoy the good life and its dangerous **curves**?

So it would seem. And what if Antonio Carcano, better known as "Tony" (Antonio, Antonio, Antonio ... *tu vuò fà l'americano, ma sei nato in Itali!*), weren't just a **lover** of **very young** street girls, as our **exclusive** pictures show?

It's a well-known fact to anyone with antennae in the right place (like the editorial staff of *Giò's Pearls!*) that the spot where the author of **love & romance** novels was snapped while sharing languid **effusions** with I., a

prostitute by trade (who refused to reveal **her real age** to our correspondent!), is notorious for **drug-pushing**.

Could it be that the master of **rosy romances** doesn't turn his nose up at the odd line of **white**? Perhaps as a pick-me-up in between his (not just literary) **travails**?

It went on like this for another five thousand words. The next piece explained why dogs always stare at their masters while doing their business. Canine defecation apparently deserved no more than two thousand words and a hundred and fifty likes, while the article that concerned Tony had garnered two hundred and thirteen. No, two hundred and fourteen. Which made Tony the king of dejection.

His first impulse was to call Giovanna. Tell her exactly what he thought of her. And no doubt inspire her to write another article. What was the point?

He reread the article. Too many brackets. Too many exclamation marks. And those words in bold. His editor would have hated it. Still, he had to admit it was effective.

Quite a few people would believe this stuff. At the very least, two hundred and seventeen people had found it interesting. Giò had turned a series of grainy photos into irrefutable proof. By combining insinuations and outright lies, she had managed to depict him as a kind of . . . pervert? A drug addict? But why? To make him lose . . . credibility?

He gave a little laugh. Tony earned his crust writing *fiction*. Fantasy. Stories. His credibility rested exclusively on his ability to come up with plots that thrilled his readers. Full stop. Giò's ingenuity was amazing. And not just hers. Someone had paid her for this ambush. These photographs, these insinuations, were good news. The best he'd had in days.

Tony realised he was amused.

The Perkmans had moved a pawn. And if they had chosen to do so, it was because his and Sibylle's moves had bothered them. Ergo, they had something to hide. Something which, twenty years later, he and Sib could find. He could not wait to show her the article. But first and foremost, duty called.

His agent's number was among his Favourites. Along with Polianna's. *Eek.*

If Polianna read this stuff . . .

"Did you see it?"

"No good morning, hi, how are you?"

"It's been picked up by all the local papers. And it's all over Twitter. And Facebook."

"OK."

"Papers," his agent repeated. "Both Italian and German."

"Bullshit has no language barriers. That's enshrined in the Autonomy Statute. Do you want to know if any of it's true?"

"I know it's not true, for crying out loud. But I *am* interested in the repercussions. For your – or rather our – work."

Tony found himself staring at his own reflection in the bathroom mirror. He needed a shave. He returned to the bedroom and crunched down another couple of aspirins.

He would think about the razor another day.

"A bit of dirt never killed anyone."

He heard a sigh on the other end of the line.

"You underestimate the problem. We need to talk. Draft a press release. Think about whether it's worth suing. We're talking slander and libel. We must—"

"Never mind the lawsuit. And you can forget about a press release. I have a novel to write now and—"

"Tony?"

"Yes?"

"Are you bullshitting me?"

"Yes."

"Whose toes have you trodden on?"

Tony smiled. "Have a good day, Mauro."

106

Twenty-Four

1.

"That friend of yours."

"His name's Tony."

The reply came out harsh. Sib had not forgotten what happened at Aunt Helga's house.

"How much do you know about him?"

"Maybe you've forgotten, Oskar, but I am over eighteen."

Oskar threw up his hands. "Of course, but I'm worried about you. Being over eighteen doesn't mean you're wise."

"Are you trying to preach to me? Save your breath."

"No," Oskar said. "It's all water under the bridge. I told you, I understand what's going on in your head. It's your life. If you want to waste it chasing after ghosts—"

"I have a couple of toasted sandwiches to make."

"The toasted sandwiches can wait. Look at this."

Oskar showed her the screen of his smartphone. Tony's face. And Irina's.

"Are you sure you can trust this guy?" Oskar lingered on the image of Irina at the side of the road.

"Did Erika trust her friends?" Sibylle said, defiant.

"It says here that he's a—"

"I was there with him at the time. The article's bullshit." Sib turned to leave.

"I haven't finished."

"What do you want, Oskar?"

"Your aunt and I were talking last night. The Yamaha's a write-off. Helga and I thought we could help you buy a new one. A second-hand one, perhaps."

That hurt. A lot. Sibylle removed her apron and threw it on the floor. "I'm taking the morning off."

"You—"

"See you this afternoon."

Sib walked across the room, to the indifference of the customers, and emerged into the open air. It was hot. This dreadful summer would never end. Her hands were shaking. Were Oskar and Aunt Helga trying to buy her silence? Had it come to this? Breathe. Concentrate.

Priorities.

It was the third time that Karin Perkman had gone on the offensive. First Rudi, now Oskar and Aunt Helga's offer and that online rubbish about Tony. It could only be her behind the *Giò's Pearls* article, just like Sib had her to thank for the accident that had cost her the Yamaha. And more besides, no doubt.

She had trodden on the cat's tail and the cat was not happy about it.

She had not told Tony about Rudi. Perhaps she should have. But she knew what he would have thought. Damsel in distress, and so on. She wasn't having that.

She walked quickly, the phone glued to her ear.

"Have you seen it?" he said.

"Oskar was very worried."

"I'd like you to—"

"There's a bus to Bolzano in ten minutes. I'm heading for the stop right now."

How she missed her Enduro.

"About the article — how's your pride?"

Tony burst out laughing. "Crushed, as a matter of fact."

"Did you really think you had a fan?"

"I have more than enough, young lady."

"Don't call me that."

Sib caught sight of the bus and picked up her pace. The driver was folding his newspaper. She signalled for him to wait for her. With a great big smile.

The driver put the gear lever in neutral.

"Hurry up," Tony said. "There's someone I want you to meet."

"Who?"

"Have I ever mentioned the Prostate Boys?"

Twenty-Five

1.

Polianna had insisted, otherwise he would. never have dreamed of accepting the honour. Tony Carcano taking on the role of evening-class teacher at the University of the Third Age in Bolzano? It was unthinkable. Not for all the world. And yet . . .

Advanced creative writing workshop.

When Tony had pointed out that there was no workshop for beginners, the head of department had told him that no pensioner with an ounce of self-esteem would ever enrol in a beginners' course, in case they ended up with a pack of novices who nonetheless considered themselves the reincarnation of Shakespeare. Tony could see the logic in that.

The day before his first class, he had panicked. He had no idea how to teach writing because he had never thought about how it worked. An idea would come to him, which he would mull over for a while, letting his imagination go into overdrive until he felt it was time to sit at his keyboard. Words would then flow of their own accord. There was no instruction guide, no secret formula.

"Forget about the magic and focus on the basics," Polianna, practical as ever, had suggested.

The basics.

Grammar, spelling, common sense. Logic. Extensive reading. And a lot of practice.

In other words, if you want to write, then write.

Almost immediately, Tony had understood that the only real difficulty in teaching these classes of ten or fifteen sprightly senior citizens lay in remaining poker-faced when it came to reading their compositions out loud.

Pensioners convinced that their national service had prevented a third world war. Ladies with stiff, backcombed hair who wrote about valiant navy captains grappling with virgins (sometimes a local variant would pop up, with valiant Alpini captains grappling with modest young maidens), but who, deep down . . .

Inevitably, he had formed a curious bond with some of the course participants. They would all go for a beer after class. Have a natter. Like a club where he was the youngest member by far.

It was Claudio, a former railwayman with a ready repartee, who had started calling them the Prostate Boys. It was a good name for the club, except for one problem, as Tony had pointed out at the time – the group included a woman: "Tante" Frida, Aunt Frida. The only representative of the female sex (and the only one on the course whose mother tongue was German) to tag along with that gang of white-haired hooligans to the bar next to the university each week.

"What you don't understand, because you're very young and very stupid," Claudio had said with a crafty smile over a glass of red wine, "is that Tante Frida here has more balls than the rest of us old wrecks all put together. Including you."

And that had been the first and only time Tony had seen Tante Frida blush. Not only because nothing but expletives or criticism of anything whatsoever had ever come out of Claudio the railwayman's mouth, but because nobody among those present had raised any objection. Tante Frida really did have balls.

"In what sense?" Sibylle asked while they were waiting for the lights to turn green.

"Tante Frida has a sense of pacing, plot and characters," Tony said. "It's the language that lets her down. She writes detective stories. Can't get enough of them. But she writes like a burnt-out carabiniere."

"I'm not following you," Sib said, confused.

"What crime writer would use the sentence 'the bullet hit him in the shoulder, and he emitted a cry'?"

Sibylle burst out laughing.

Amused, Tony expanded. "I fear it's an occupational hazard. For decades, Tante Frida was the prosecutor's office's nightmare. To paraphrase Claudio the railwayman, otherwise known as 'the Choo-choo Poet', she was the ballsiest lawyer in Bolzano and the surrounding area. When she announced her retirement, there was more than one party around here, trust me. But do you know what I like most about that adorable old lady!"

"No idea."

Tony parked the Mustang in Via Duca d'Aosta, a short walk from the austere courthouse building.

"Tante Frida served six years in jail. Murder. A girl from the Puster Valley who married the wrong man. Tante Frida stabbed him with a knife three times. Then she just watched him die and called the carabinieri. The judge sentenced her to twenty years. In jail, Tante Frida began to study. For the eighth-grade exams, then the school certificate. But it wasn't enough. She enrolled for a degree in Law. Meanwhile, she read the paperwork from her own trial. It got her thinking. Until that moment, she'd felt she'd done something wrong and deserved to be punished. But things change in prison. Who was truly the guilty party? The man who had beaten her every night? The man who had raped her for years? Or the woman who, one fine day, decides she's had enough and sticks a knife in his belly?"

"So she appealed and turned murder into self-defence? Extraordinary."

"She did even better than that. She unearthed so many errors in the magistrate's work, and so many irregularities in the trial proceedings and the carabinieri's statements, that she left prison with a clean slate and fulsome apologies from the state. Wave hello, Sib."

On the third floor of the building, a woman was smiling down at them. Sibylle greeted her.

"If it's war the Perkmans are after . . ."

Twenty-Six

1.

Tante Frida's office was exactly as Sibylle had imagined it while they were waiting for the lift. Practical and full of natural light. Elegant. But carelessly so. Rather like the outfit Tante Frida was wearing.

Sibylle felt intimidated in her presence. Tony had told her that Tante Frida had balls. Not that she had this kind of charm.

It was not about her clothes or her bearing. Tante Frida oozed a singular energy. Wisdom, perhaps. Or perhaps the unflappable tranquillity of a woman who has been to hell and back and emerged unscathed.

She had a steely handshake and piercing blue eyes.

"And how is my favourite mutt?"

Freddy licked her hand.

Tante Frida led them to her desk. Stacks of files, a top-spec computer, not a single ounce of dust, and, on the floor beside it, a tabby cat. It stretched out, glancing at Sibylle, then at Freddy. Freddy stopped wagging his tail, dropped his head, squinted and glared. The cat yawned.

"Out, Severino," Tante Frida said. "Out."

The cat departed. The dog grumbled something or other after it. The cat did not rise to the provocation.

Tante Frida shut the door, sat down and put on a pair of bifocals which, rather than ageing her, somehow added allure. Sibylle became even more painfully aware of the shorts and the blouse tied above her belly button, which she had decided to wear that day in spite of the bruises after the fall from her motorbike.

"So, Tony, let's hear about this mess you've got yourself into," Tante Frida said.

2.

By the time Tony had finished explaining everything, a shark-like grin had appeared on Tante Frida's face. Aside from a tub full of piranhas, perhaps, there was nothing scarier than Tante Frida on the warpath. And the name Perkman had whetted her appetite.

"Do you know them?"

"My dear, I've known the Perkmans for ages. Everybody knows the Perkmans. Except for this young man over here. But, after all, who are the Perkmans? Timber, ski lifts, and, naturally, electronics. Shares here and there and everywhere. And since Karin took over the firm, they've invested heavily in renewables. That family have always had a thing about the environment. So that's the Perkmans. No big deal."

"Tante Frida, you're embarrassing me. And I know you're doing it on purpose."

"Then sue me. I wanted to show my young friend how . . . how your head can sometimes be in the clouds. In case she hadn't noticed."

"Have you ever met Karin?" Sibylle said. "Have you ever spoken to her?"

"A cold bitch. Like her father."

"Has she ever broken the law?"

Tante Frida put a hand to her mouth to conceal a condescending smile. "Ah, the innocence of youth. Everyone breaks the law. Only some end up behind bars while others have me as their lawyer. Like you, young lady."

"Me?"

"Yes, you. You've just become my new client. The client of the firm

I've left to my niece, Isabella, strictly speaking. But I think I have time for one last fling. Which means you're also lucky enough to be my *only* client. Any objections?"

"I can't—"

"The expenses are taken care of. This so-called novelist friend of yours has put up with my literary drivel for years. I'd say that pays off the debt more than amply."

Sibylle blushed. "I don't want – I – I can't accept."

Tante Frida took her hand in hers. "Shall I be brutally honest with you? Would you like that?"

"Yes, of course, but I won't change my mind."

"First of all, you're going to be my hobby. Since I retired, I've been so bored. Except for Wednesday nights. Tony, you know how much I enjoy your classes, don't you?" she added flirtatiously. "But it's June now – no classes till October – and my niece can manage perfectly well on her own. Am I making myself clear so far?"

"Yes."

"Secondly, and this is the crucial thing, you'll get nowhere without me."

"Tante Frida is right," Tony said. "She has experience with this kind of issue. So far we've been stumbling around like bulls in a china shop."

"Sibby Longstocking," Sib muttered, biting the tip of her thumb. "And they all fall down."

Tante Frida burst out laughing. "I like you more and more. And Tony forgot to mention that I have what he would call connections. In other words, it will be much easier for you to obtain information with my help. I might even save you from doing something very silly and very dangerous."

"I can't," Sib said.

Tante Frida removed her glasses. Her face softened. "Put your pride away. If you're serious about going all the way, if you really want to dig until you get to the truth, then you need to put your pride to one side. Pride should be measured out with care. Save it for the real battles. Not for minor details like this."

"I . . ." Sib twisted a lock of hair around her fingers. "It's not a minor detail. For you . . . for both of you, money is a detail. But for me it's – it's money. Do you understand? And pride . . ."

Tante Frida's tone was at once brutal and gentle.

"Pride is like the knife I rammed into my late husband's stomach. A double-edged sword. It can become a prison. Like the prison that prevented me from running away from that piece of shit. Because I had been taught that the most a woman could aspire to was to be a wife – good, meek, always smiling. Even when she's treated like a punchbag. It's the kind of pride one should steer clear of." There was a twinkle in Tante Frida's eye. "Or you can use it to say 'enough!'. Now, do we have a deal?"

"Thank you, signora."

The lawyer clapped her hands.

"As a new client, you're entitled to call me Tante Frida. I'll ask around. Call in some favours. I'll let you know what I find out. Personally, I think you're chasing after ghosts, but I must admit that what you've told me does arouse some suspicion, so do be careful and . . . Tony? Where do you think you're going?"

Tony was in the process of standing up. He froze, perplexed. "I thought we'd finished."

"Don't we want to discuss the small matter of libel?"

"What libel?"

"Ah, so you really are a coke-head pervert?"

Tony shook his head. "The Perkmans are powerful, yes. And they're clearly behind Giò's scoop. We're all agreed on that, aren't we?"

Tante Frida simply nodded.

"Yes," Sibylle said. "We've trodden on the cat's tail."

"And I'm also certain," Tony concluded, "that Polianna will burst a blood vessel when she sees that picture in a local newspaper. Local, you understand?"

Tony studied the women as though expecting a reaction. They stared back, perplexed. "No serious journalist would ever take this rubbish seriously," he added.

"I wouldn't be so sure."

"The Perkmans are powerful, of course, but just here. In Alto Adige. I . . ." Tony stammered, embarrassed. "I mean . . ."

At last Sibylle understood. She smiled. "You have readers all over the world."

Tony shrugged. "If this is the worst the Perkmans can do to me . . ."

Tante Frida removed her glasses and looked at him. "Pray it is, Tony. Pray it is."

Twenty-Seven

1.

The St Bernard didn't let the lead go slack for a single moment of the journey.

There were bushes, flowers, tufts of grass, tree trunks, mushrooms and pebbles to be sniffed, catalogued and watered, as though Freddy was preparing for a Prostate Boys entrance exam.

Tony would happily have let him romp about freely if it weren't for what Wolfie had told him about the foxes in the area. In the Bolzano region, rabies was considered extinct, so Freddy had not been vaccinated. "Sorry, old boy. But we must be grateful for small mercies."

2.

Hannes's junkie fantasies, all that talk of ethereal worlds, ghosts and monsters under the bed had left Sibylle feeling uneasy. Tony realised this from the way she asked him once too often what it all meant. So he felt obliged to tell her about Ricky Riccardo. "Ricky Riccardo is a guy from Shanghai. One of the good ones. He keeps away from bad company and isn't afraid of spending his time with books. He toes the line. On graduation day, he decides to bend the rules and treat himself to a solitary grad ball. Ricky Riccardo is a fan of Castaneda's, so he gets himself some peyote for a celebration. You know what that is?"

"I've read Ginsberg."

"I don't know much about Ginsberg, but what I do know is that ever since that evening Ricky Riccardo has been standing out on his balcony – every day, at all hours, come rain or shine – staring into space and stroking his cat. A cat that died years ago. 'Bye, bye, Ricky Riccardo.'"

"Point taken."

Sib never mentioned ethereal worlds or ethereal people again. Instead, when he voiced his intention of taking a stroll through the woods to find the spot where Gabriel had carved the hummingbird smile, she urged him (again and again, until Tony was flattered by her excessive concern) to be careful.

"You could get lost."

Tony had shown her a map of the area. "I just want to check if my shit detector still works."

"A map is one thing, the land another," Sibylle had insisted. "And what the hell is a shit detector, anyway?"

Tony had smiled. "Hemingway. According to him every good writer has an inbuilt shit detector that starts flashing whenever it gets a whiff of it. Apart from when Hannes came out with that Ricky Riccardo-style stuff, my shit detector has kept quiet. Which means that, in the clearing where Wolfie found Betta, there should be a tree with the hummingbird smile carved in the bark."

"You've just won the prize for the most absurd decision of the year," Sibylle had declared. "And why do I get the feeling you're hiding something from me?"

"Because you're as intelligent as you are sexy." Tony had managed at once to make her blush and to avoid having to give her a straight answer.

It only took a couple of hours for Tony's good mood to go up in smoke. At that point he began to curse himself, Hannes the cowboy and Ernest Hemingway.

When they reached the stream, Freddy, a city dog through and through, opened his eyes wide and began to drink avidly, amazed to find such bounty left unattended.

Tony, on the other hand, was exhausted. The excess greenery that had awakened Freddy's senses was stifling him. Firs, pines, ash trees, brambles. Nothing but green, accompanied by an orchestra of insects that left his temples throbbing.

A sudden macabre thought made him grit his teeth: Freddy was performing his noisy ablutions in the same water in which Betta and – unless the map was lying – Erika had drowned. The stream flowed right out of the Kreuzwirt lake, where Sib's mother had died.

Tony swore and shook off his rucksack. He tied Freddy's lead to a fir tree a few steps away from the water so that the St Bernard could carry on refreshing himself, and turned his attention to the task he had trekked all this way to carry out.

In truth, Sybille wasn't alone in feeling uncomfortable about the fantasies of Hannes the cowboy. However illogical his plan to find the clearing where Betta had erected her tent might prove, he had an inkling that tracing the carved hummingbird smile with his fingertips would help him sweep away the sense of mystical woo-woo that Hannes had bestowed on him. Maybe he would discover something that would give the investigation a push forward. He had always found dreaming with his eyes open to be the most effective way of seeing things from a fresh perspective.

Macabre thoughts, fatigue and the stifling heat aside, this was not a bad spot. The stream, the clearing, surrounded by ferns over a metre tall, the compact wall of trees, a luxuriant bush, an anthill. And, barely visible, a second, hidden path. Tony frowned. He checked. This path was not marked. Sibylle was right. *A map is one thing, the land another.*

He put the map down and pictured Betta coming down this hidden path. He imagined Gabriel and Hannes following in her footsteps years later, staggering along with nothing like the young woman's confident stride. Then again, had she not died with an astronomical level of alcohol in her blood? But, he reminded himself, shifting a stone with the tip of his boot, Betta had managed to put up a tent, so she couldn't have been drunk on arrival. Unlike the two junkies.

Tony had a vision of Betta listening to the same rustling of foliage he could hear now. Breathing the same faintly sharp air. He imagined her starting to drink. And, for a moment, he felt his imagination beginning to take flight. But no. Hard as he tried, he could conjure nothing but an image of the young woman sitting on the ground, knocking back vodka. There was no Eureka moment. No revelatory details revealed themselves in a flash of blinding light. That was not how it worked, in any case.

Like all writers, Tony knew well that he was not the true craftsman of the stories that earned him advances, awards and adulation. They had a life of their own – all he did was jot them down. There was no "ready, steady, go" formula to get him started. And there, in the clearing, along with a couple of billion insects, a few million pine needles and a large St Bernard who was enjoying life to the fullest, stood a writer with a large portion of egg on his face.

It's the heat, he told himself.

He kneeled by the stream, took a breath, closed his eyes and plunged his head into the water. Heaven must be very much like this feeling. When he got back up, Tony realised two things. Firstly: even if he grew a Hells Angels-length beard and managed to get into a fight with Joyce – God rest his soul – he would never approach the great wisdom of old Hemingway. Secondly: his shit detector was working just fine. Hannes the cowboy had not lied.

The tree on which Gabriel had carved the hummingbird smile was right in front of him, just across the stream. The symbol was still visible after all these years.

Tony drew closer.

It looks like a serpent's head, Sib had said the first time he had seen the hummingbird smile. He was not all that sure he agreed anymore. Now, it looked to him like some kind of flint arrowhead, or, better still, a danger sign written in an alien language. The grooves were deep: two parallel vertical lines, two more lines at the bottom and two horizontal notches immediately above, like a pair of eyes. Dead eyes. Why could he not stop these unhealthy thoughts? It had been a terrible idea to come all the way out here alone. He was spooking himself. Maybe it was time to—

A sound, sudden and terrible, chilled the blood in his veins and at the same time filled him with disbelief. It upset him. Could Freddy really growl like that?

4.

Growling was the correct but imprecise definition. Freddy was growling, whining, quivering and urinating all at the same time, his muzzle pointing towards the bush next to the anthill. His eyes were focused, his muscles tense.

"What's the matter, boy?"

Freddy did not even spare him a glance. The bush. Nothing else existed for the St Bernard.

Tony broke off a branch, judging it to be long enough. He crossed the stream and, leaning over as far as he could, brushed it against the foliage of the bush, shaking it.

Nothing happened. He tried again, harder, with the same result. There was nothing there but twigs, leaves and ants busy doing whatever it is ants normally get up to in the woods. Even so, Tony felt on edge.

He took a few steps forward, and when he was just a couple of metres short of it a fox emerged from the bush. Tony darted back with a cry. The fox bared its sharp teeth, covered in froth. It had yellow eyes, like the devil. Saliva was running down the sides of its muzzle as it jerked its head erratically.

Rabies, Tony thought.

"Erika!" the fox croaked. "*Erika!*"

Ready, steady, *go*.

It only lasted a few seconds but it was a "ready, steady, go" Tony would never forget. The fox's eyes became chasms overflowing with darkness. A darkness that *bent* the world. Around its body, the ground sank like a taut sheet on which someone had placed a bowling ball.

Tony staggered.

The panting in his ears was not his, not even that of the fox, but the sound of backwash – backwash coming from the animal's eyes. There was an ocean of ink inside them. The ground *tilted*.

The bowling ball grew heavier. Tony stumbled but did not lose his balance.

A part of Tony, the part from Shanghai, was telling him to go to Freddy, who kept growling, calm him down and get out of there.

Another part, the typist part, could not help but take note: a shape was emerging from the ocean of ink – Erika, wearing the mud-soiled Maturaball dress. The typist part of Tony knew that Erika was there.

This was an ethereal place. Ethereal places were system errors. Wormholes through which people like him would sneak in to *steal* plots. The time had come to settle scores. Erika had emerged from one of these wormholes to make him pay.

Erika's coming to get you.

You're on Route K, my boy. Remember. K.

Freddy howled and Tony abruptly returned to reality. He hurled the branch at the fox. And missed. The animal retreated, glaring at him with resentment.

It coughed. "Krrrka! Ka! Krrrka!"

Not *Erika*.

"Krrrka! Ka! Ka!"

Its body went into a terrible spasm. Only the whites of its eyes were showing. Its open jaws snapped at the air. Freddy growled again.

Tony turned his back on the fox.

"Sing with me, Freddy." Tony began slapping his thigh, beating time. "Remember, Freddy? 'Another One Bites the Dust'. Freddie Mercury used to make thunderclaps disappear, remember?"

For a moment it seemed to work. Freddy stopped thrashing about. His lead sagged. There was contact between the eyes of the man and those of the dog. Both terrified.

"We like Freddie Mercury, don't we? Freddie Mercury, not Freddy Krueger," Tony muttered, realising he was wary of approaching the St Bernard.

Was he afraid? Afraid of Freddy? What the hell was happening? *Whatever happens to ethereal people when they end up in ethereal places*, Tony told himself. He reached out to stroke the dog's muzzle. Freddy sniffed the tips of his fingers.

"Good boy, Freddy. Good boy. We're going now, now—"

"Krrrka! Krrrka! KA! KA!"

The fox was closing in.

Freddy started bawling again. Tony gripped his jaw with his right hand. "Pum. Pum. Pum. Remember the bass line, Freddy?"

In his pocket, along with his phone, Tony had one of those silly multi-purpose knives favoured by part-time mountain dwellers. Without letting go of Freddy's muzzle, he opened the knife with his teeth, cutting his lip in the process. The fox grew agitated at the smell of blood.

"Ka! Ka! Krrrka!"

Tony tried to ignore it.

"There is no Milwaukee protocol for animals, Freddy, OK? So think about Freddie Mercury. The song. The good magic. I'm here with you, OK? No need to be scared."

The fox was trembling. Drooling. Screaming its terrible "Krrrka! Ka! Kkkaaaa!"

If the fox were to bite Freddy . . .

Tony let go of the muzzle and twisted the lead around his right hand, ignoring the pain caused by the strap cutting into his flesh. With his left, he raised the knife to the sky and prepared to strike. The blade flashed, slicing through the lead.

The moment Freddy felt the tension relent, he gathered all his energy to pounce. Tony dug his heels into the ground and pulled on what was left of the lead with all his strength. A hundred and ten kilos of pure killing instinct strained to tear at the rabid fox.

The muscles in Tony's shoulder tensed up in spasms, the pain almost unbearable. He was propelled forward. He was afraid he wouldn't be able to hold on for much longer. The collar did its job, Freddy ran out of breath and backed down. Tony tightened his grip, ready for another jolt.

There was no need. The fox had vanished.

Freddy howled.

Twenty-Eight

1.

The Black Hat was at its busiest between one and two. Farmhands, craftsmen and office workers from Kreuzwirt and Sand in Taufers would walk in complaining about the heat, cracking jokes about Oskar's broken air conditioning, ravenous and in a rush. The "Can you make me a quick toasted sandwich?" hour.

Sib usually dreaded it. She found it dull and stressful. Today, however, she was thankful not to have to exchange small talk with the customers.

Tante Frida had told her to put her pride aside, and it was good advice. Nine times out of ten it was pride that got Sibby Longstocking into trouble. However, swallowing her pride came at a cost: a big lump in her throat.

Before the June 8 business and the "I'm-coming-to-get-you-Erika" business, Sibylle had been focused on her plan. To save enough money for university, work her socks off and make her lifelong dream come true – designing motorbikes.

She had all the necessary paperwork. Even the talent, according to some of her former teachers. And, naturally, doubts. Engineering, sure, but where? If she chose Trento, would her German accent present an obstacle or lend her exotic appeal? Or Innsbruck: would she be treated like any other student, or would the dialect inflection that came out whenever she felt under pressure mark her out as a peasant freshly down from the mountains? Details, details . . . Sibylle was sure that this was her path. She had realised it when, at the age of eleven, she had got her hands on the scooter of one of the Kreuzwirt boys. By fifteen she was already an ace at tuning her schoolmates' mopeds. At sixteen, she fell in love with the Yamaha. But knowing it and making it happen were two different things. Age was not the problem. Sib was capable of exercising patience when she set her heart on something. Two years would go by quickly. The problem was money. Where could she get it?

Aunt Helga had come to her aid. Oskar had a vacancy for a waitress. Part-time. It was the ideal gig. But if her school grades dropped, Oskar would fire her. Sibylle was one step closer to achieving her dream.

It had been hard at first, especially in the evenings, when the perverts at the Black Hat could be relied on to let their hands wander. Keeping the arsehole slasher in full view had helped her get used to her surroundings. Her wages and tips had allowed her to buy the Yamaha and begin to amass her university fund.

Sib hadn't given much thought to her job at the Black Hat or what had prompted Oskar to give it to her. Aunt Helga and Oskar loved her.

What else was there to say?

Sib never considered that she had taken Erika's place. A part-time waitress in the same bar. Above all, it had never occurred to Sibylle that Helga and Oskar might be giving her handouts. Swallow your pride, Tante Frida had said.

But who said that she had to enjoy it?

"Hey, Niki."

Only one person called her that – Niki, as in Niki Lauda: Willy Daum. Lucky Willy. Sixty-nine years old and always exhibiting a mouthful of dentures. Always smiling. And why not? After all, Willy was the lucky one.

Former postman, former rising star of motocross, occasional mechanic, keen drinker of orange juice (never seen drinking anything but freshly squeezed orange juice) and, in his spare time, used motorcycle salesman to blonde girls. It was Willy who had obtained the Yamaha for her at half the listed price, taught her a few tricks to transform it into a fire-spitting dragon and showed her how to ride it properly. Sib had not yet thanked him for the tip about bouncing like a spring if she came off her bike.

"The usual?"

Willy beckoned her over. And since Willy was the least dangerous person in the universe, Sib obeyed.

Twenty-Nine

1.

A million years later, the dog and his owner emerged from the thicket. Scratched by briars, bruised, paws (Freddy's) and the rest (Tony) covered in cuts.

Tony felt the urge to kneel and kiss the tarmac. But he'd had enough madness for one day. Instead, he hugged the St Bernard.

If anybody walked past and spotted him on his knees, clinging to the dog's neck, his face buried in the animal's filthy coat, and considered his attitude somewhat unorthodox, well, they could go fuck themselves.

Freddy had wanted to save his life. The St Bernard had been prepared to leap on the rabid fox to do so. Because Freddy was a stupid lump with a brain the size of a canary's. A stupid, stupid dog who did not know that if the fox had bitten that idiot owner of his, he would have faced, at worst, a race to Emergency and a ridiculously long needle stuck into his backside. But if the fox had bitten Freddy . . .

"OK. It's over." Tony sighed and stood up. "And we've still got some pride left, right?"

He looked around. He no longer had any idea of where they were. The map, the knife, his T-shirt and his rucksack were still by the stream. He checked his pockets. Keys, wallet. The screen of his phone was cracked.

Tony calculated that the strip of tarmac under his feet was bound to be Route K (*don't forget, K is dangerous*) because they had not trekked far enough to be clear of the valley. The Mustang was parked in a long-stay lay-by along the 621-K, so it was just a matter of finding it and putting an end to this dreadful day. But was the lay-by to his right or his left?

"Tony says left. Does Freddy have any objection?"

2.

"I heard you had some trouble."

News certainly spread like wildfire.

"Rudi cut me off. It sent me flying but I'm still in one piece."

"He said it was you who suddenly came at him. Says he wants to report you."

"He won't."

"He said he would."

"And you believe him?"

Willy shrugged. "How many bruises?"

"A couple. But the bike is a write-off."

"So I heard."

"From Oskar?"

"From your aunt."

"It's just a bike."

Willy smiled. "Don't ever say such things in my presence."

Willy's motocross career had ended in 1972. But not on the track. Willy never had an accident while racing. In July that year, Willy was trying out his cousin Manfred's Moto Guzzi down the 621-K when he was betrayed by an oil stain. He broke his pelvis and cracked his head. The doctor said it was a miracle he survived. Hence Lucky Willy.

He had a thick skull, but the pelvis fracture had not healed as expected. Willy had a lopsided walk, especially when it looked like rain. A real shame. Without that mishap, Lucky Willy would have been a great motorbike pilot.

"Sorry," Sib said. "I've got a few problems. I'm – I'm on edge."

The Black Hat was empty apart from Oskar, half asleep behind the counter, and a couple of pensioners absorbed in reading *Dolomiten*, the local paper. Tony was on page seventeen, under the headline "Media Star". It was a far less scathing article than the one on Giò's website. No doubt for fear of lawyers, Sib thought, not without pleasure.

"And there's more on the way." Willy indicated the poster of Jo Zorn by the door. The country singer, holding the guitar Johnny Cash-style, was staring at the horizon. "Ever heard one of his songs?"

"A couple."

"Jo Zorn was one step away from becoming the kind of star who goes on television and fills stadiums. He died before making it. A local boy. Josef Zorn, Jo to everyone. I saw him strumming his guitar when he was this high. He called it 'the devil's bride'. And you know what they say, if you dice with the devil—"

Sib pulled away.

Willy smiled at her with infinite gentleness. "At least Jo died before getting old. He spared himself a lot of trouble. I'm just Lucky Willy, the one who could have made it but instead—"

"What are you trying to tell me?"

"I have fully functioning eyes and ears. Ears especially. And especially when someone answers the phone and starts to whisper."

Thirty

1.

It turned out they had been walking in the right direction. Half an hour later, Tony glimpsed the Mustang's chromium plating glittering behind a thicket. But, no, luck was not on their side yet.

While Tony was busy dancing the tango with Miss Rabies, some joker had been getting his kicks. Flat tyres, front and back, and a nice new inscription etched with something sharp – a knife or a key – on the bonnet.

Tony opened the door. Freddy curled up on the back seat and immediately fell asleep. Tony wound down the window to let the air circulate and shut the door. Then he examined the engraving on the bonnet.

SUKKS

Not sucks. *Sukks.*

A classic example of creative spelling.

Tony let out something akin to a sob. Despite its sorry state, his phone was still working. He called the breakdown service, gave his location, repeated it a couple of times since the connection was very poor, and said goodbye just as the mobile died. *Sukk this.* And, at that moment, all his accumulated tension exploded. Tony burst into the kind of laughter that gets you into trouble with teachers at school: uncontrollable and uncompromising.

He chuckled. "We're following a Mustang, Sukks model, on Route 66, Sheriff."

Tears began to streak down his face. There was no way to stop. His stomach hurt. But he still could not stop.

". . . remarkable performance in *Bullitt* by Steve McSukks."

And, of course . . .

Tony raised his arms to the sky and, imitating the voice of the announcer at PalaOnda, the indoor sports arena in Bolzano where he would go to cheer on the home team, yelled at the top of his lungs, "All rise for Tooony SUKKS Caaaaarcanooo!"

He could almost hear the crowd of supporters chanting "Su! Ukks! Su! Ukks!" as he suddenly realised his bladder was about to burst. It's a fucking hysterical reaction. That damned fox, Freddy and . . . Another image came to his mind. The culture pages in *La Repubblica* reviewing his book with a singular, blaring and thunderous:

SUKKS

His laughter forced him to double over, clutching his stomach. I'm about to wet myself, he thought. If I don't stop I'm going to Pollock my trousers and Polianna—

"Signore?"

Tony raised his hand. "Just   just a minute . . ."

He could not catch his breath.

"Are you alright? Is everything OK?"

Tony wasn't so much laughing now as braying. "I'm fine," he stuttered, teetering on the brink of a coughing fit. "Fine."

He forced himself to stand upright by clinging to his car.

Praying to the god who watched over idiotic writers, he glanced at the inseam of his trousers. There was no stain. Hemingway would have been proud of him. Hemingway, the lion-slaying, womanising author of the immortal masterpiece, *For Whom the Bell Sukks* . . .

Tony turned his final laugh into another spasm of coughs and splutters.

"Do you need help?"

"I've called the breakdown van. But thanks for stopping."

Tony held out his hand. The Good Samaritan had a strong handshake. He smiled. There was a gap between his front teeth and he drove a red pickup.

Thirty-One

1.

As indicated by the sign outside, the Black Hat was also a dance hall. There was a stage for a band at the back of the room and live music every Friday. The rest of the week, however, the Black Hat was simply a bar. But God help anyone who told Oskar this.

God help anybody who called what he described as the office a cupboard. A few square metres carved out between the (no less shabby) performers' dressing rooms and the storeroom (almost as large as the bar, for some reason). It always made Sibylle feel claustrophobic. There wasn't even a window. Just a desk with a computer, a poster of Hank Williams and a chair.

It was never a good sign when Oskar asked you to join him there. The same went for finding him amid the account books, pen in hand, with that contrite look on his face.

Don't you dare. Don't you dare cry. Don't give him the satisfaction.

"Listen." His voice trembled. But only a little. "This hurts me more than you. You've seen the accounts yourself. I've done the maths three times. Unfortunately . . ."

Sib darted him a look that silenced him.

"Unfortunately . . ."

Oskar bent his head without finishing.

Sib had no trouble doing it for him.

. . . *Unfortunately, you went to see Lehrerin Rosa. You spoke to Hannes the cowboy. Unfortunately, you ask too many questions. You can't just accept that a body was fished out of the lake. You didn't accept the new Yamaha. That was a real slap in the face. You should have taken it.*

You should have taken it.

She wished she could snatch the account books and hurl them to the floor. Grab the computer and smash it into Oskar's face. Scream out all her contempt. But that would achieve nothing except make her burst into tears. And she would not give him the satisfaction. Not him, nor Karin Perkman.

"Unfortunately, I've trodden on the cat's tail," was all she said.

Thirty-Two

1.

"Four flat tyres. One's bad luck. Two's fate, but four is—"

"Vandalism."

"Bastards."

The stranger adjusted his beret. He was about one metre eighty tall, with broad shoulders and the look of a red meat eater who earned a living in the open air. The gap between his teeth and the dimple in his chin gave him the look of a man who could be good fun when the mood took him. "I agree, Signor . . ."

"Rudi. My name is Rudi Brugger."

Where had Tony heard that name before?

"Did you call the carabinieri? This car must be worth a fortune. Is it vintage?"

"That's right."

Rudi whistled, impressed. "It's a nice little number. You know, you look like someone famous. What did you say your name was?"

"Carcano. Tony."

Rudi took half a step back, a graceful, almost balletic movement. "You're kidding! The writer? The one from Bolzano?"

Mauro, his agent, had said that 92 per cent of his readers were women. Tony had never trusted that statistic. When E. L. James made her triumphant entrance into the world of publishing, a lot of men out there had discovered they enjoyed reading about broken hearts and

S & M liaisons in office corners. Still, it was hard to imagine this hulk of a man tackling *Midnight and a Kiss* or *The Moth Huntress* . . .

"In flesh and blood. Call me Tony, alright?"

Rudi gave him a slap on the shoulder. To the delight of Tony's bruises and scratches. "It would be an honour."

Rudi climbed into the red pickup, and came back out waving a copy of *Two*, Tony's first book. He looked so happy that for a moment Tony found himself returning to the theory of ethereal worlds.

An hour ago, in the forest, he'd come face to face with a jawful of frothing, foaming teeth (*Route Krrrka! Ka!*), and here he was now in a lay-by with his vandalised Mustang and an unlikely fan who was gleefully showing him a copy of his novel. He could only imagine that he'd somehow landed slap bang in the Wonderful World of Oz.

"*Two*'s my favourite," Rudi said. "*The Happy Gypsy* is not bad, maybe a bit long. And *Midnight* is really good. As a matter of fact, as far as I'm concerned, *Midnight* is a close second after this one. The policeman who seems like a bastard at first but then turns out to be a wonderful single father. What's the little girl's name? The one obsessed with matching the colours of the rainbow to her father's feelings? Daddy's red. Daddy's—"

"Lara."

"That's right – Lara! Such a sweetie. And then she goes against her family's wishes just so she can—" Rudi stopped. "Sorry. I'm a big fan."

"So I see."

"Still, *Two*'s the best. Hands down. You don't mind me saying that?"

"No, I'm flattered."

"Can I be cheeky and ask you a question?"

"Of course."

"Even if it's kind of personal?"

"Try me."

Rudi's expression suddenly altered. He no longer looked like a friendly carnivore who tells jokes to cheer you up. He just looked like a carnivore full stop. "How do you sleep at night, Mr Writer?"

"Excuse me?"

Rudi began to read. "'He opened up in his body and in his heart. His mind became a throb of pleasure as he shyly penetrated her, and at the same time . . .'"

Rudi had not opened the book at a random page. There was a bookmark and the passage he was reading out was underlined. Who would take the trouble of highlighting passages in one of his novels? It was not Rudi's carnivorous expression that frightened Tony. What really scared him was the bookmark and the underlining.

"I got it from the Sand in Taufers library. The public library, you understand, Mr Writer? Now if it was just you and me, we're adults, right? Talking about where and how you dip your biscuit is normal. Between adults. But a library is also for . . ." Rudi waved his hand in the air. His voice grew shrill. "I've seen this book in the hands of *young girls*. Children, practically. What do you call this stuff?"

"Can you take a step back, please?"

Rudi struck him in the chest with the book. Not hard. Just a firm tap. "This is pornography," Rudi said. "This is filth. Por-no-gra-phy."

"Step back. I'm serious."

"How do you sleep at night, Signor Carcano? Happy and warm like an egg up a hen's arse? Do you drift off counting the zeros in your bank account? From now on, if I were you, I'd sleep with one eye open. You never know, somebody might open you up just like—"

The sound of a car horn. The breakdown van. "See you around, Mr Writer."

Rudi said hello to the breakdown van driver. A joke, a goodbye and a handshake. Then he climbed into the red pickup, opened the window and leaned out towards Tony.

Smiling, he told Tony something that left him breathless.

Thirty-Three

1.

It was not a picture-postcard lake.

Nothing to do with the mountain lakes that were the dream of any photographer. The Kreuzwirt lake did not strike a pose. Rather, it looked like a well with open borders. As though, on the day He decided to create it, God had been in a rush. He had stuck His finger into the peat, then filled the impression with water. Tick. What's next on the list?

The lake without a name was not large. About twenty metres across, no more. But it was deep. And despite the source that fed it all year round, its waters never managed to be truly clear because of the mud in the peat. Towards the middle, this opacity approached total darkness.

Still, all in all, God had done a good job. The lake had its charms. Especially once your nostrils grew accustomed to the smell of the peat bog. Moreover, unlike mountain lakes, which are photogenic and full of poetry but essentially dead, the Kreuzwirt one was swarming with life. Frogs, toads, newts and, beyond the shoreline, earthworms, butterflies of all shapes and sizes, and birds.

Sibylle could not remember how long she had been sitting at the water's edge, across from where Dr Horst had dragged Erika's body out of the lake.

Never had she felt as alone as she did now. Alone and angry.

Are you happy now? You've fucked up my life. For the second time.

"Erika the Bitch."

Normally, she would have put on her helmet and hit the gas. That would be enough to calm her down. But the Yamaha was a write-off. And now that Oskar had fired her, the chances of buying a new one any time soon were next to nil. Let's be serious, she thought.

The Yamaha was the least of her problems. She had to eat. Pay her bills. Her savings for university would melt away like snow in the sun. In a couple of months she'd have to pack her bags and sell Erika's house.

Who was she kidding? If only it were that simple. Nobody in Kreuzwirt would ever give her a job, nobody would ever buy the house surrounded by blackberry bushes. They wouldn't take it off her hands even if she gave it away with a ribbon on top. Erika's house was destined to suck her dry for eternity.

That's what happened to those who went up against the Perkmans.

Unless Sibylle chose to forget everything. Because the Perkmans were good people. This whole business would end immediately if Sibylle wanted it to. All she had to do was get up, clean off the peat mud and go and ring the doorbell at Krotn Villa.

Karin and Michl would listen to her problems. They would comfort her. Sibylle would make amends. She'd admit she was wrong. Stupid things enter the heads of stupid girls like Sibylle the Stupid.

Karin and Michl would accept her apologies, dry her tears and burn the picture of Erika with the hummingbird smile. All would be forgiven.

Take the pill, Sib.

It's bitter but it will make you feel better.

You'll be able to keep the house. Buy a motorbike. Perhaps even aim higher than a second-hand Yamaha. You'll meet a nice local boy. One without so many strange ideas in his head. One who'll take you skiing in the winter and to the sea in the summer. A husband without issues. Every so often, you'll read one of Tony's books and feel a small pang of sadness. It'll pass soon enough, you'll see. And when Sibby Longstocking shows up, when you feel suffocated at night, when some kid draws the hummingbird smile on your front door, you'll get on your nice new motorbike and go for a ride in the woods, confident that no red pickup will come out and cut you off. Little by little, with a bit of goodwill, one step at a time, the world will become smaller and smaller. Its borders will shrink. Until all that's left is Kreuzwirt with its geraniums at the windows.

A little place for a happy little Sibylle.

2.

At dusk, Sib decided it was time to go home.

Thirty-Four

1.

They were very kind.

A courtesy Toyota and an XXXL T-shirt that hung loose on him. The tyres would take a couple of days, they didn't have any in that size. They weren't equipped to do a paint job but they could recommend a guy who . . .

Tony had cut them short. He had slipped a couple of banknotes into the oil-stained hand of the breakdown driver, scribbled his home phone number on a piece of paper and asked for directions to the nearest vet.

Dr Pirone had disinfected Freddy's wounds and offered to do the same with Tony's. Then he had given the dog his first anti-rabies jab. Freddy was not all that keen on it, but endured the injection with the stoicism typical of his breed. The vet booked him an appointment for the following week. And another one for the week after that. After that, Freddy would be safe from Miss Rabies. Tony thanked him.

Still in Sand in Taufers, he found a mobile phone shop and bought a replacement handset. While driving to Kreuzwirt he called Polianna to reassure her. They would be late for dinner but no need to worry. They were having a great time. Everything's OK and the sun's shining. Don't worry. He tried to contact Sibylle twice but there was no reply.

He left the Toyota in the Black Hat car park just after eight. The sky in the east was a revolting expanse of coagulated blood. So much the better. Neither Tony nor Freddy was in the mood for a romantic sunset.

Thirty-Five

1.

Someone was smoking outside Erika's house. A figure sitting on the steps, hunched over. The tip of the cigarette lit up his face.

"Wolfie."

The former gamekeeper looked at her for a few seconds without seeming to focus. His eyes were bloodshot. It was the first time Sib had seen Wolfie drunk.

"Hi, sweetie. I'm told you're having more bad days than good."

"Really shitty."

Wolfie indicated the rucksack. It was sturdy and had seen all sorts. "And it's not over yet. My fault, I'm afraid."

Sib tensed up.

Wolfie tried to stand, but stumbled and fell back down. "Can't hold my drink. Do you mind helping me?"

Sibylle did not take the hand the man was holding out. "First tell me what you're doing here."

"Stubborn. And blind. Not exactly small stuff."

"In Kreuzwirt?"

"On this earth, my girl."

"Did Karin send you?"

Wolfie propped himself up until he resumed a standing position. He staggered but did not fall. "We all owe something to Friedrich. He was a good man. The deeds of the fathers will end up in the pockets of their offspring. Isn't that what they say?"

"What's in the rucksack?"

Wolfie threw the cigarette butt on the ground and crushed it with his boot. Then he bent over and picked it up. He narrowly avoided falling forward. If he had, Sib would have left him to it. He slipped the butt into the pocket of his khaki shirt and indicated the rucksack once more. "Open it."

Sibylle obeyed gingerly. There was a pickaxe inside. "Were you supposed to break my bones?"

"No. Don't—"

"Not yet?"

Wolfie lit another cigarette. He spat on the ground. "After seeing what chemo did to my poor Margherita I find these damned things disgusting. It's like swallowing burnt shit. But I'm not stopping. Each one brings me closer to where she is now. I miss her. I miss those times. Everything had its place and every place had its thing. Margherita was my right place. Now I feel odd. An old, odd sock."

Some other time, Sibylle would have been moved by his confession, voiced without a trace of self-pity, a simple expression of raw, profound grief.

Not now. Not with the pickaxe in her hand. "Do you think I can't smash your head in, Wolfie?"

"You'd be doing me a favour, sweetie."

Sib felt the urge to do it. To raise the damned pickaxe and shatter that drunk old man's skull. He missed his beloved wife? There was a Sibby Longstocking express ready to take him to meet her. "First you," she said, "then that bitch Karin."

Wolfie chuckled. "You wouldn't get anywhere near her. Rudi would stand in your way first. Or Michl. Or else . ."

"The good people of Kreuzwirt."

Disgusted, Sib dropped the pickaxe. "What did you come for?"

"Sooner or later, you pay for your sins."

"What sins?"

"All of them, without exception. That's why I'm here. To atone. And leave you a reminder."

"A message from Karin?"

"Michl. He came in person. He always frightened me. More than Karin. Maybe because he's a doctor. I've never liked doctors." Wolfie scratched his badly shaved chin. "Karin is a rabid fox. Like the one that bit your mother. Somebody gave her the illness, so what can she do? Nothing. But Michl, he's the only one who could ... My poor, poor head ..."

Wolfie had to lean against the wall. Sib felt sorry for the old man. She grabbed him and helped him sit on the ground. She went into the house and returned with a glass of water.

"Thank you."

Sib crouched next to him. "What could Michl do that frightens you so much?"

"Leave without consequences."

"Wouldn't Karin allow him to?"

"Perhaps, perhaps not. Perhaps they're truly in love, as they say, or perhaps he just enjoys watching us jump through hoops. That's what scares me about them. Karin speaks and you jump. Karin speaks and ... I'm here. With that stupid stick, threatening a girl."

"Otherwise what? What would they have done?"

"It's not mine. Do you understand, sweetie? The house."

2.

No-one stopped them. No-one even seemed to see them. A petite young woman dragging an old man with a limp rucksack on his shoulders. And yet Sibylle and Wolfie passed many Kreuzwirt residents on the way. We've become invisible, she thought. Or maybe it was just her. Like Erika, before she drowned.

147

Sib took Wolfie home. She helped him open the door and lie down on the double bed. And as she threw a blanket over him, she saw him grab Margherita's picture and put it on the pillow next to his.

She wished him goodnight.

Wolfie did not answer. He was asleep.

Sibylle left, the pickaxe over her shoulder.

Thirty-Six

1.

Tony sat at the bar. "Bourbon. Jim Beam."

"Sibylle isn't here," Oskar said. "And we don't serve people who are driving."

"The dog's driving. The Big Jim is for me. I wasn't looking for Sibylle."

Oskar poured it for him. Tony downed the bourbon in one gulp, remembering Rudi's final words to him.

Have a good evening, Signor Carcano. You and Erika.

Not Sibylle. *Erika.*

And that had terrified him. But it had also given him an insight.

"You know what they say in these cases, don't you?"

"No, I don't."

Tony winked at him. "Krrrka."

"Excuse me?"

"It's fox language," Tony said. "It means: I have three questions for you. Or perhaps a couple more, I don't know, that depends on you. Besides, it's a nice number. So I have three questions for you. Hold on tight, here's the first: do you love Sibylle?"

Oskar removed the glass and the bottle from the bar. "We don't like drunkards here."

"The dog's driving. I'm asking the questions. Number one: do you love Sibylle?"

"Then you'll leave?"

"At the speed of light." Tony put a banknote on the bar. "Keep the change."

"She's like a daughter to me."

"Question number two: who's Rudi?"

Oskar rubbed his knuckles. "Why do you want to know?"

"Rudi. Big, strong. Dimple on the chin. Excellent taste in books, but a filthy temper."

"He's Peter's son."

The smell of disinfectant. Essence of rose. The care home with the stupid name – Aurora. Lehrerin Rosa doing the crossword. Rudi, Peter's son. The Peter who had built the greenhouse for Signora Perkman. Why had he not worked it out sooner?

"The custodian at Toad Villa?"

"Yes, that's him."

"I'll bet he lives in the house that Friedrich Perkman gave to his father. Because Perkman was a man who—"

"Who took care of people. Yes."

"And what else does Rudi do for the Perkmans? Does he just give the silver a polish every now and then or—"

"That's none of your business. Or mine."

Tony pushed away the empty glass of Jim Beam. "Would you mind giving me a mineral water? Still, please. I hate bubbles. And no lemon. I have enough acidity as it is."

Oskar remained motionless.

"Believe me, Oskar, I'm certain – I mean it – that you love Sibylle. And I know for a fact that, despite her dreadful temper, Sib feels the same." He tapped the bar with his finger. "Water for the thirsty, please."

Oskar gave him a glass of mineral water.

Tony drank it in a single gulp. He had not realised how dehydrated the events of the past few hours had left him.

"And this is a problem. At least for me. Because this gorgeous big puppy here has grown fond of the girl. And he doesn't want to hurt anybody."

"Are you threatening Sib?"

"Actually, I'm threatening you."

Oskar burst into an uproarious laugh. Tony would have done the same in his shoes. There was at least a twenty-kilo difference between him and the owner of the Black Hat.

"You know," Tony said with a mocking smile, "in my district, back in the good old days, there were a lot of tough guys like you. People who carried a knife in one pocket and a strong desire to beat up little shits like me in the other. Or perhaps just make them bleed a little. So you had to be very fast, and I was. Like lightning. Only sometimes speed wasn't enough. So you learned. Do you want to see what those bullies taught me, Oskar?"

"Say what you have to say and don't let me catch you in my bar again."

"Alright. But first you have to tell me why someone who runs a place like this would go and stuff himself with burgers and fries at a *brattaro* by the side of the road. Or do you not serve burgers and fries here? Maybe back in '98 you didn't have that hot plate over there. Cocaine? Pills? What did you go to Hannes the cowboy for? And, above all, what would Sibylle think of you if I asked her this question?"

Oskar turned pale.

Tony went in for the kill.

"Maybe you went there for the girls. Girls who'd run away from home and needed money. Girls like Erika. So, let's be friends again and you can answer the third and most important question: did you lie to me when you said you loved Sibylle?"

Oskar clenched his fist, the veins in his neck swollen. His eyes were narrowed and his nostrils quivered.

Tony did not bat an eyelid. "Sure that's a good idea?"

The fist came to rest on the bar. Oskar helped himself to a large dose of Jim Beam.

He downed it without shifting his hate-filled glare from Tony's face. "Cocaine. In '98, the Black Hat was going under. I was thirty-three years old, I had zero money in the bank and I had to find a way to keep this place afloat. I had to cut down on staff. But not Erika."

"Why not?"

"Because of the way they treated her. I felt sorry for her."

"Who?"

"Everybody."

"Gabriel, Betta, Karin?"

Oskar shook his head. "They were kids. I didn't blame them. They'd fall out and forget it all by the next day. I blamed the adults. Laughing behind Erika's back. All that business with the tarots. Erika was truly convinced she could read the future. And they indulged her. So they'd have a story to tell."

Tony raised an eyebrow. "But they paid her?"

"It was a way of putting her in her place."

"So you cut down on staff, and the workload increases. You go to the *brattaro* on 621-K to restock on cocaine. And you find Erika. And then?"

"Things got better."

"Not for Erika."

"No. I meant for the Black Hat."

Tony gave a sarcastic laugh. "Perkman never leaves his friends in the shit, right?"

"He suggested turning the Black Hat into a dance hall. There was plenty of room. It just needed a small investment. He also helped me organise the first concerts. Publicise them in the local papers."

"That's all?"

"If you made Perkman angry, you made Peter angry. If you make Karin angry . . ."

Thirty-Seven

1.

When Sibylle announced that she was going to live in the house Erika had been bequeathed by her mother, Aunt Helga wasn't too happy. Her sister's old place needed quite a lot of work, probably too much. Sib risked blowing all her savings.

Sib asked Oskar's advice. After a quick inspection he, too, had his doubts. He could take care of the wiring and Sibylle could even get away with keeping the bathroom tiles, as there were some wonderful products around for tackling mould. But the door and windows needed replacing because the frames crumbled as soon as you touched them. And that would cost a great deal of money. As would repairing the roof, which leaked in several spots.

"Sib, are you sure you want to take on all this work?"

It was like with the Yamaha: when Sibylle set her mind on something, there was no talking her out of it. Asking for favours here and there, and with a small bank loan, she made Erika's house habitable again. It wasn't perfect. It was very draughty. The water heater worked every other day and the gas cylinders under the kitchenette scared the hell out of Sibylle. Moreover, it cost an arm and a leg to heat it in the winter. But it was hers.

She had always felt safe within those walls.

Now, the house surrounded by blackberry bushes had become a trap. She had seen many foxes caught in such traps, in the woods.

Eventually, almost all of them, owing to hunger, thirst and pain, would yield to despair and start gnawing at the trapped paw to tear it off and run away. A ghastly sight.

Sibby Longstocking could not help laughing. The fox is wise and does not end up in the obituaries. Do as the fox does, bite at your ankle, tear off your paw and flee far away.

Sib raised the pickaxe and let out a cry. The sound of the first window shattering warmed the cockles of her heart.

Thirty-Eight

1.

A blonde young woman, identical to Sibylle in every way, except that Sibylle had never done anything quite like this, was dancing around the outside of Erika's house, smashing the windows with some kind of large stick.

"*Di Erika kimpt di holn!*" she was screaming. "Erika's coming to get you! The bitch is coming!"

"Sib?" Tony called out in disbelief.

The young woman stuck the pickaxe into the ground. "Oskar," she said, as though that explained everything.

"What about Oskar?"

"He got a call from Karin. So now I don't have a job. We've trodden on the cat's tail, right? Wolfie, on the other hand, was supposed to leave me a reminder. Except that he was too drunk to do it. So I made myself my own reminder." Sibylle laughed. A laugh that reminded Tony of the sound the rabid fox had made. *Kkkka! Krrrka! Ka!* Even Freddy, next to him, seemed frightened.

"One thing at a time, please. Oskar fired you because Karin asked him to. So far, I'm with you. Then it all becomes a bit of a muddle. Why are you trying to demolish your own house?"

"Because Wolfie was too drunk to do it." Sibylle's voice grew shrill. "And I'm stupid. And so are you. Because you still don't get it. The Perkmans own *everything*. And everyone."

"Sib, please—"

"*Please?*" Sibby Longstocking barrelled into him like a high-speed train. "I don't have a job anymore, I don't have anyone anymore. And the bike . . . That son of a bitch Rudi wrecked my fucking bike. I don't even have that anymore!"

Tony felt his stomach lurch. "You said it was an accident."

"Rudi cut across me with that truck thing he drives."

"Rudi."

Sibylle put her head in her hands and went back to chanting, "*Di Erika kimpt di holn! Di Erika kimpt di holn!*"

Tony followed his instincts. He put his arms around her. Sib tried to free herself. Tony would not let her. Sibylle burst into tears. Tony could feel them through the fabric of his T-shirt.

"Erika's dead. She's the one person who can't hurt you anymore. Don't be angry with her," he said, stroking her hair. "Why didn't you tell me about Rudi?"

Sib swallowed her pride. "I didn't want you to think I couldn't take care of myself."

"I'd never think that, Sib."

"Really?"

"Of course not."

A duck called. Freddy whimpered. The tears stopped. Sib's breathing slowed down.

Tony was about to pull away from her, but she held him tight. "Wait another minute, OK?"

"OK."

"It's nothing sexual, alright?"

"It never even occurred to me."

"I just need to wipe a bit more snot from my nose. When I cry a lot of it comes out."

"You really know how to make a man feel needed, Sib."

Sibylle giggled. "And how was your day, Kleenex man?"

"In a word, it sukked."

156

Still rocking her, Tony told her about the fox, then about the Mustang and the meeting with Rudi.

"The message is clear," he concluded. "Leave Kreuzwirt. You should have got out long ago."

"Do you want to give up?"

"Not a chance," Tony said. "The time when the Carcanos kept their heads down is over."

These were not his own words. Repeating them made him shudder. A powerful anger jolted through his body, like a high-voltage electrical discharge. Sibylle must have felt it, because she pulled away from him and looked at him quizzically.

"All I'm saying is that you need a safe place where you can lick your wounds. You could come and stay with me for a few days. I have a guest room I never use. If you'd feel weird about it then there are hotels. I'll pay, obviously. What's important is that you—"

Sibby Longstocking gave him a push. "Forget it, Mr Macho. I'm not going anywhere."

But Tony wouldn't budge. "The Perkmans strike where they know they can hurt you. The bike, the job, the house. But especially your pride. Because they know you'll never ask for help. But you're no longer welcome in Kreuzwirt. It could become dangerous for you to stay here. That's why I want you to pack your bags and come to Bolzano. I would have asked you sooner if you had told me about the accident. And . . ."

A breath.

Two.

"What I'm trying to tell you, Sib, is that even if you give up, the Kleenex man here will carry on alone. All the way."

"Why?"

Tony looked up at the sky and uttered a sentence from twenty years earlier. "Because there are no more stars."

Thirty-Nine

1.

Milani was waiting for him outside the editorial office. It was the evening of March 23.

He forced him into the Citroën, filled his head with bullshit and dragged him into one bar after another. He called it the Jim Beam Tour.

Late that night, totally plastered, they found themselves beside a country road on the outskirts of the city. Tony lying on the ground, Milani a little further away, pissing on a row of dried-up vines, emitting gurgles of pleasure.

"You'll get used to it," Milani said. "You just have to learn the trick. Get it down you without tasting it."

Tony managed to turn his head just enough to avoid vomiting all over himself. When he was done throwing up, Milani pushed a cigarette between his lips and lit it.

"What's that song?" Tony asked later.

Milani glanced at the Citroën parked next to them. A rhythmic melody was coming from the car radio.

"'Criminal'. Fiona Apple."

Tony had seen the video on MTV. A bewildered-looking young woman glaring straight into the camera. And Fiona Apple looked like . . . "Erika," Tony mumbled. A frightening comparison. "Her name is Erika. Her name is not Fiona Apple. Her name is Erika."

"I'm almost certain your dead girlfriend never recorded a song. I repeat – 'dead'. If you want to be a journalist you have to know your verb tenses," Milani said. "Her name *was* Erika. Your head's all messed up, isn't it?"

"Who says I want to be a journalist?"

"Because you've got a chip on your shoulder." The photographer chuckled. "I saw it the very first day. You want to pick a fight with the whole world."

"What's the song about?"

"About how she feels guilty about having been raped. Crazy stuff, right?"

Tony felt the taste of the peat bog on his lips. "There are no more stars," he muttered.

"What?"

"They've gone. The stars. Erika told me."

Milani burst into a phlegmy laugh. "You're even drunker than I am. The stars are still there. It's the planes that have disappeared. I haven't seen one all day."

"Planes?"

"The things with the little lights. That fly. Know what I mean?"

2.

"Milani was right. On March 24 the bombings in Serbia began. Civil aviation had already been banned from the airspace above Alto Adige. Walscher and Krauts could sit back and watch a real ethnic conflict live on TV. I got him to take me home. The newbie was waving the white flag. Milani said he understood. He apologised."

"Why?"

"At the time I thought it was for involving me in that business. But now, having reached the conclusion that it was Friedrich Perkman who ordered him to keep close to me, I think it was because he felt guilty. About me and Erika. The next day . . ." A crooked smile. "The next day

I signed up for the forklift operator course. I didn't get a job at the steelworks – I found a position at another firm instead. I couldn't bear the thought of seeing my father. We argued so much I ended up leaving home and enrolling at university, which he'd always said was a waste of time. Alongside the forklift job, I worked as a barman every so often, to cover my bills. That was my life for a few years. Books, forklifts and 'What can I get you?'"

Sib gave him a friendly slap. "I know all about that."

"One day, I went to the cinema to see a comedy. At one point I noticed a young man and a girl in the back row. While everyone else was laughing, they were holding hands and crying. It was the same feeling I'd had when I saw Erika by the lake. Except, that day, in the cinema, I finally understood her. I understood what I'd read in your mother's eyes: that nothing made sense." Tony gave a bitter laugh. "Neither grief, nor joy, nor struggle – nothing. It was all a big joke. For me, for those two who were crying while everybody else was laughing – for Erika. I was furious and scared stiff. I didn't want to be swallowed up by this horror and there was only one thing I could do to stop that from happening. Write."

Tony saw his reflection in Sibylle's eyes and he did not like what he saw. He looked too much like Freddy with the rabid fox.

"If reality was a sky without stars, then I would write about love conquering all. If life and death were meaningless, then I would make up stories with a happy ending. If the world was a lie, then I would cheat even more. I would spit in the face of that damned sky. That's how *Two* was born. When I finished it, I told myself that Erika would have liked it. That was the last time I thought about your mother." He looked at Sib for a long time. "I sent it to an agent. To get rid of it, more than anything else. He accepted it and told me not to hold out too much hope. That was fine with me. I had a different purpose in mind. It took three years for the book to be published, but when it reached the bookshops . . . *Bang.*"

Sibylle was crying. Her eyes were clear. Alive. Infinite.

Tony gently brushed away a tear. It was warm. "You're in danger here. Let me help you, Sib."

"For Erika's sake?"

"I want to write you a happy ending."

"I like books that end with a kiss."

"So do I."

Tony could smell Sib's perfume and, under that, the scent of her body. She was so close that, for a moment, the blue of her eyes seemed to penetrate him. Caress her. Give her peace. It lasted only a second, but it was second in which he could *breathe*. Then a sound from the bushes startled them. A hedgehog shuffled out into the moonlight then returned to darkness. Freddy emitted a kind of "wow!" Sib smiled, Sibylle withdrew, and Sibby Longstocking stuck her tongue out at him.

"Now go," she said. "Before . . . we all fall down."

"Will you come?"

"Not today, Mr Kleenex. But I promise I will. Let me just pack my bags. And say goodbye to someone."

Tony waited for Sib to go inside, then got into the Toyota and started the engine.

The Toyota made it onto the road. Two hundred. Maybe three hundred metres.

Then stopped dead. "Shall we do some camping, Freddy?"

Tony and Freddy spent the night behind the blackberry bushes, waiting for Karin Perkman to make a move. At dawn, Tony woke the St Bernard and together they went back to the car. Tony felt destroyed. He put his head on the wheel and fell asleep. Ten seconds or maybe an hour later, Sib's voice startled him. "Don't you want some coffee?"

A cup changed hands. Tony felt ridiculous.

He cleared his throat. "The moment for the kiss has passed, right?"

Sibylle laughed. It was good to hear her laugh. "You don't have great timing."

Forty

1.

At 8 a.m., Tony delivered Freddy into Polianna's care. At 8.10 he came out of the shower. At 8.15 he was already on the move. By 8.30 he was standing outside the bank.

Impatient.

2.

Sib had also slept fitfully that night, confused because of Tony. She had seen him watch over her. She had been tempted to let him in, or at least send him home to sleep in a proper bed.

But his presence had reassured her. Just like his hug.

Sib was sad. For Erika. About what Tony had told her. For herself. For Wolfie? Also. And Rudi? And Oskar? Puppets in the hands of the Perkmans.

Sib was confused. Had she really felt the urge to stop Tony's mouth with a kiss? Should she dismiss it as a fleeting moment? Or one of Sibby Longstocking's crushes? Or the emotional rollercoaster of everything that was happening?

Sometimes she thought it was. Other times, she thought the opposite. Sadness, confusion, happiness. And fear. Of what Aunt Helga would say. But when her aunt opened the door, saw the rucksack and the suitcase and threw her arms around her, Sib's fear vanished. "Thank God, my darling. Thank God."

"I'm sorry . . ."

"No, I . . ."

Sybille gently pulled away from the large woman. "I understand." They went in and sat across from each other at the kitchen table. "But I have to know."

"Why?"

"Because otherwise I'll always be the daughter of Spooky Erika."

Helga indicated Sybille's rucksack. "Will you come back?"

"I don't know. Tell me about Erika. Please."

"It was hard for her. That nickname. She'd laugh about it. But I could see it hurt her."

"Karin? Gabriel?"

"Everybody."

"Oskar, too?"

"No, he was very fond of Erika." Aunt Helga was fiddling with her apron. Something Sibylle had seen her do a thousand times. "That's what Kreuzwirt is like. You know that."

Yes, she knew. But for the first time, Sib noticed the way people referred to Kreuzwirt as though it were not a town, but a living entity. A person.

That's what Kreuzwirt is like. Kreuzwirt doesn't want tourists. Kreuzwirt calls a spade a spade. Kreuzwirt always helps its friends. Every now and then, Kreuzwirt murders somebody.

"You once told me you used to work for the Perkmans."

Aunt Helga nodded. "For the lady, actually. Frau Christine. She was a wonderful woman. She came from a very old family. Friedrich was so in love with her. It's hard to imagine a couple more in love. I was at their wedding, you know."

Helga went to get an old photo album and started leafing through it.

"When was it you worked for Signora Perkman?"

"In '78. Before Erika and the twins were born. I did the cleaning. The turret hadn't been built yet, but the library was already there. Signora Perkman enjoyed reading. Poetry, novels. There were books for every taste. Every Saturday, she'd go to Innsbruck to buy new ones. But not those that were locked up. The forbidden section."

Old, very valuable books.

That was what Lehrerin Rosa had said.

"What do you mean, 'forbidden'?"

"No-one was allowed to read them. They barely even let me near them to dust them. Horst and Perkman said they were mainly science books. But I never believed them."

"What about Horst? What do you know about him?"

"Same as everyone else."

"He came to Kreuzwirt in '73, is that right?"

"Yes, with Michl. Such a beautiful child. Quiet, clever. Very clever. Who his mother was or why she wasn't with them was a mystery. In '73, Horst had problems. And Perkman—"

"Gives everyone a helping hand. Always the same story," Sibylle said, annoyed. "Got a problem? Perkman solves it. Oskar never stops telling me."

Helga hesitated.

"Or is it a lie?"

"Actually . . ."

"Please."

"Oskar hated Perkman."

3.

Left alone in the vault, Tony took a break. His hands were shaking. It was the anger. Except that it was not his anger.

It was his father's.

Giuseppe Carcano died in May 2006, a few weeks after *Two* was published. When Tony went to the funeral with his mother, it was at the top of the bestseller list. After the ceremony, one of his father's friends handed him a note. An appointment. Giuseppe had left something for him. Something his mother must never know about. Tony was expecting it. Because his father was a practical man, who never allowed his son to go out without a payphone token, and who would never have left his family at the mercy of events. Once, in 1988, amid all that was happening in the Alto Adige at that time, the bombs and the helicopters, Giuseppe had taken him aside and, for the first time, spoken to him man to man. He had told him he was right to run away when the older boys were angling for a fight, that it was a good thing, that Our Lord had said to turn the other cheek.

And Our Lord is Our Lord, OK? But . . .

Tony opened the safe deposit box. His father's .22. Small and chunky. Ugly. Tony turned it over in his hands. *A man,* Giuseppe had said, *must always defend his family. It's all that matters, alright?* Tony checked the safety catch and put the magazine in, the way his father had taught him. He released it and remembered his mother's screams when she discovered the pistol. *What do you want to do with that? Get yourself killed? Do you want your son to grow up without a father?*

Giuseppe had made the pistol disappear in the Eisack. Thrown it into the river. Or so he told his wife. Tony had not believed it for a second.

His father was a practical man. One who never allowed his son to go out without a payphone token. One who would never have left his family unprotected.

Tony hid the .22, handed a banknote to the employee, who deactivated the metal detector, and left with a nod of goodbye.

4.

"Oskar had big plans at your age."

"The Black Hat?"

Aunt Helga cut a slice of strudel and served it to her. "Oskar bought the land in 1986, even before applying for the licence. And that's where he went wrong. He was naïve. That's why he failed."

"Failed?"

"The Black Hat was supposed to be a hotel. It was Oskar's dream. He wanted to build Kreuzwirt's first hotel. He was too young to remember how Friedrich had persuaded the people of Kreuzwirt to give up on tourism. And he was stubborn. Just like you. Don't you like the strudel?"

Aunt Helga was an excellent cook, and her cakes were better than anything you could buy from a *pasticceria*. This was the first time Sibylle ate just to keep her happy.

"Perkman went to him and offered to buy the land. Oskar refused. He wanted this hotel at all costs. But the licence was delayed. There were technical problems. Things like that. Perkman came back and offered to buy the land for three times what it was worth. An astronomical sum. Oskar accused him of putting spokes in his wheels. He said that if he bothered him again he would call the carabinieri. Perkman did not reply. He sent Peter."

Sib's fork stalled in mid-air. "Rudi's father?"

"Yes. Peter made him an offer on Friedrich's behalf. Perkman would leave him the land on the condition that, instead of a hotel, he built a dance hall. A compromise. Oskar gave in. The documents came through less than a week later. Only, Oskar had to wait two months before signing them. Because of his broken bones. Do you understand what I'm trying to say, honey?"

"If Perkman was the kind who took care of his friends," Sibylle said, "then what did he do to his enemies?"

Helga did not reply. She had found the photo she was looking for.

Friedrich Perkman. Much younger than the man in the wheelchair Sib had seen in town a couple of times, when his illness was already at an advanced stage.

Bushy moustache, still bearing.

On his right, Dr Horst. Round glasses and just a hint of the paunch that dominated Sibylle's recollections of him.

And Signora Perkman. In folk dress. No woman from South Tyrol would have dreamed of wearing white on her wedding day, back then. It would have been unthinkable.

"Frau Christine."

Slim. Radiant. In love. With a cascade of curly blonde hair.

Sib's phone startled them. Tony.

"Tante Frida's found Gabriel."

"Where?"

"You won't like it."

Forty-One

1.

"How do I look?"

The man sitting in the shadows simply grunted.

She was not concerned. She had come across quite a few lunatics in her time.

She had started "the life" at twenty. The pregnancy had come totally out of the blue. A guy like any other – she met him in a bar. A one-night stand. Never saw him again. Then, the sting in the tail. There was nothing like a scan to open your eyes to reality. No money. No job. No prospects.

The only thing she owned that was of any worth was her body. So she put it up for sale. The first time, she cried. He got frightened and apologised. She told him to go to hell. Insulted him. Slapped him.

But she accepted the money.

Then it became a habit. The trick was to make your mind go blank. Compile a shopping list. Think about the little girl's marks at school (she had grown so quickly) or . . .

As she got closer to thirty, her client numbers began to fall away. They preferred younger, more toned girls. Her assets were losing value, and so, as economists on TV put it, she identified a gap in the market, starting from a simple basic assumption: men were deluded. They would come to her for a quickie or in order to obtain what they could no longer get from their wives (and who could blame them . . .?). In any case, they all wanted to be in charge, right? *Wrong.* Clients paid to delegate command to someone stronger than them. So why not make it more ... explicit?

A gap in the market: a great expression. Fewer clients, bigger profits. Piece of cake.

<h2 style="text-align:center">2.</h2>

"Do you like me?"

The man stood up from the chair and adjusted the wig on her head. He took her chin and gently turned her face left and right.

"Let's start."

It was not the first time this guy had come to see her. He paid. Without making a fuss. But deep down she was afraid of him. What he asked for was ... strange. Well, no stranger than what her clients generally requested (her favourite paid her to force him to give her presents). It was the way he asked that made her anxious. And the fact that he was a drug addict. The signs were unequivocal. Still, he paid well and the clutch in her Fiat Punto was on its last legs. No point in being picky.

The man removed his shirt and kneeled by the bath, filled to the brim. Cold water. To please him, she had even added ice.

Impatient.

"What are you waiting for?"

She took him by the hair, long but not dirty (even though he was an addict, he was scrupulous in his adherence to the house rules, which is why she acted as though she did not notice his vices), pulled it just enough to hurt him a little and plunged his head into the water. She counted. One, two, three ...

At sixty, she pulled him back up.

"Again. Two minutes."

One minute was alright. Even two minutes. When he asked for three, she hesitated.

"It's not safe."

The tattooed man indicated the jacket on the bed. "There's another hundred in there."

"It's not about the money."

"I'll raise my hand if I can't take it anymore."

She shook her head. "No, you won't. And I'll end up in the shit."

He stared at her. His pupils were small and darted around. He was stoned.

Completely stoned.

"Two hundred."

"It's not—"

"*Three hundred.* On top of the usual price."

A handsome sum. She gave in. She grabbed him by the hair and pushed his head into the water. He started to thrash about. Bubbles floated up to the surface. She had to struggle to keep him under.

At eighty seconds, she let go. He was crying. A pathetic sight.

"Why?" she asked.

"I want to know what it feels like. Again, please."

She'd once been forced to tackle a client armed with a knife. She had repeatedly been in situations that would have made many of the police officers she had come across during her career lose their cool. Now she understood that there was something worse than a knife or the contemptuous looks of the police. The man's smile, for example.

"No. That's enough. Time's up." She removed her blonde wig and tossed it aside. She proffered her hand, palm up. "Three hundred. As promised. Then get out. And don't come back."

Gabriel looked at the wig on the floor and started to tremble. "What have you done to her?" he shouted. "What have you done to her?" Then he leaped at her, grabbed her by the throat and squeezed.

Forty-Two

1.

"Did he kill her?"

"Almost. She had a knife concealed on her. She was no amateur. After she stabbed him, she called the carabinieri and they arrested him. They arrested them both actually, but she was released. That was in 2008. Ever since, Gabriel has been a guest at Via Dante."

Tony frowned. "I didn't think the Bolzano jail was meant for serious crimes. Don't they send them to Padua?"

"You're right. And yet your friend, Signor Plank, is there, behind bars. And that's not the only oddity in his file," Tante Frida explained.

As well as attempted murder, Gabriel was also convicted for possession with intent to supply, assault, theft, burglary, petty theft, robbery, aggravated robbery, armed robbery, assault on a public official, as well as a host of lesser crimes which nevertheless were included in the file Tante Frida had managed to obtain. Many of the offences had been committed in prison.

Brawls, in particular.

"He spends more time in solitary than in his cell. I've even found a diagnosis. Paranoia with dissociative delirium. Mad as a hatter. And a menace to society."

"But," Sibylle said, "with that kind of diagnosis, shouldn't he be in a psychiatric institution?"

"Normally, yes," Tante Frida said. "Especially as he's a drug addict.

But Gabriel's lawyer never played the mental illness card. I've had a quick glance at the trial papers and, if you ask me, the man was totally incompetent. The judges have always given his client the maximum possible sentence. And he has never – I mean never – asked for leave to appeal."

Tony raised an eyebrow. "Strange."

"It's not strange. It's impossible. Especially as I know the lawyer in question."

"Did he provide any explanation?"

Tante Frida smoothed her turquoise skirt. "His name is Johannes Kaufmann. The *second-best* brief in the whole of Alto Adige."

"So it wasn't incompetence."

"Not in the least. It was what we hacks call 'intent to harm'. Someone doesn't want Plank to get out of jail."

"Kaufmann is somehow connected to the Perkmans, right?" Sibylle said.

"They're his only clients. Except for Gabriel – if you really believe someone like him can afford Kaufmann's fees. So I saved myself a phone call."

"We have to speak to him," Sibylle said. "Not Kaufmann – Gabriel. If the Perkmans—"

Tante Frida raised a hand. "The Perkmans want Gabriel behind bars. Out of the way. But they want him out of the way *within their territory.* If he were transferred to Padua or Trieste, they wouldn't be able to control him. And here's another thing. If you want to see Plank, you have to go through his lawyer. And nobody has managed it in ten years."

"But Karin doesn't want him dead," Sibylle murmured. "It's the same as with Martin. Why? Martin's her brother. And Gabriel is a drug addict. If Karin had wanted him dead, she could have found a million ways to kill him. An overdose. A road accident."

A pickup that cuts you off in the middle of a forest, she thought. Or a murder dressed as suicide. "So, either Gabriel knows something," she added, "something Karin also wants to know—"

"Or something that could land the Perkmans in trouble," Tante Frida added.

"Exactly."

"Or else," Tony said gloomily, "it's something he's done. Something for which death would be . . . too mild a punishment."

The two women looked at him.

Tony tried to elaborate. "Up to now, we've thought of Martin as Erika's possible killer. But we actually have very little evidence. You said it yourself, Sib. Martin kills Erika, Horst and the Perkmans cover it up, then imprison him. Right? And, so far, Karin's behaviour has done nothing but confirm this theory. The incident with the pickup, the photographs with Irina, Rudi's performance with the Mustang, Oskar firing you. And that business with Wolfie. As Tante Frida says, the Perkmans have their share of skeletons in the cupboard. There's no question about it. What we still lack, however, is the *why*. We don't know why Karin's acting this way. So maybe we're on the wrong track. And this makes me wonder: what if Karin is *punishing* Gabriel? What if Gabriel killed Erika?"

Sibylle twisted a lock of hair around her fingers. "But why? And why lock Martin up all this time?"

"Maybe Martin saw something and can't keep his mouth shut. It would also explain why Gabriel isn't in an institution for the mentally ill. There, they have psychiatrists who would listen to what he has to say. Whereas in prison . . ."

"Nobody's interested in the ravings of a convicted criminal."

"Exactly. You want a motive for Gabriel? I don't believe in motives, they almost never make sense, but . . . it could be the same as for Martin – madness. Or perhaps Gabriel was in love with Erika and she turned him down once too often."

"You're forgetting that Martin has a record – Gabriel doesn't. Or at least he didn't back then. His problems with the law came after Erika's death, not before. Then there's the incident in '88. It was Martin who attacked Betta, not Gabriel. And Martin fell off the grid the day after

Erika's death, while Gabriel ended up in jail nine years later." Sib shook her head. "In any case, we have to go and talk to him. Without Gabriel we have no evidence."

"That won't be easy with Kaufmann and the Perkmans on alert," Tante Frida said. "You can tread on the cat's tail once, but twice . . ."

Despite the heavy, leaden air in Tante Frida's office, Tony grinned. "I know that look of yours, Tante Frida. It means you've already come up with a solution."

The woman brought her hands up to her chest and fluttered her eyelashes. "You really can read the thoughts locked in a girl's heart."

"Listen, there are people who'd pay good money to make fun of me. Have you come up with a way to bypass Kaufmann and talk to Gabriel?"

"You won't like it."

"I've heard that before. Tell me what I have to do."

Tante Frida exchanged a complicit look with Sibylle. "Why do men always have to be so self-obsessed?"

Forty-Three

1.

Matteo Zanon was a bureaucrat, but he liked to portray himself as a good father.

His children (thankfully not his biological ones) had committed quite a few misdeeds, so they had to be punished, of course, but he was a firm believer in rehabilitation. And this didn't just mean bars on the windows and poor-quality food. Every now and then it meant turning a blind eye. Like a good father.

That was why he had agreed to Tante Frida's request, pretending not to notice the obvious subterfuge involved. Passing a prostitute off as a "fiancée" was the oldest trick in the book.

But when Tante Frida insisted that the young woman in high heels and miniskirt was not to be searched, alarm bells had started to ring. Tante Frida then swore that not only would there be no bloodshed, but no-one would ever find out – least of all Kaufmann.

Zanon had his doubts about the latter promise. Kaufmann was a slippery son of a bitch with eyes and ears everywhere. But since Zanon was a good family man and owed Tante Frida a couple of favours, the visit was approved.

Still, he felt uneasy.

Of all his children, he had to admit, Prisoner 66-55-321 was the one he liked least. To put it bluntly, Zanon found 66-55-321 frightening. And this was a slip of a girl. If 66-55-321 laid his hands on her . . .

Zanon escorted the young woman from his office to the cell block. They turned left, then right, walking past the education labs and classrooms.

"Wait here," he told her when they reached their destination. "The camera inside is out of order. As you can see, there's a button next to the door. If things don't go to plan, press it. Is that clear?"

The young woman nodded.

"Please repeat it."

"There's an emergency button. The camera is kaput. I've got it."

The warden made to leave. He stopped and swallowed a Maalox. Then he turned back.

"Is this really necessary, signorina?"

2.

The bars on the windows made her feel claustrophobic. Not to mention the smell. A mixture of sweat, dirt, food and testosterone. Or the prisoners' remarks.

As she followed Warden Zanon, Sibylle had tried to keep her eyes on the floor and focus only on his voice as he explained the house rules. Even so, Sib had ears. She could not miss the silence.

The silence that she left in her wake. It made her feel *dirty*. And sad.

The room was bare. A bed, a chair. The smell of chlorine made her eyes water. She sat on the bed. The mattress sank. The springs squeaked.

Sib sprang back up to her feet. Much better to stand.

Is this really necessary, signorina?

Yes. It was.

Three paces ahead. A wall.

Three paces back. A wall.

Her gut told her to give up. To press the button and get herself out of there. Out in the open air. To get rid of those clothes. Go back to being Sibylle. And never find out what Gabriel could tell her. About Erika. About Martin.

Gabriel was the key. Without Gabriel, all they had was a fistful of air. The Perkmans would win, as they always did. And Erika would die again.

The sound of footsteps approaching. Sib switched on the voice recorder hidden in her handbag.

Forty-Four

1.

He was wearing a pair of shapeless jeans and a white T-shirt. The two guards made him sit on the bed. They did not say hello to her or even deign her with a look.

One of them – stocky, with a moustache – removed the prisoner's handcuffs. The man rubbed his wrists. There were nasty marks. And not just where the steel had cut into his flesh. There were bruises on his muscular, tattooed arms. A large, dark one under his chin. And heaven knows how many more concealed under his clothes. Sibylle remembered what Tante Frida had told her about Gabriel, who, even in prison, had not wasted any time getting into trouble.

"Did the warden tell you about the button?" one of the guards said.

Sib nodded.

"Out loud, please."

"Yes."

2.

All that remained of the little boy in the Polaroid who wanted to become an astronaut were the glasses – though these had different frames. Other than that, Gabriel could have been someone else entirely.

Not only because of the muscles, the long hair and the tattoos doodled everywhere. It was the sense of menace that oozed from every pore.

He sighed and looked up at her. "I knew you'd come, girl."

His voice was that of someone having a friendly chat. But his eyes . . .

Remember, he's crazy. Be careful, Tony had said to her. *If he says anything that scares you, anything at all, even if he just gives you a funny look, drop everything and run. If you can't beat them, beat it. Alright?*

Sibylle took the chair and sat down, only too aware of the distance between her knees and those of the prisoner. Not even a metre and a half. "Thanks for agreeing to—"

"Or should I say, 'boy'?" Gabriel asked, interrupting her. "Are you a man or a woman? I guess the question doesn't make much sense to you, does it?"

"I don't understand."

Gabriel motioned imperceptibly towards the camera.

"It's off," Sibylle said, trying to keep her voice calm and relaxed.

Gabriel winked. "What do you want to talk about?"

"Erika."

He took off his glasses, stared at them, then put them back on. "What did you do with her?" he said. "You've picked a blonde to come and see me. Who looks like her. What did you do with her?"

"I don't understand," Sibylle said. "What do you mean?"

"Who's watching us? Kaufmann? Or has Karin left the villa and come all the way here?"

Gabriel took a crumpled packet of Marlboros out of the pocket of his jeans. "Do you mind?" The tone of someone making small talk.

"Go ahead."

Gabriel showed her a match, then lit it by striking it against the wall. "They won't let us keep lighters, but matches are fine. Crazy, don't you think?"

Give him slack. Let him talk.

Sibylle adjusted the handbag on her lap. She hoped the mic was powerful enough to pick up everything Gabriel was saying. "A bit strange. Yes."

A deep drag.

"Or is Horst out there?"

"Dr Horst is dead."

"Yes, Josef is dead. But as far as I know, Dr Michl Horst is still alive and well. Do you know him? Nice guy. Everything's always on his terms. Very reserved, elegant. They say the ladies like him. Karin certainly likes him." Gabriel pointed the cigarette at her. "You've done an excellent job. Blonde, curly. You look just like her. Like Erika. An ethereal person for your ethereal world. But if you think that's enough to take me in, you're very much mistaken. Are you armed, boy?"

"No, I—"

"What have you got in that bag? A knife? A gun? The way you're holding it, I'd say a gun. Or would you rather kill me with your bare hands? But that's not your style? And I doubt you'd manage to get me down on my knees. I'm not the type. But you don't want to kill me, do you?"

Sibylle bit her lip. "What's an ethereal person?"

Gabriel expelled smoke through his nostrils. "Ethereal people are the key. And the lock."

"Are you also an ethereal person?"

A laugh. "I am the hunter. If I was an ethereal person, I wouldn't be here. I'd be sitting where you are."

It made no sense.

Still, Sibylle continued. "And me . . . who do you think I am?"

"You have many names."

"Tell me one."

"I'll tell you the one I've given you. You're the prey."

Sib gave a start.

"You don't like it, do you?" the prisoner said slyly.

"Why . . . the prey?"

He leaned forward, whispering but continuing to smile. "Because sooner or later, boy, I'm going to crush that pretty little head of yours and send you back where you came from."

There was a flicker in Gabriel's eyes which almost made Sibylle push the panic button. But she did not. She stood up and let her hair down. "I'm Sibylle, Erika's daughter. I don't know who you think I am, but you're wrong. I'm not your prey."

"Sibylle? The baby?"

"Yes." Sib remembered what the drug-dealer cowboy had said. "I am not the Wanderer."

Gabriel squinted. "If you're really Sibylle, who told you about the Wanderer?"

"Hannes."

"That arsehole never could keep his mouth shut. What else did he tell you?"

"Who *is* the Wanderer?"

Gabriel glanced at the camera and moistened his lips. He threw the cigarette on the floor and let the smoke contaminate the room.

He watched the swirls rise to the ceiling and disperse until the cigarette burned out.

He looked annoyed. "What game are you playing?"

"I'm trying to understand," Sibylle said. "Ethereal people are the key, the lock, the door. What you're saying makes no sense to me."

"The key, the lock, the door. The key, the lock, the door. The key."

Gabriel took off his T-shirt.

Sybille pulled back. All she had to do was turn and push the button. But she did not.

There were tattoos on Gabriel's torso, and a huge scar across his chest. It went from shoulder to shoulder, from his navel to his throat.

The hummingbird smile. Carved in his flesh.

Gabriel ran his finger over it. Then dug his nail in. Blood oozed from the small wound. "The key," he said. "The door. They're important. But what's more important is what comes out of it. The Wanderer. He takes people and devours their souls. He makes them kneel. He wears them like a pair of gloves. He uses them. Then he gets rid of them. And kills again."

A sob.

Sibylle looked away from Gabriel's scars. From the finger that would not stop digging.

The man was crying. "And kills. And kills. Again and again."

Sib felt pity. Then horror. Then pity again. But there wasn't much time. They would never get another opportunity like this.

"Until a hunter arrives? Like you?"

Gabriel pushed his nail in all the way.

He moaned.

"Grahame knew it and so do you," he murmured. "Because I know who you are." Sibylle drew closer. She stroked his hand, then took it. Gabriel did not protest.

"I'm Sibylle. I'm not . . . the Wanderer. Or whoever else you think I might be. Look at me. I look like—"

"Erika."

Gabriel pulled away abruptly, rejecting the contact. He rubbed his face with his hands. "They're killing me day by day. Solitary. Then the showers. There's always somebody waiting for me. And the medicines. The medicines. Kaufmann. Karlo. Michl. The Perkmans."

"And the Wanderer?"

"He never comes here. I thought you were him. I hoped you were."

"So you could kill him?"

"To get it over with."

"Do the Perkmans know about the Wanderer?"

Gabriel said nothing.

"What do they want from you?"

Gabriel brought his mouth close to Sib's ear. "They're watching us."

"No. The camera is out of order."

"You don't understand."

"I understand, but you have to help me—"

Gabriel grabbed her by the throat. He lifted her and shook her like a rag doll.

"You?" he roared. "Do you understand?"

Sibylle struggled and lashed out blindly. She kicked and punched. Nothing. Gabriel was too strong. Sibylle was utterly defenceless.

His eyes flashed. "Do you know about the dead girls? Do you know about the island in the middle of the clearing? Do you know about Mirella? Don't lie to me. You know nothing."

"Please . . ."

Gabriel let go of her. Collapsing to the floor, Sibylle fought for breath, trying to edge closer to the panic button. Her head was spinning. Black stars were dancing before her eyes.

"Do you know what this is?" Gabriel shouted, digging his fingernails into his flesh. "Do you know what Grahame did to his son? Do you know?"

"I want to know about Erika. About the hummingbird smile someone removed from the lakeside. I want to know about the Perkmans, about what's behind this, and—"

Gabriel tore the camera off the wall and hurled it to the floor. She heard swearing outside.

The voices of the guards calling her.

"Signorina? Signorina?"

Sib ignored them. "Please," she said, "help me."

The rattling of keys. More swearing.

"They're coming," Gabriel whispered. "Mirella. The wind took Mirella away. Like all the others."

The door was flung open. Brawny arms seized Sibylle. A light-blue uniform came between her and the prisoner.

"What does it mean?" Sib cried.

Gabriel hurled the guard against the wall. Two more, holding batons, rushed into the room.

"If you really are who you say you are, look for Mirella."

The two guards raised their batons. Gabriel roared. More blows. The prisoner bent over. He fell. They did not stop hitting him. The last thing Sibylle heard before the guard with the moustache managed to drag her out into the corridor was Gabriel's laugh.

Forty-Five

1.

Tante Frida gave her a glass of grappa and was not content until Sibylle had drunk it all. It made her stomach burn. Tante Frida poured her some more.

"If the Perkmans want something from Gabriel," Sib said, as soon as she had a little colour in her cheeks, "they won't get it." The sound of the batons thudding into the prisoner's body were still echoing in her ears. Gabriel's cries, his laughter. "He'll never give up," she added. "Never."

"You sound very certain."

"Gabriel thinks he's been endowed with some kind of superior power. He's a total fanatic."

Tony shook his head. "He's insane, and it could be his sense of guilt and not fanaticism. Don't forget the prostitute. He got her to wear a wig and asked her to drown him. Then he tried to kill her. A curly blonde wig. Ring any bells?"

"I felt sorry for him. He didn't frighten me."

"No sympathy for the devil, Sib, or we'll really be in trouble."

"Who's Grahame? Who's Mirella?" Tante Frida asked, bringing the conversation back to more solid ground.

"No idea about Mirella," Tony said. "But Grahame was a writer. Kenneth Grahame. His most famous novel is *The Wind in the Willows*. A children's book. Martin's favourite, according to Lehrerin Rosa. Remember, Sibylle?"

Sib nodded, reaching out for the voice recorder. She let the recording play as far as "*Do you know what Grahame did to his son?*"

"Do you know?"

"Grahame's son died young," Tony said. "He killed himself. He was twenty years old."

"Suicide," Tante Frida murmured.

None of them said it out loud, but all three were thinking about Erika in the lake surrounded by the peat bog.

"Is Gabriel saying that Grahame killed his son?" Sib said.

Tony fidgeted on his chair. "And how would he know the details of something that happened almost a century ago? I think he meant that Grahame did to his son what Perkman did to Martin. He locked him up in the house. Securely."

"Locked up?"

"Grahame wrote *The Wind in the Willows* for him. He loved him, but not enough to challenge the morality of the times, which viewed difference as something to be hidden away. However – and I don't mean to defend him – you must realise that Grahame could have locked up his son in an asylum and forgotten all about him. Instead, he kept him with him. If anything, he showed more sensitivity than most of his contemporaries."

"Fat comfort. And it didn't exactly work out, since in the end he committed suicide," Tante Frida said bitterly. "And what was so terrible about that poor boy?"

"He was blind in one eye. And he probably had some other disability. Nobody knows. The very concept of disability back then was rather nebulous. Unemployment was considered a mental flaw, just to give you an example. The point is . . . what did Lehrerin Rosa call Martin?"

"'My little mole.'"

"Mole is the main character in Grahame's book."

"That's all very interesting," Tante Frida said, "but something else is puzzling me. Gabriel mentioned dead girls. Plural."

She reached out for the recorder. Gabriel's voice filled the office again. "*The wind took Mirella away. Like all the others.*"

"Aren't you letting your imagination run a bit wild?" Tony protested.

"Didn't you pick up on it?"

"We're dealing with a maniac."

Sib first looked at Tony, then at Tante Frida. "Wait. Stop," she said. "What am I missing?"

"Gabriel mentioned women, plural," Tante Frida explained. "He said that the Wanderer, whoever he is—"

"Not whoever," Tony protested, "*what*ever *it* is. To Gabriel, the Wanderer is a kind of monster who devours people's souls. In other words, Gabriel is out of his mind. Tante Frida, can you really believe that—"

Tante Frida silenced him with a severe look.

"'He kills and kills.' That's what he said," Sibylle murmured, shuddering. "Do you think there could be other victims?"

Tante Frida adjusted her glasses on her nose. "I'm not saying anything. This is just speculation."

"Where I was born," Tony muttered, "speculation rhymes with 'oops, my mistake'. Let's go easy on the flights of fancy, shall we?"

"All I'm saying is that it's something to bear in mind, that's all. In any case, we must find out who this Mirella is. If she's alive, dead, or both."

Sibylle gulped down her second glass of grappa. This time, the bite in her stomach was followed by a pleasant warmth. "How can somebody be alive and dead at the same time?"

"Missing persons, unidentified bodies. Right up my street."

"It sounds a little vague," Sib said.

"I appreciate your doubts, but do you know what all these years of work have taught me?"

"To be patient?"

"That solutions are seldom to be found where you go looking for them. The needle is never in the haystack."

"And," Tony muttered, "we don't even have a haystack."

Tante Frida opened a drawer and took out a couple of sweets. She offered one to Sib and the other to Tony who, unlike the young woman, unwrapped his without even looking at it and put it in his mouth. It tasted of strawberry. A flavour he hated.

"Don't be taken in by films, my boy. In real life, more often than not the police don't find the culprit."

"Are you trying to keep up the troops' morale, Tante Frida?"

"More often than not, the police get in our way."

Then, noticing that the sweet was still in Sib's hand, she added in a reproachful tone, "What's life without a little sugar, Sib?"

Forty-Six

1.

The moment they left Tante Frida's office (after spitting out the sweet into a handkerchief in a less than elegant manner), Tony told Sibylle that he was going to pop over to Sand in Taufers to pick up the Mustang and return the courtesy Toyota. The garage had contacted him while she was with Mr Out-Of-His-Mind.

"I'll come with you."

"You're tired. You need a rest. Besides," Tony added with an enigmatic smile, "I've already warned Polianna."

Sib turned abruptly while the lift was taking its time to arrive. "Polianna?"

"My nanny. She'll get pissed off if you call her that, so don't let it slip out. 'Home help' is the term my accountant uses."

Sib enjoyed his attempt at humour. The encounter with Gabriel had left her feeling drained, and even Tony looked rather pale. The only one who appeared to be immune to the strain was Freddy, who was wagging his tail happily.

"She's waiting for you downstairs," he said. "She'll take you home. I'll be back in a jiffy. Too many emotions for today."

"Can't you take me yourself?"

The doors opened. The lift made them both feel claustrophobic.

"It's better you meet Polianna on neutral ground. She's a little possessive. Keep schtum about that, too."

"What do you mean, possessive? Is she like a girlfriend?"

Tony burst out laughing. "More like a mother. You said you would abandon Kreuzwirt. Was it a lie?"

Sib indicated the rucksack on her back. "Don't—"

"And you're exhausted. Polianna will take care of you. I just need to pick up the Mustang. I'll be back before you know it."

They were blinded by the sunlight.

Polianna was standing as straight as a pole a few metres from the Toyota. She was carrying a bag over her shoulder, wearing an ankle-length skirt, and had a scarf tied around her head.

If Polianna doesn't slaughter me first, Sib thought, as Tony introduced them.

The woman seemed to be scowling, and Tony was clearly on tenterhooks. It would almost have been funny, if Sib had not felt she was about to be grilled.

"Polianna, will you take care of Freddy?"

"Of course."

"Any problems, give me a call."

"There won't be any. Put on your seat belt. Don't drive too fast."

Tony got into the car, waved goodbye and vanished into the traffic.

Polianna's first words to Sib were, "Are you trying to hurt my boy, signorina?"

"Pass, ask me another."

The woman strode off towards the bus stop.

Thanks, Tony. Thanks a million.

Forty-Seven

1.

"You're not a purist, are you?" The mechanic indicated the new tyres on the Mustang.

As a matter of fact, Tony thought, a true connoisseur would indeed turn his nose up, but finding original tyres would have taken a great deal of time.

"So long as it goes, that's enough."

"About that," the mechanic said, nodding towards the inscription and handing him a greasy note. "This is the address of a friend. He can take care of it. The tyres are one thing, but . . ."

Tony slipped the piece of paper in his pocket. "Actually, I think 'Sukks' gives it a touch of personality."

"It's your car, boss."

He muttered this in the tone of one obliged to deal with a lunatic, though it did not prevent him from accepting Tony's money. He handed him a receipt, somewhat dismissively, advised him to report the incident to the insurance company and the carabinieri (Tony had not done so, it would have been pointless), then said goodbye and went about his business.

Back behind the wheel of the Mustang, Tony headed to a DIY store just outside the town. He bought a carpenter's hammer, a large number of nails of various sizes (better to cover all the bases) and ten-millimetre-thick plywood boards. With some difficulty, he managed to cram everything into his car and drove to Kreuzwirt.

In the block of flats where Tony had spent his childhood, no-one ever needed to call on a plumber, an electrician or a carpenter. All you had to do was ring the Carcanos' doorbell, and bingo. Thanks to his father, Tony was the only pupil at the Martin Luther primary school who could tell a Torx from a Robertson, or knew the difference between a wire stripper and a wire cutter, and how to spell "reamer" correctly. Even so, he did not have half his father's talent. He lacked his touch. Still, Tony thought, as the Mustang darted across the shadow of Krotn Villa, he was sure he could fix some plywood over the windows of Sibylle's house to prevent animals and rain getting in, without making too much of a hash of it. It wouldn't prove much of an obstacle for burglars or determined intruders, but it might dissuade the local kids from any acts of bravado.

When Tony arrived at the house surrounded by blackberry bushes, he saw that someone else had had the same idea. And he did not like that one bit.

Especially since he had left the .22 at home.

2.

"I've been rude. Forgive me."

Sib looked up from her plate. When Polianna had offered her the first sandwich, Sib had accepted out of pure politeness, even though she was convinced that after what had happened in the prison she would not be able to swallow a thing. And now she was finishing a third.

"I . . ." Sib wiped her mouth with the back of her hand, realised what she had done and blushed.

Polianna smiled. "These are Tony's favourites. Cooked ham, roast veal, olive pâté and cheese. I use goat's cheese, but don't tell him. It's the secret ingredient."

"I'll take it to my grave."

"You're a sweet girl. I'm sorry I went after you like that."

Sibylle smiled. "Signora, Tony told me you're very—"

"Polianna, please, not 'signora'."

"Tony said you're a little protective towards him, Polianna."

The woman pulled a face and, for a moment, Sib feared she had put her foot in it.

"A little. Maybe, yes. And you, are you going to hurt my boy?"

"We're not . . ." Sib searched for the right words but Polianna beat her to it.

"You don't have to be, in order to hurt somebody."

"No. I wouldn't do it deliberately, anyway."

"Tony is no longer the little boy who used to run and hide in the library, you know? I remember it well. He's learned to give some and take some. He was always arguing with his father. And in some ways he hasn't changed. Did you know that I'm the one who gave him Freddy? And it was I who persuaded him to teach that creative writing class. His mother asked me to. We were very close. It was she who told Tony that he could afford a housekeeper to keep his fridge stocked while he was writing. You should have seen the state this place was in before I set foot in it."

"A mess?"

"On the contrary. Very tidy. But in an unhealthy way. Fanatically so. Tony had built himself a kind of—"

"Fortress. Complete with moat and alligators."

"Do you know what Tony's days are like? Alarm clock goes off at six, coffee, walk with Freddy, another coffee, new novel until midday, snack, radio news, short walk with Freddy, third coffee of the day, correct drafts, light supper, sunset with Freddy, DVD or a book, goodnight."

"I thought a writer's life was more exciting. Autographs, admirers . . ."

Polianna burst out laughing. "Tony and the limelight don't mix. He doesn't even have launches. He writes and writes. That's all. And that's dangerous."

"Why? After all, it's his work. And he enjoys it."

"He loves it. But he's running the risk of . . ." Polianna searched for the right word. Sib found it. A man in a T-shirt and a dog on the lead. Alone, amid the apple orchards. A bit too pale, a bit too set in his ways, a bit too angry. A man who wrote happy endings so he could spit at the starless sky.

"Getting lost."

Forty-Eight

1.

Oskar stopped hammering as soon as the Mustang appeared in the driveway. He put the hammer down on a rung of the ladder, wiped his hands with a rag, then walked towards the car.

Tony turned off the engine and got out, ready for confrontation.

"I'm sorry about Sib," Oskar said, crossing his arms.

"Are we talking about her house or her job?"

"I had to."

"Did Karin Perkman call you?"

"Michl. Where's Sibylle?"

"In Bolzano. Does this bother you?"

Oskar shook his head. His earring glistened in the sunlight. "She's an adult. It's good to take a break every now and then. Even if your fling isn't destined to last very long."

Tony felt the impulse to burst out laughing. *Fling.* The semantic damage of TV soaps. "I don't think you know Sibylle half as well as you think, my friend."

"I want to ask you three questions, Tony."

"I've heard that before."

"Do you care about Sib?"

"That also rings a bell."

Oskar poked him in the chest with his finger. "Answer me."

"I would never hurt her. Now take your hand off me before I ram it down your throat."

"I guess that will have to do."

"That's my motto. Second question?"

"Do you want to see what Sibylle has avoided by leaving Kreuzwirt?" Oskar did not wait for a reply. He lifted his T-shirt and revealed a ten-centimetre scar. The cut had been neat and precise.

"Peter?" Tony asked, remembering what Sib had told him about Oskar's plans to build a hotel in Kreuzwirt. "Was it him?"

"This one dates from 2000. Peter was in treatment at the time. They said he was through, but he held on for four more years. You know what they say about the proverbial bad penny, don't you?"

"Then Rudi. Or Martin, perhaps?"

Oskar pulled down his T-shirt. "Martin was shut up in the villa, and Rudi ... I know you've had a run-in, but Rudi's tough guy act is just that. An act. A show. I know what I'm talking about. Rudi's alright. He has friends, he likes the cinema. Sometimes, we go fishing together."

"And he has good taste in books. Who are you trying to kid, Oskar?" Tony said, belligerently. "Rudi tried to kill Sibylle."

Oskar's reply left him speechless. "Then where's the body?"

"The – the body?"

"Did he want to kill her or just give her a fright?"

Tony felt the blood rush to his head. "That's bullshit."

He was about to turn away and leave. He had nothing more to say to this bald fraud.

Oskar stopped him by grabbing his arm. "Rudi ruined your car. And scared the wits out of you. Don't deny it, you shat yourself. But ask yourself what he could have done if he'd actually laid his hands on you."

Tony shook himself free. "Why don't you try asking Hannes the cowboy?"

"I'm not looking for trouble. I just want you to understand. Rudi only does what the Perkmans tell him to. If they say to give you a fright, he dons the psychopath mask, puts you through five minutes you won't forget, then goes back home to watch a film, or drops by the Black Hat for a beer. On the other hand, his father, Peter . . ." Oskar shook his head. "About the hotel – Perkman ordered him to slap me around a little. Maybe break one of my teeth. Nothing more. That's what Rudi would have done. But his father broke my elbow in three places and enjoyed every second of the torture. Peter was the kind of arsehole who runs over a dog just for the pleasure of watching it die."

Tony grimaced in disgust. "I can think of a couple of medieval treatments for someone who goes in for this kind of thing."

"And in any case, in 2000, Rudi was a forty-kilo thirteen-year-old – clothes included. Do you think a skinny boy would have been able to do this?" He pointed at his chest, the scar now covered with the T-shirt.

"Who was it, then?"

"Michl."

Tony felt overwhelmed by dizziness.

Michl?

"I was blind drunk, so it was the perfect moment to attack me. While Michl was cutting, Karin was laughing. They were both laughing. She was there to enjoy the show."

Michl.

Karin.

"Why? Why did they do it?"

"Kreuzwirt is like an animal. Old. Nasty. It has trouble adapting to change. It can't bear it. Everything has to remain in its place. For eternity. And I wanted to leave once and for all. Close the Black Hat and disappear. I couldn't take it anymore."

"Erika was another one who didn't know her place, right?"

"You're beginning to understand."

"And what was her place?"

"At the bottom of the food chain. Reading tarots was alright. Being spooky was alright. But being seen in the bright light of day, asserting her . . . difference, that wouldn't do. Erika was too much for this town. Too alive, too free. Kreuzwirt is like a hamster cage, and you're the hamster. Keep running in your wheel and no harm will come to you. But don't you dare get off."

"A place where nothing changes except the names of the actors, right? Rudi takes over from his father. Karin from Friedrich. And Michl is the hamster, like Horst before him."

It was as though in Kreuzwirt time had got stuck in a muddy rut. And if anybody dared try to break it out . . .

"You said you had three questions. There's one more to go."

"Will you make Sibylle drop this business?"

"She won't give up."

"Then keep close to her."

"And *you* need to stop playing the obedient hamster. If you know something, then speak up. Don't wait for someone to hurt you."

Oskar turned to look at Erika's house.

When he turned back, he seemed to have aged by twenty years.

"There was someone with Gabriel," he muttered. "Whenever I saw him. To – to buy stuff."

"You weren't clean back then?"

"No."

"Cocaine?"

"I'd slipped up again. I'd buy it from Gabriel, not from Hannes. I don't know . . . it didn't seem so bad to get it from someone I knew. Sometimes, Gabriel was with a woman. His girlfriend."

Tony shuddered. "Was her name Mirella?"

"She told me it was Yvette. Yvette Fontana. But Gabriel called her Leah. She'd get pissed off whenever he did. A skinny woman. Almost certainly an addict."

Leah – or "that cow", as Hannes had called her.

"What about the name Mirella? Does it mean anything to you?"

"Never heard it."

"Is there no-one in Kreuzwirt with that name? Somebody connected to Gabriel?"

"Have you found him?"

"He's in jail. Attempted murder."

"I didn't know that."

"But you're not surprised."

"No."

"Is that all, Oskar?"

"In 2000, this scar was a message for me. Now it's a message for you. From Erika. Save her daughter, take her away. As far away as you can."

Forty-Nine

1.

Sib woke up and for a moment panicked, convinced she was still in the cell. The bars on the windows, the reinforced doors. The nauseating smell. Luckily, it did not last long. She was in Tony's house. In the area he still called Shanghai. She remembered the sandwich with the olive pâté and the goat's cheese. But don't tell Tony. She was safe, not in Via Dante. No bars on the windows.

What time was it? The light that filtered through the shutters was oblique. The clock on her phone told her it was just after five in the afternoon.

Sibylle stretched.

When Polianna had realised how tired she was, she'd cut the chatting short and taken her to the guest room, which overlooked Castel Firmiano. A nice, inviting bed, two wardrobes ("All the space you need," Polianna had said, eyeing the unbelievably crammed rucksack Sibylle had brought from Kreuzwirt) and a small desk with an office chair. While Polianna was showing her the room, Sibylle had surprised herself by wondering how many other women had slept in that bed. Or in the one in the adjacent room. *His business. Don't be so childish.*

Polianna had left her phone number for her.

"The fridge is full. Just remember to change Freddy's water. St Bernards suffer in the heat. In any case, if you need anything, don't hesitate to call me. I live in the building across the street."

Left alone, Sibylle yielded to curiosity. Tony's apartment was spacious, but apart from the latest air conditioning system (it's for Freddy, she thought, smiling, he bought it for Freddy) and a kitchen that looked like something out of a spaceship, it seemed a home like any other. A few reproductions of famous paintings, a couple of posters, a stereo, a mirror next to the front door, Freddy's bed, a sofa and books. Tons of books. They were everywhere. The walls of Tony's fortress. A yawn reminded her how badly she needed to rest, so she picked one of Tony's novels from a bookcase and took it into her room. She was slightly embarrassed that she'd never read a single line of his books.

She lay down on the bed still dressed. After three pages, she was asleep.

2.

A couple of hours later, once the moment of confusion was over, Sibylle got up and left the room, barefoot, dishevelled, her mouth all mossy, and her sense of reality not quite in focus yet. Freddy was snoring like a motorboat, the flow of the air conditioner stroking his coat.

"Did you have a good sleep?"

Sib jumped.

Tony put his mobile on the sofa and smiled. "I didn't mean to startle you."

"You could have woken me up."

"I didn't want to."

"More emails from nutcases?"

Tony shook his head. "I'm starting to regret asking Chiara to spread the word in the lunatic community."

"That bad?"

"The guy convinced he's the Antichrist is the best of the bunch."

"The world is a strange place," Sibylle said. "How long have you been here?"

"I had a chat with your former employer. A peaceful one, don't worry."

"Give me a summary."

"He told me not to hurt you."

"Funny. Exactly what Polianna told me."

Tony grimaced. "Was it tough?"

"After Tante Frida? Are you joking? Tell me the truth: you have a weakness for bossy women, don't you?"

"For bossy women and—" Tony stopped.

Ones that wake up dishevelled.

And twist their hair around their fingers.

Who don't realise how brave they are.

And who . . .

"Women who can cook," he concluded, getting up. "What can I say, I'm a Neanderthal. Fancy a coffee?"

Sib followed him through to the kitchen.

"Did you know that in 2000 Oskar wanted to abandon the Black Hat?"

"No."

"And did you know that Karin and Michl sliced him up?"

Fifty

1.

A slow day for Madama dell'Angelo. Her last client, a sales assistant at H & M who dreamed of marrying a colleague who never got his name right, had left at ten in the morning. Satisfied and, as ever, hopeful. Since then, nothing. Madama dell'Angelo had used the free time to do some online shopping, update her Facebook profile (kittens and incorrect quotations), add a couple of artificial spiderwebs to her new statue of the Santa Muerte, which had arrived in Bolzano directly from a Korean factory for just €29.99, call her mother, who had caught a summer cold, and have a cheese sandwich and a low-calorie drink for lunch. When she decided to close up and go home, at about five in the afternoon, she heard the bell above the door ring and looked up.

A man and a woman. He was about forty – she, younger. Long blonde hair. Madama dell'Angelo adjusted her turban and the chains she wore around her neck, and concealed a satisfied smile. Couples were her favourite. Especially those going through a bad patch: *mismatched couple, earnings double.* They would turn to her as a last resort to put back together something that was not there anymore. And this meant a good few consultations. And add-on rituals.

And the odd amulet to keep under your pillow.

And . . .

She invited them to sit at the small table in the middle of her shop, lit a couple of candles and shuffled the tarots. Meanwhile, she studied their body language (the young woman on tenterhooks, the man giving it the classic "I'm here for her sake") and asked a few questions to extract information.

"The Devil. A burning passion has now fizzled out," she said, showing the first card.

The young woman put a hand to her face.

"Don't worry, darling. Let's see what the Arcana has in store for you. Getting the Devil is not always a bad thing. Take the veil off your eyes. Don't believe what you read."

"There are a lot of charlatans around," the man said.

"But you've come to Madama dell'Angelo."

Madama dell'Angelo always referred to herself in the third person. New card. Temperance.

"Serenity and calm. Can you see the golden amphora? It represents reason. Reason is often a harbinger of—"

"Harbinger? Did you really just say that?" The man looked first at her then at the young woman beside him. "Good God. *Harbinger*," he repeated in disbelief. Then he blew out the candles. "Do you have any idea what my editor would do to me if I submitted a manuscript with a word like that?"

The young woman stood up and locked the door. Then she drew the curtain over the only window in the shop.

The man took the pack of cards from her hand and began laying them out on the table. "My turn now."

Two vertical lines made up of three parallel cards. Two on a slant at the base. Two more, horizontal, higher up. The hummingbird smile.

Madama dell'Angelo removed her turban, revealing a cascade of voluminous dark hair. She always knew it would happen sooner or later. That sooner or later someone would come.

"Aren't you curious to know your future, Yvette?"

Unlike Madama dell'Angelo, Yvette Fontana, alias Leah, did not speak in the third person. She waved away the smoke released by the blown-out candles. "No need," she said. "You're here about Gabriel and Mirella."

Fifty-One

1.

It was Tante Frida who had given Tony and Sibylle Madama dell'Angelo's address. Once the elderly lawyer had discovered Gabriel's girlfriend's true identity, tracking her down had been child's play. Not only did Yvette Fontana have an unusual name, but she and Gabriel had been stopped by the police in 2007, both suspected of selling cocaine in the car park of a nightclub in Appiano. The charges fell through, probably because they managed to get rid of the merchandise in time, but anything that ended up on the police database stayed there for eternity. "And don't mention privacy to me, Tony, or I'll start screaming."

"I didn't say a word."

After treatment for drug addiction and a series of occasional jobs, Yvette Fontana, a Psychology graduate, had reinvented herself as a spiritual guru. Her shop, in Via Cassa di Risparmio in the centre of Bolzano, the former workshop of a tattoo artist, was registered as a therapy room.

Tony had enjoyed the irony.

2.

"Gabriel had fire in his belly," Yvette began.

"We met in 2003, in a nightclub. He came up to me to sell me some MDMA. I'd never tried it before but I'd heard of it, and I thought, why not? We got chatting. He was witty, intelligent. I fell in love. It didn't take him long to give me the habit. A story that's dull as hell."

"You were together for quite some time."

Yvette smiled sadly. "I liked being with Gabriel. It was exciting. At least at first. I'd always been a bit of a square – getting a degree because my family wanted me to. But with Gabriel I felt like we were Bonnie and Clyde. Even if we often slept in homeless shelters or on the streets."

"Was Gabriel violent?" Sib said.

"No, not with me. Never. But he had his issues. Erika. Her death. You must already know about her, since you're here. Gabriel had a photo of her. He'd say he'd make Kreuzwirt pay. He told me he knew straight away that she'd been murdered. He used to tell me what people called her."

"Spooky Erika?"

"That was the least of it. According to Gabriel, they were envious. He said Erika was free, brilliant. But Gabriel spoke like a man—"

"In love?"

"Obsessed," Yvette said. "There were many rumours about Erika. Gabriel said that some were true. That she would roam in the woods at night, for instance. That you could see her talking to animals. And not just when she was a child. And then there were *other* rumours. If a man left his wife, it was Erika who had seduced him. That kind of thing. Paying her to read tarots was a way of treating her like a whore. When she went to work at the Black Hat, there was even more talk. Erika said she didn't care. But Gabriel knew she was upset. That's why she clung to her tarots. To feel special."

"So upset she'd commit suicide?"

"So upset she ran away from home."

Sib wiped sweat from her temples. Despite the fan hanging down from the ceiling, the air was sweltering.

"And came back pregnant. Did Gabriel know who the father was?"

"No. Gabriel used to say that Erika was the loneliest person he'd ever met. That's why he decided to make Kreuzwirt pay. In a . . . in a crazy way. By wearing a blonde wig and going around drawing that damned symbol on the walls of the houses. It was his way of rattling everyone's nerves. Psycho stuff. And yet I always found him somehow romantic."

"Was Gabriel the voyeur who broke into people's homes?"

"No, that wasn't him. He would have told me. You must realise, until Erika's death he was just like any other boy. It changed him. After that, he started to torment Kreuzwirt. His father soon noticed, asked to be transferred and took his family away. Gabriel told me that when the poor man discovered the wig, he totally lost it: he thought his son was gay."

"Broad-minded people," Tony muttered.

Sib shrugged. "Kreuzwirt."

"They left, but the damage had already been done. Gabriel was scarred. He had nightmares about Erika, the lake, the town. When he grew up, he started popping pills. First so he could sleep, then so he wouldn't sleep, and finally because he couldn't do without them. He was obsessed. By Erika and by the Von Junzt. Sometimes he was jealous. Of a dead woman. Crazy, I know."

"What's the Von Junzt?"

"*Unaussprechlichen Kulten.* It's a book. Von Junzt was the author. I thought you knew."

Unaussprechlichen Kulten.

"Unspeakable Cults."

"Never heard of it."

"Once, Gabriel took me to see Kreuzwirt for myself. We didn't go into the town, just stayed on the slope, among the trees. He showed me that big house – Krotn Villa. He said it had a library and that he used to go there as a child, with Erika, Betta and Karin. That's where Erika found the Von Junzt. Gabriel said it was full of pictures. He found them scary, but Erika didn't. That symbol, the hummingbird smile, that's where she got it. Naturally, when Dr Horst found them peeking at those books he flew off the handle. He fired the cleaning woman who hadn't locked the cupboard where they were kept Erika's aunt."

Sib stared. "Helga? Was her name Helga?"

"I don't know. Maybe."

Lies. How many lies had Aunt Helga told her?

"From that moment on," Yvette continued, "Erika started laying the cards following that pattern. The hummingbird smile. She said it was a lucky symbol, because hummingbirds bring luck. Erika loved animals. Gabriel used to say that she was brilliant at imitating their cries. Did you know that?"

"Yes."

"Years later, Gabriel got hold of some faded photocopies of the Von Junzt, full of underlinings. He told me they were from a first edition and that there were sections missing, but they were more than sufficient to show that Erika had been wrong."

"About what?"

"The hummingbird smile was used for summoning the Wanderer. That's what he called him: the Wanderer. Or sometimes He Who Comes and Goes. Also 'the ghost'. Or else Tommy Raggiodisole. Gabriel said that Horst had been imprudent to leave that book unattended. He thought he should have burned it. That symbol . . . do you know about ethereal worlds?"

Tony shifted uneasily on his chair. "Very little."

"Gabriel used to say that there are many worlds. Some are copies of ours, but with small differences. The symbol of the Olympics is made up of six circles instead of five, Yvette is blonde instead of dark, or else the Adige flows through Rome, and—"

"The Foxes can afford players from the National Hockey League."

"There are hinges between these worlds. They hold back evil so that it doesn't overflow, and at the same time their purpose is to act as a reservoir. Because, according to Von Junzt, evil is necessary for the world to function. Without death there is no life. Without mourning there is no rebirth. Without war there is no peace."

"Let me get this straight," Tony said. "The universe holds evil back in these hinges, but then, every so often, it sprays some here and there to make everything slide better? That's crazy. That's stupid."

"Gabriel's words exactly. The universe is stupid. A stupid, blind fool who keeps repeating the same mistakes. But it's the only one we've got. Ethereal places are the spots where the worlds are closest together. Most people can't see them. Some – those who are more sensitive – sense their presence. Ethereal people, like Erika, swing between worlds. Usually, ethereal people are special individuals. That's what Gabriel used to say. They live their lives unaware of the power they have to scratch beneath the surface of things. Because, in order to do that, you need keys."

Yvette indicated the tarots on the table. "Ethereal people are the door and the key and the lock. It's what Von Junzt talks about. About how using certain symbols allows you to reach other worlds through fragile spots in reality. Erika had started to play with one of those symbols. One of the worst. The hummingbird smile. Through which the Wanderer could pass."

"So the Wanderer isn't a person?"

"Tommy Raggiodisole isn't from around here. He's a nightmare. The hummingbird smile is used to access the hinges directly. That's where the Wanderer comes from."

The dripping of some kind of water-feature hourglass. In the distance, a car horn.

Tony's sudden laugh. "Very suggestive. OK. But now let's get back to Mirella. To Martin Perkman. To Gabriel. And to Kenneth Grahame. Have you ever heard this name?"

"*The Wind in the Willows*. Of course. Gabriel would mention it almost as often as the Von Junzt. He said these two books were somehow connected, although he never explained how. Did Gabriel talk about Martin? Yes, often. Betta and Karin, too. Especially Karin. He hated her. He said she was the one who had started most of the rumours about Erika."

"We understood they were friends."

A more than eloquent grimace appeared on the woman's face.

"And Mirella?"

Yvette became gloomy. "Mirella Buratti is her full name. I remember her mother on TV, launching appeals. It was January 2008. Gabriel said the Wanderer had killed her. That was a strange time. Gabriel had almost stopped taking drugs, just a few amphetamines so he wouldn't sleep. But no more hallucinogenics or anything like that. He stopped dealing. He wanted to find that girl and dealing was a waste of time. Naturally, he didn't succeed. A few months later he assaulted that prostitute and . . ."

Yvette fiddled with her necklace. "It was Gabriel who broke up with me. He said being with him was dangerous. It happened just after he met up with that pretty boy."

"What pretty boy?"

"Michl Horst. A doctor. Karin Perkman's boyfriend. I don't know what they said to each other."

While Michl was cutting, Karin was laughing.

". . . I only know that at the end of that meeting, Gabriel burned all his notes, a load of maps covered in scribbles, notepads, exercise books – and the photocopies of *Unaussprechlichen Kulten*, too. He put me in the car and drove me to a treatment centre in Trento. He dumped me there and said we'd see each other again."

Yvette studied them both.

Her eyes were filled with tears. "I'd call it love. Wouldn't you?"

Fifty-Two

1.

"What do you think?"

Sibylle and Tony were taking a walk with Freddy in tow. Every so often, they would come across a daredevil on a mountain bike, a jogging fanatic or a fellow dog lover, but even though sunset was drawing to a close, the heat was such that it discouraged all but the most determined from leaving the house.

"I'm calling bullshit on the Tommy Raggiodisole rubbish. And don't even get me started on that 'ethereal worlds' and 'hinges of the universe' nonsense. As for the universe being stupid – I withhold judgment, because there are so many idiots around that you do start to wonder. But if that's what you call love, I think I can live without it."

"He broke up with her before hurting her, so in a way he was protecting her."

"From himself? Well done," Tony said. "Don't forget it was he who made her a slave to that stuff in the first place."

Sibylle gave a pebble a kick.

"Sorry," Tony said. "It's just that certain things give me rage."

"Apology accepted." Sibylle thought about the boy from Shanghai who spent his days stroking an invisible cat. "Are you saying Tommy Raggiodisole is an extra in your friend Ricky Riccardo's world?"

"Along with winged horses, the tooth fairy and the Smurfs."

"What about Mirella? Do you know if Tante Frida has any news?"

"I tried calling her, but she was a little . . ."

"Abrupt?"

"Laconic. She told me to let her do her beeping job. The beeping was underlined several times. Better to leave her be. When she's in an obsessive phase, her Puster Valley blood emerges." He laughed. "Tante Frida has access to the police database. If Mirella Buratti ever existed and her disappearance was reported, like Yvette said, then she'll definitely find her. And don't ask me if accessing the police server is legal. We don't want to know, right?"

"*Nix.*"

"In any case, if the newspapers mentioned Mirella and her mother went on television, we don't need Tante Frida's help to find her. I'll get down to it as soon as we're home. But, Sib, until we get our hands on some solid proof, I'm asking you to remain sceptical." Tony stopped and his tone softened. "It's always best to use the conditional. OK? The key word is *if.*"

"And the Wanderer?" she said. "And the evidence gathered by Gabriel? Could that be the reason Michl went to talk to him in 2008, giving him such a fright that it made him leave Yvette and disappear?"

"What evidence? Up to now we have only rumours. Tread carefully, Sib. Above all, this does not mean that the Wanderer, or anyone like him, really exists."

In other words, Tony thought, feeling his frustration rising in the heat, despite all their efforts, they were going round in circles.

"Do you never go out on a limb?" Sibylle said, teasing him.

Tony gave her a crooked smile. "You want the truth?"

"Shoot."

"As far as I'm concerned, this Tommy Raggiodisole business amounts to an admission of guilt."

"For having killed Mirella and possibly some other girl?"

Tony let his eyes wander over the vineyards and Castel Firmiano. A little further south, the Adige was flowing calmly.

"This is where we return to the magical world of *if.*"

Fifty-Three

1.

Sibylle rushed into Tony's office in the middle of the night, making him jump.

"I know who he is!"

"Who? What?" Tony said, confused. "What time is it, Sib?"

Only then did Sibylle notice the chaotic state of the room. There was paper strewn all over the place and the printer was busy spewing out even more. "What's going on?"

"Tante Frida has done her homework."

"Is all this stuff about Mirella?"

Tony rubbed his eyes. "Yes, in a way."

"Why didn't you call me? And what does 'in a way' mean? You know you can be truly unbearable when you put your mind to it?"

"I thought you were asleep."

"Well, I wasn't. Are you going to answer me?"

"One thing at a time. Who were you talking about?"

"Tommy Raggiodisole. I saw your DVDs. And your books. There are massive gaps in your pop culture." She smiled. "And yet it's a film from your generation."

"From my generation?"

"From when you were my age."

"*Fight Club*? *The Matrix*?"

"*The Exorcist*."

"That film came out before I was born, *little girl*," Tony protested.

"*The Exorcist III* came out in 1990."

"I was *eleven* years old."

Sibylle opened her eyes wide. "Really?" she said, teasing him. "Only *eleven*? Perhaps you'd better start using anti-ageing cream."

"Very funny."

Sib sat on the small sofa, crossed her legs and pretended not to notice how hard Tony was trying not to ogle them. She even pretended she wasn't enjoying it.

"Tommy Raggiodisole – or Tommy Sunlight," she said, "is the name of a character created by William Peter Blatty."

"Should I know him?"

"Yes, of course. He was a genius. He wrote the book *The Exorcist* is based on, and directed *The Exorcist III*, which was based on his novel *Legion*."

"So we're looking for a writer obsessed with horror, are we?"

Sibylle grabbed a magazine and hurled it at him. "Idiot."

Tony dodged it. "Bring me up to speed. Because I'm really not following you. Might be an age thing."

"*The Exorcist III* is the true sequel to *The Exorcist*. Have you seen it?"

"The first one. Nearly died of fright."

"Mr Kleenex the Lion-hearted, is it? It was hugely successful, so they shot a sequel that wasn't endorsed by Blatty. A few years later, he wrote and directed a film based on *Legion* – in other words, the real *Exorcist II*. There are many differences between the film and the book, the main one being the name of the baddie. In the film, he's called Patient X, in the book Tommy Sunlight."

"And that's Tommy Raggiodisole."

"Do you know what *Exorcist III* is about?"

"The little girl with the swivelling head, who vomits green mush, grows up and becomes an escort. She meets corporate raider Richard Gere and falls in love."

"The demon Pazuzu is back in town, killing loads of people. And the police have a devil of a job finding him."

"Of course – he's a demon."

"And because, to quote Gabriel, he 'wears people like a pair of gloves.'"

"A brilliant way to fool Forensics, but I don't think it'll help us."

A feeble joke, Tony had to admit. He looked around. Now it was his turn to update Sibylle.

Where to start?

Fifty-Four

1.

"Let's start with reality. Let me present Mirella Buratti. Look."

Click.

2.

The woman in the clip was clasping a handkerchief. She was visibly anxious.

She had applied make-up for the interview: a little foundation and eyeliner, except that the latter was smeared in places where she had tried in vain to hold back her tears.

The clip was from a TV news programme from January 2008. An appeal. The woman's name was Grazia Buratti. Her daughter, Mirella, had been missing for forty-eight hours.

A picture of the girl filled the screen. Mirella's chubby face smiling under a cascade of blonde hair.

3.

Tony froze the picture.

"Mirella," he said, "was twenty-three when she disappeared on

January 11, 2008. The next day, the 12th, her mother contacted the police but since her daughter was of age they had to wait forty-eight hours. On the 13th, there was still no trace of her, and word reached the newspapers. The story ran for a couple of days, then nothing. There were sightings, but they didn't lead anywhere."

"She was never found?"

"Never. We have the report on her disappearance. But Tante Frida didn't just stop at Mirella." Tony opened his arms to indicate the chaos in his office. "Missing persons from Alto Adige: 1999 to the present day. There are more than three hundred. Given the total number of residents, that's huge. She also sent me a file with similar cases that were solved. Accidents, elopements, people who got lost in the woods and were found dead . . ."

"How many?"

"At least three times as many."

"Three times?"

"That's right. The reason I didn't call you was because I tried taking a trip in the world of *if.*"

Sib frowned. "The world of *if?*"

"I tried to think as though there was some truth behind the story of the Wanderer and Gabriel's other fantasies. I put reality aside and started to speculate, as Tante Frida would say."

"Go on."

"I wondered: what do Erika and Mirella have in common? Very little. They come from different places, speak different languages, and led very different lives at different times."

"But they're both young, female and blonde."

"Of course, it's a bit of a stretch, but I was travelling in the world of *if,* OK?"

Sibylle nodded.

"I've tried to narrow down the search to those three parameters. The mess you see here is the result. Seventy-four blonde women under thirty have gone missing in the past twenty years."

"I didn't think there were so many in the first place."

"Neither did I," Tony hastened to say, already beginning to regret sharing his thoughts with Sibylle. "For the time being, none of this means anything. There's nothing to say that Mirella is actually dead – maybe she went to live in Hawaii. In truth, we don't even know for sure that Erika was murdered ... We have a strong suspicion that she was, but no hard evidence. And I haven't even taken Betta into consideration."

"You don't think her death is connected with this?"

"I think our only certainty is that Mirella truly disappeared, and that the person who aroused our suspicions is totally off his head. Do you know the expression 'unreliable witness'?"

"I looked into his eyes. Gabriel wasn't lying. And he's not crazy."

"There's a diagnosis that states the exact opposite."

Sibylle began looking through the files.

4.

Anne Liebermann, 24.

Student.

Went missing on November 22, 2009. Last seen at 1.40 p.m. at a bus stop in Bruneck, wearing a red hat and a pale-blue ski jacket. She was listening to music and moving her head in time. She looked calm.

In the picture, the young woman was hugging a tree and smiling.

Marianna Caiani, 29.

Office worker.

Went missing on July 3, 2011. Last seen coming out of the paint firm where she worked at 3.05 p.m. She was wearing chinos and a dark blouse. She said goodbye to her colleagues, but seemed distracted. She got into her car, a cherry-red Mini, and there has been no sign of her since. The Mini was never found.

In her picture, Mariana was at a Christmas market, wearing a reindeer hat.

Lucia Macchi, 28.

Unemployed.

Went missing on September 15, 2006. Last seen coming out of Domino, a nightclub in Aldein. She had an argument with the bouncer who was concerned about her evident state of intoxication. Further investigation revealed that the young woman was actually a casual worker at the nightclub, with no contract.

Lucia's expression, in the picture circulated by the investigators, seemed one of defiance.

Helena Gamper, 22.

Student.

Went missing on August 15, 2010. Last seen by her mother in Moos in Passeier. Helena was heading to the municipal pool for a swim with close friends. She never reached them.

In the photograph, she was sitting astride a Vespa.

Julia Unterkircher, 23.

Factory worker.

Went missing on September 6, 2015. Last seen at 7.15 p.m. by a distant relative in the centre of Brixen. She said she was waiting for a taxi. The relative offered to give her a lift, but Julia declined and the man went about his business.

The photograph showed a tall young woman in a Pusteria Wolves hockey team T-shirt.

Student . . .

5.

"Sib?"

Tony shook her gently.

"Do we really want to believe that a lunatic could have murdered seventy-four people and got away with it?"

Sibylle did not reply.

Her eyes were haunted. All those lives vanished into thin air.

Tony continued. "Let's pretend the killer is some kind of evil genius and that the police are a bunch of imbeciles. Just think how long it would take to single out a victim, murder her, get rid of the body in an effective way – *extremely* effective, in fact, since not a single body has surfaced. Calculate the time it takes to erase all trace of the victim as well as your own tracks. Shall we say a year? Six months? Let's say three. Seventy-four multiplied by three makes two hundred and twenty-two months, or eighteen years. A woman disappears every three months for eighteen years and nobody notices?

Sib glared at him. "Don't make fun of me, Tony. He didn't necessarily kill all seventy-four. He may have killed a tenth of them, or even two or three and the others just ran away from home, or—"

"Exactly. The parameters are too broad. More than half the women in Alto Adige are blonde. This undermines any calculation from the word go."

"I can see that," Sib said, annoyed. "Every morning in the mirror. OK. Message received. Let's not jump to conclusions."

"One thing at a time. Let's step back from the world of *if*. We've found Mirella. Let's start with her. I think it's worth asking her mother a few questions. The rest is just a theory."

Sibylle began to gather the files. "Anything missing?"

"The supporting materials."

"Like what?"

"Newspaper articles that lead nowhere, pages and pages of transcripts, minutes and more minutes."

"Print it all."

"All of it?"

"All the files. Not just the blondes."

"Sib, it's late. We have to—"

"I'm not sleepy, and I don't have anything to read."

"It's hundreds of pages. Maybe thousands. It's impossible to print everything."

"Is that a tablet, over there?"

Tony linked it to the computer. "You risk losing sight of the crux of the matter."

"I want all the files Tante Frida sent you. Without exception."

"Sib . . ."

"Explain something to me, Tony. Please." She paused and glared at him with defiance. "If you're so sure you're right, if you really think this is all a waste of time—"

"It is."

"Then why are you so terrified?"

Fifty-Five

1.

Grazia Buratti lived in a social housing block of flats built in Via Milano in the 1980s and 1990s. Someone had stuck a sticker showing a psychedelic Jesus on the entry phone. Third floor.

The woman served them home-made peach-flavoured iced tea. It was too sweet and left a bitter aftertaste, but it was cool and refreshing. Tony and Sibylle thanked her.

Through the open window you could hear the shouts of children playing football in the courtyard. A combination of Italian, Albanian, Arabic and Tigrinya.

The missing young woman's mother sat opposite them in a small living room cluttered with pictures of her daughter, sacred images of questionable taste and a dusty television. Her eyes were bloodshot and shiny under heavy lids. Gnawed fingernails. The perfume of her deodorant could not disguise the smell of a body in dire need of a bath.

In a corner, a router connected to an old computer was emitting the odd flicker.

"I use it to keep Mirella's memory alive," she said, catching Tony's glance. "I want those who screwed up to remember her for ever."

"The police?"

"Damn them. They never even looked for her. Never. Not properly, anyway. From the very first day, they told me she'd run away. As far as they were concerned, the matter was closed. They had better things to do. As though my Mirella wasn't important."

"You don't believe she ran away?"

The woman clenched her fists. "Not in a million years. We had a great relationship. Mirella had a job at the Hunting and Fisheries Office. She was looking for a place of her own. Why would she have left?"

"Did she have anyone? I mean a boyfriend or—"

"That's exactly what the police asked me."

"And she didn't?"

"No."

"She might have been seeing someone without your knowledge."

"I knew everything about my daughter," the woman said in the exasperated tone of someone who has repeated a story a thousand times. "I knew she had a crush on her boss, Dario Rossini. And I knew there was a Signora Rossini. I advised Mirella to come to terms with it and move on, because some things are best left alone, but we didn't argue about it. There was no need to shout at Mirella: she was a reasonable girl."

"The police . . ."

Her left eye twitched. She rubbed it as though trying to gouge it out of its socket.

"The police, the police . . ." She dropped her fist on her thigh. "One day I found him right outside my apartment. He must have followed someone in. Mirella's boss. Dr Dario Rossini. Don't ask me what he's a doctor of. An insignificant little man. He accused me of ruining his life. As if I could care less about his reputation."

"Did he seem dangerous to you?"

"That little man?" She gulped down the rest of her tea. "He couldn't have hurt a fly. Nothing but talk."

"Appearances can be deceptive."

"The police turned his life inside out, like a sock. That's why his wife left him. She discovered his affair with my daughter and walked out on him. But they couldn't pin anything on him. That's when they stopped looking. They said Mirella had run away from home. Idiots. I can hear them whispering whenever I go to the police station. They call me 'the madwoman', but I know Mirella is dead. I can feel it. I just need to mourn over my daughter's body. Give her a decent burial. Be able to—"

Her voice broke.

"So you think she's dead," Sibylle said gently.

"Come with me."

They followed her to Mirella's room. There was an oil portrait of Kurt Cobain hanging above the bed. Judging by the brushstrokes, it had been painted by the young woman. On the floor, in the gap between the wardrobe and the window, there were two more paintings.

Jim and Jimi. Morrison and Hendrix.

A few coloured candles were displayed on a cluttered bookshelf, next to a Thun ceramic angel. *How to Fight Shyness. I'm OK, You're OK. Fitness for the Lazy. You Can . . . If You Want to!* A couple of natural diet books. Crystals, aromatherapy oils and a book on feng shui, but no tarots or anything like that, Tony noted. In a corner, under an ironing board, there was a foam rubber mat, rolled up and secured with an elastic band. A blouse with a diamond pattern lay folded on the ironing board. There were photographs on the walls.

Mirella with her arm around a friend. Mirella sticking her tongue out. A dreamy-looking Mirella immortalised in front of a sunset by the sea. Even on the beach she wore socks and baggy T-shirts. Mirella with more friends – always female, never male. Mirella, who fell in love with her boss. Mirella, who hung her accountancy diploma next to the painting of Kurt Cobain.

Mirella, who . . .

"Do you really believe," Signora Buratti said, "that a girl like this would leave at the drop of a hat?"

Fifty-Six

1.

Her name was Alessandra, but the badge pinned to her chest said "Alexandra". Alexandra worked in a perfume shop in the city centre and was in charge of the health section. Products for acne, irritated skin, self-tanning. She had told them over the phone that she could only spare a few minutes or her boss would get pissed off. And that she was on a temporary contract.

At the appointed time, she waited in the street. After a brief introduction, she took them to a table in a café not far from the shop.

"Grazia said you often go and see her."

"I like her. But she hasn't been the same since her daughter went missing. Nothing like when Mirella and I were at school together. She's a wreck now, but once upon a time she was a force of nature."

"Were you and Mirella close?"

"Yes, very."

"Did you know about Rossini?"

Alexandra grimaced. "That pig? He just fucked her. That was all he wanted. He would never have left his wife. Besides, Mirella had somebody else. I told Grazia. I also told the police, but I have no idea who it was. I never met him, and she never told me outright, but some things you can just sense."

"What do you mean?"

The young woman adjusted the thick smock that the perfume shop staff had as their uniform. Tony did not envy her in the least. In this heat, it would be like going around in a diving suit.

"Mirella was suddenly more radiant. More beautiful. She started to take better care of herself. She even lost weight. Not that there was anything wrong with that, since Mirella had always been on the chubby side. She got her hair cut. Short, like Valentina from those comic strips. It didn't particularly suit her, but she liked it and it was enough to make her look . . . sexier. She was a bit more self-confident and that gave her a little something extra. And she dumped her circle of friends, all her former schoolmates and—"

"Friends like you?"

Alexandra toyed with her coffee spoon. "At first, I was upset. But the day before she left, she dropped by and gave me this. I thought it might interest you."

A paperback. Kenneth Grahame's *The Wind in the Willows*. A very worn copy.

"Was it hers?"

"That's what she said. And now you're going to ask me about the doodle, aren't you? Everyone else does."

"What doodle?"

Alexandra showed them the first page of the book.

Every journey is a new beginning.

Next to Mirella's flowing signature was a doodle: the hummingbird smile.

"Who else?" Sibylle said. "You mean the police?"

"They took photos of it, they took down my statement and that's the last I heard from them." Alexandra stood up and anxiously checked her watch. "No, I mean the other guy. The one with the long hair and the tattoos."

Fifty-Seven

1.

Under the jet of the air conditioning, Sibylle was absorbed in the materials collected by Tante Frida. Sitting at his desk, Tony was busy chewing at a black Bic. He had dozens of them scattered around the house. He said that writing by hand helped him concentrate. It was partly true and partly superstition. He had written the first draft of *Two* with a biro like this one.

"What are you thinking?"

Tony was startled.

"Did I frighten you?"

"I was thinking. I sometimes—"

"Abstract yourself?"

"Great writers abstract themselves," Tony said. "I just absent myself for a while."

"And where the hell were you?"

"Mirella's room. Tell me what books you read, and I'll tell you who you are. Mirella read a lot of self-help books. *How to Lose Weight in a Hundred Days. Change Your Life by Moving Your Furniture Around.*"

"I prefer Stephen King."

"I've always found them much more disturbing than Stephen King."

"You don't look like the macrobiotic diet type."

Tony smiled. "I'm a writer. Writers read."

"How silly of me – I thought writers wrote. Why do you find them disturbing?"

Tony stood up and took a rather bulky volume from the bookcase. "A hunting manual?"

"Research for a novel I never wrote. I was just thinking about some ... parameters."

"Young, blonde women under thirty."

"Not exactly."

The biro returned to Tony's lips. He sat down. Even though his eyes were directed at Sibylle's legs, he wasn't really looking at them. He was huddling in some corner of his mind again. "Do you think I'm a cynic? Be honest."

Sibylle was taken aback. "I could use a lot of adjectives to describe you, but definitely not cynical."

Tony blinked and returned to the office overlooking Via Resia.

After a few seconds' lag, he looked away from Sib's legs. "The authors of these manuals are. They know perfectly well that adding a few drops of lemon juice to your diet won't change your view of the world. And you certainly won't find the love of your life or have a successful career just because you stick a piece of quartz on your bedside table. They're manipulators. They use people's vulnerabilities to ... well, to make money."

"In a way, all artists do that. Through writing, painting or music, they manipulate readers' emotions and earn their living. You're no different."

"Wrong. To quote one of the horror films you like so much: 'I'm selling the sizzle, not the steak.'"

Sibylle clicked her fingers. "Easy! *Halloween*, Rob Zombie's version. The second one. Carpenter hated it, but I didn't mind it. It's a line from Dr Loomis, played by Malcolm McDowell, the guy from *A Clockwork Orange*."

"You see? My pop culture knowledge isn't so deficient."

"Maybe not, but you're good at avoiding questions. You're not cynical, but you are *avoidive*. Does the word 'avoidive' exist"?"

"I don't think so."

"Well, they should invent it."

Tony pressed the biro against his chin. "Low-cost answers. That's what these guys sell. They're offering the steak, only the steak doesn't exist. I sell the sizzle. Fiction. A few days in the company of stories to give you breathing space. That's what my readers are after. And I'm happy to provide it." He began to wave the biro in the air, as though conducting an orchestra only he could hear. "What do the guys who write these manuals offer? Change. Change the way you dress and do your hair. Change the way you see yourself. And above all – and this is something I can't stand – these gurus are always urging you to divide people into 'positive' and 'negative'. Naturally, they suggest that you distance yourself from the negative ones."

"What's wrong with that?"

"The fact that they presume," Tony said abruptly, "to tell you who's negative."

"You make them sound like a bunch of Charles Mansons."

Tony smiled. For a moment he was once more the little boy who had escaped the bullies by hiding in the library.

"An apt example. Creating dependency. That's what they want. And that leads to isolation, to exclusion from groups you were close to. Your family, for instance. Have you ever seen one of those documentaries where a lioness stalks a herd of antelopes? She never darts into the middle of the herd. No, she waits for one of the antelopes, the weakest one, to cut itself off. This is all a bit pop psychology, but you did ask what I was thinking. So now you know."

"Do you think Mirella's new boyfriend was some kind of manipulator?"

"Let's remember to take everything with a pinch of salt. But yes. Mirella may have been seduced by a very cunning predator. And vice versa."

"Vice versa?"

"We go hunting for what I like. Young, blonde women. These parameters don't actually relate to the victims. They tell us what our hypothetical – and I stress *hypothetical* – Wanderer likes."

"Are you thinking of Gabriel?"

Frustrated, Tony hit his knee with his pen. "I've been thinking about this over and over again. At first glance, Gabriel fits perfectly. Insane, violent, morbidly drawn to Erika's death, and he has a penchant for blondes. But can you really picture Mirella with someone like Gabriel?"

"As a matter of fact, no. Gabriel could have charmed someone like Yvette, but Mirella . . . Mirella was your typical good girl who went out with her female school friends on Saturday nights. She lived with her mother and had a crush on her boss."

"Exactly."

"And yet you have a theory."

"It's just a theory."

Sibylle huffed. "Do you really have to say this every time?"

"Yes, because speculation rhymes with—"

"Who then?"

Tony took a while to answer. The biro went from his lips to the desk then back again. "An intelligent man. Capable of manipulating others. Knows how to handle people. With a certain charm, you understand? But at the same time cold. Very cold. Someone who watches, studies, waits. Who doesn't act on impulse."

"And with a weakness for blondes."

"Am I mistaken or is Karin Perkman blonde? Let's play the birthday game, Sibylle. How old was Michl Horst in '99?"

Sib provided the answer without hesitation. Ever since she had found the photo of Erika in her letterbox, she had been doing nothing but calculating dates of birth.

"He was born in '72. In February, if I'm not mistaken, or perhaps—"

Polianna opened the door to the office. She was pale. "There's someone who . . ."

Who frightens you, Tony thought. And anyone who frightened Polianna was looking for trouble.

The man came in unannounced.

"It's a pleasure to meet you, Signor Carcano."

Fifty-Eight

1.

Tall, with short, grey hair. A military crew cut. Glasses with thin wire frames. A cold expression. A mocking smile. He was wearing an expensive-looking linen suit.

"Edvard Bukreev."

A Russian accent.

Alto Adige and the Trentino region were full of Russians. Historically, Merano had been a destination for the Tsarist aristocracy. And Lake Garda had practically been colonised by the nouveau riche who had proliferated after the fall of the Soviet Union.

But what was a Russian doing in his home?

Tony signalled to Polianna that everything was alright. Even if that was not strictly true. This man stank of money. A lot of money. It was not just about his clothes but his bearing. The rich – those whose wealth is calculated in stock exchange fluctuations and not in cash – carry themselves as though nothing can touch them. And they bring trouble.

Like the Perkmans.

Polianna left the room and closed the door.

"Signor Bukreev," Tony said. "I have no idea who you are or how you found me, but please take a seat."

Sibylle, still standing, went to the window, putting the maximum possible distance between her and the newcomer. She crossed her arms. She missed her arsehole slasher.

"I apologise for intruding like this," Bukreev said. "I tried to contact you by email. In vain. So I came in person."

Chiara the bookseller, Tony thought. The emails. Along with the madman who addressed him as "Dear Mr Antichrist", Tony remembered having deleted at least three messages from a Russian who wrote like Tolstoy. The fact that he was here, in his home, made him shudder.

The Russian continued. "You're not the kind of person who yields to pressure, are you, Signor Carcano?"

"What do you mean?"

Bukreev indicated a shelf above the desk. "The foreign editions of your novels. Others would find it scary to keep them in the room where they work. Success can pile pressure on those on whom it is bestowed."

"On the contrary, I find them reassuring," Tony replied. "Like bad reviews. It means I'm not a genius. Geniuses die young and broke, while I want a long, comfortable life."

"And yet you've gone up against Karin Perkman."

"You read the gossip rags, do you, Signor Bukreev?"

"I read anything I find useful." Bukreev turned to Sib. "Signorina Knapp, I presume. Now I understand why the non-genius here present has decided to put his long, comfortable future in jeopardy. You're a gem, if I may say so."

"If you don't tell us why you're here," Sibylle replied, "this gem is going to kick you."

The Russian seemed to get the message.

He opened his briefcase and took out a sheet of paper. "Here."

It was an ordinary photocopy on ordinary paper. From the looks of it, the reproduction of a page from an old book. At its centre, the hummingbird smile.

Sibylle handed the paper to Tony.

"Have you heard of Friedrich Von Junzt?" Bukreev said. "The *Unaussprechlichen Kulten*?"

"No," Tony lied, "but I'm a big fan of Sophie Kinsella. Have you read anything by her?"

Bukreev closed his briefcase and put it down next to him. "Strange man, Von Junzt. Died in 1833 at the young age of forty-one. An anthropologist, we'd call him nowadays. But also an astronomer, a mathematician and an opium addict. Something that makes him irresistible to us, don't you think?"

Tony did not reply. His silence did not seem to bother Bukreev, whose icy face was showing signs of life for the first time. "This symbol . . . You asked an ignorant bookseller, Chiara, from that bookshop—"

"Carnival, in Via Andreas Hofer."

"Exactly. The young bookseller put feelers out among the community of those interested in such things. 'Anybody know this symbol?' The question circulated and eventually it reached me. I am that anybody." The Russian indicated the photocopy in Tony's hand. "That's why I tried to contact you, and why I am here. The symbol comes straight from the Von Junzt masterpiece, the *Unaussprechlichen Kulten*. This is a photocopy of a page from – alas – a second edition of the book. It's rare enough, though not as rare as the first printing, of course, and was edited by the Düsseldorf scholar shortly before his premature death. Von Junzt was murdered. Presumably for having divulged things then considered unfit to be divulged."

"What nonsense."

"You think so?"

"People in 1833 didn't die because of a book."

"In the twenties and thirties, not to mention the forties, anything written by Oppenheimer, Heisenberg and Fermi was considered top secret. Anyone who read as much as one word risked being murdered by the secret service."

"This is a pure exercise in rhetoric on your part. Fermi and company dealt with very concrete things."

"Concrete and terrible, I agree."

"You make it sound like a threat."

"On the contrary, Signor Carcano. Mine is an offer of help. You want to learn about the Von Junzt and I am here to tell you what I know."

"Why?"

The Russian pretended not to hear the question.

Tony was about to repeat it when Bukreev took a thick stack of photocopies from his briefcase and handed it to him.

"What is it?"

"Take it, it won't bite."

Tony did.

"It's a photocopy of the second edition of the Von Junzt, from my personal collection."

"Don't you have a first edition?" Tony said mockingly. "Too expensive?"

"As far as I know there's only one complete copy of the first edition."

"In the Perkman library?" Sibylle said.

"In the Horst library," the Russian replied.

"Did you know him?"

Bukreev assumed his impassive mask again. "I met him once. I made him an offer for the first edition, but he laughed in my face. After he died, I offered three times as much to Friedrich Perkman, but he wasn't all there anymore . . ."

"In what sense?"

Bukreev crossed his legs. "There are three types of people interested in this kind of book. Those who treat cancer with bicarbonate of soda, those who slaughter hens at midnight to summon the devil, and those able to appreciate the *intrinsic* quality of such texts."

"Intrinsic? Meaning?"

"Owning a first edition Von Junzt is tantamount to owning a work of art. A so-called safe asset. I'm a businessman, Signor Carcano, not someone who slaughters hens."

"What about Perkman?" Sibylle said. "Did he dance with spirits in the moonlight?"

"Perkman implied that he truly believed in its bizarre contents."

"Do we mean the same Perkman who, back in the seventies, sensed that the future was in electronics?"

"People change, Signorina Knapp. Especially as they get old and sick. Besides, who says that computers and ancient legends can't be interconnected? Von Junzt's ideas about overlapping universes could be seen as the forerunners of Schrödinger or Tomonaga's theories. And the Wanderer could be a good metaphor for Paul Dirac's studies on antimatter."

The turn the conversation was taking was threatening to give Tony a headache, so he decided to steer it towards more concrete ground. "If you read my housekeeper's recipes in front of a mirror at midnight, they also conceal amazing esoteric and scientific discoveries. Stop pulling my leg, Bukreev. How much is a Von Junzt worth? A first edition, I mean."

"I offered Perkman seven million euros."

"Seven million? Are you kidding me?"

Bukreev indicated Tony's bookcase. "I see you have a passion for Hemingway. How much would you pay for a copy of *The Old Man and the Sea*?"

"The cover price, I guess."

"And what if it were an American first edition?"

"No idea."

"Current estimates are pushing twenty thousand dollars."

"What are you trying to say, Bukreev?"

"What all collectors know. That books often have strange backstories, and their worth is partly based on that backstory. Imagine I was proposing to sell a copy of *The Old Man and the Sea* that John Fitzgerald Kennedy had in his pocket on November 22, 1963. A copy stained with the blood of King Arthur. Its value would be inestimable, don't you think?"

"I'm asking you once again. What is it you want from us, Signor Bukreev?"

"You asked what this symbol was, and I'm here to tell you what I know."

"I'm all ears."

"According to Von Junzt, the symbol is a portal to Evil. An invitation that allows Evil to be incarnated. The key to lure the Wanderer."

"For a cynical businessman, it seems to me you belong to the second category rather than the third, Signor Bukreev. Should I be hiding the dog or do you only slaughter hens?"

Bukreev stood up. "Keep the photocopies. You never know what could come out of them." A smile. "And say hello to Zingerle for me."

"Zingerle?"

"He's recently had a baby girl and I haven't yet had a chance to congratulate him. My respects, signorina. I wish you a long and comfortable life."

Fifty-Nine

1.

In her dream, Sibylle met her mother.

Erika was wearing a long red dress. They were not in the house in Kreuzwirt, but in Tony's apartment. Erika was barefoot.

There were black water stains on the floor.

Erika had brought with her the smell of the peat bog and the lake. Her skin was cold. Even so, Sibylle let her hug her. She let Erika's hands stroke her.

"You should add some lemon juice to your diet, sweetheart." Sibylle broke away from the embrace. "You should stay away from negative people."

Tommy Raggiodisole was wearing an evening dress, red and stained in mud. "You should get over the past."

White eyes and a mouth like a lioness. "And get your hair cut. You'd look much better with short hair."

Sixty

1.

Alto Adige was full of Zingerles, but there had only ever been one Ignaz Vinzenz Zingerle Edler von Summersberg. Born in Merano on June 6, 1825, died in Innsbruck on September 17, 1892 – he was the only one Bukreev could have meant. It was not instinct that brought Tony to this conclusion, but simple logic.

2.

With a name like that, Ignaz Vinzenz-and-so-forth had only two options in life: to become a merchant, like his father, or else embark on a career as a theologian, like his uncle, who had made it as far as the Vatican. Instead, Ignaz became a philologian, a Germanist and, above all, an expert in myths and sagas. In other words, he spent his entire life swimming in the same waters that the Russian tycoon so enjoyed. And Perkman, before he died. And Horst, too, since – apparently – the Perkman library was in fact the Horst library.

There were photographs of Ignaz Vinzenz Zingerle that showed a man with a good-natured face and a flowing beard. The kind of person you could picture entertaining a brood of grandchildren with stories by the fire. While smoking a pipe, just to keep to the stereotype. Ignaz Zingerle's only living descendant had set up a website about his illustrious ancestor. Thomas Zingerle – for that was his name – lived at the foot of the Plose slopes, a stone's throw from Brixen, in an attractive villa surrounded by vineyards. Life must be treating him well.

Ignaz's descendant – clean-shaven, dark hair – signalled to Tony to cut the engine. He was pushing a pram. Inside it, a newborn baby girl was sleeping peacefully. His third child, he told Tony.

3.

Thomas Zingerle led the way to the villa, a modern building with large windows, plunged into the cheerful chaos particular to a family of five – and happy. "I've dreamed of writing a biography of Ignaz for years, but I'm afraid my literary talent stops at composing invoices."

"What do you do?"

"Animal feed. Ignaz would not have been proud of me."

"Why? Did he hate farming?"

Thomas Zingerle (*Just Thomas*, he had said over the phone, *the tradition of never-ending names should be confined to the nineteenth century*) showed Tony into a room crammed with objects, books, diaries and photographs. A kind of museum. "I followed in my father's footsteps, while Ignaz was a rebel. His father wanted him to be a merchant or a theologian, but he had other ideas. All because of a book. That one." He indicated a volume.

Tony smiled. "Fairy tales. By the Brothers Grimm."

"His nanny read them to him. When Ignaz was a little older, he discovered that the two brothers hadn't made up a single word of what they had written. They had simply collected stories people had been telling for centuries. So he decided to do the same. This is his first published book."

Sagas from South Tyrol.

"An inquisitive man."

"And an intelligent one," Thomas said. "There are many of his notes here. The Grimms had correspondents who wrote down local legends and sent them to them by post. Ignaz did not agree with this method and developed an avant-garde approach of his own. Not only did he go to talk to his sources in person, but in his books made a clear distinction between his own thoughts and those of his interlocutor. Nowadays, this is pretty much standard procedure, but he was one of the first to put it into practice."

Thomas took a period photograph from a cupboard drawer. Two men in ridiculous knickerbockers and feathered hats, with rucksacks on their backs. They were smiling, standing next to a mule loaded with sacks and a large chest. One of the men was Ignaz. The other was much younger, with a Kaiser-style moustache and a proud expression.

"That's Fritz Giraldi. Fritz was a *Welschtiroler*, so—"

"From Trento, an Italian born under the Kaiser's flag."

"He was the guide who escorted Ignaz whenever he set out to hold his interviews. Fritz knew the mountains like the back of his hand."

Tony pointed to the rifle resting against the shoulder of the man with the moustache. "He was a hunter."

"That's why Ignaz picked him in the first place. Then, despite the gulf in social class and education, they became great friends."

"Did they go hunting together?"

"No, the rifle was for protection. Judging by the letters Ignaz wrote to his wife, Alto Adige was a rather dangerous, primitive place back then. But that's not why you're here, is it? You said on the phone that you were interested in the *Unaussprechlichen Kulten*."

Tony showed Thomas Zingerle the stack of photocopies given to him by Bukreev. He had spent all night poring over them, not understanding a great deal. Not only because the print and the old German made it hard to read and decipher, but because of what Von Junzt (an opium addict, according to the Russian, and Tony had seen this confirmed by the first few lines) had written. Obscure formulae and senseless abbreviations, delirious passages about plateaus concealed behind the veil of reality. Tony had found one long passage highly entertaining, he had to admit – an invective against Schopenhauer (*he confused Mayan with Aklo!*) – but the rest . . .

The Wanderer. Hinges that oozed evil. Worlds in precarious equilibrium.

Ricky Riccardo, if you're out there, give us a shout.

Even now, Tony could not stop wondering why Bukreev had suddenly showed up at his home. He could have been a wealthy eccentric in search of an audience for his strange tales, but Tony did not believe that. Bukreev was a businessman, and businessmen always have their eyes on some prize or another. So he tried to do a quick search on him. He seldom appeared in the database of the newspapers Tony subscribed to, and always in connection with large investments in methane pipelines or contracts for roads and bridges. A guy like that, Tony thought, always wanted something.

The question was: what?

He had not found an answer.

However, as the first light of day filtered through the shutters to find him rereading the *Unaussprechlichen Kulten* for the third time, he came across a symbol on page thirty-two that had nothing to do with Von Junzt's delirium.

A stamp.

What had Bukreev said? That books have odd backstories. Exactly. The stamp on page thirty-two was the mark of the library of the Sabiona convent in Klausen, not far from Bolzano. And so, as he took Freddy for a walk while Sibylle was sleeping the sleep of the just, Tony had tried calling.

A very nice, very early-rising nun had told him that the book he was enquiring about, a second edition of the Von Junzt, was no longer held at the convent. It had been donated in the early 1980s to the Orthodox Church in Moscow and was now in the private collection of a certain Edvard Bukreev.

"How did this second edition of the Von Junzt end up in the convent library?"

"It was donated by Ignaz Vinzenz Zingerle shortly before his death. Zingerle had two copies of the book and thought the second edition would be of interest to the abbot at the time."

"Two copies of the *Unaussprechlichen Kulten*?"

"Besides the second edition he gave the convent, Zingerle owned an extremely rare first edition which he kept for himself, naturally. Unfortunately, it was stolen. No-one knows by whom or how. The only thing we know for sure is that at present the first edition of the *Unaussprechlichen Kulten* is in the Perkman collection."

"But if it's stolen goods, how can—"

The nun burst into an uproarious laugh. "How naïve you are, Signor Carcano!"

4.

"Did Ignaz ever mention *The Wind in the Willows*? The book by Kenneth Grahame? In connection with the *Unaussprechlichen Kulten*? I know it might seem silly, but . . ."

Thomas gave him a knowing smile. "How could he have? Ignaz died in 1892 and *The Wind in the Willows* was published in 1908."

That's what happens, Tony thought, when you abandon reason and start drawing parallels between things that have no logical link.

"Bukreev. It was he who sent you here, right?" Thomas said craftily.

Tony's face flushed.

Thomas burst out laughing. "Whenever there's talk of my ancestor, you'll always find Bukreev lurking somewhere. Exactly because of this theory that links the *Unaussprechlichen Kulten* and Kenneth Grahame."

"So there's something in it, then?"

"In the forties, a German scholar called Michael See came up with a bizarre theory that linked Ignaz and Grahame. Some adventure my ancestor allegedly had, shortly before he died."

"What kind of link?"

"A *Pinocchio* kind of link."

Tony thought he had misheard. "*Pinocchio*? By Collodi? That *Pinocchio*?"

"Do you really know about the Von Junzt and have no idea about *Pinocchio*?"

Sixty-One

1.

Her eyes stinging from being hunched so long over the tablet, Sibylle was beginning to wonder what the hell she was looking for. The tax number and driving licence of whoever it was who had made Mirella disappear?

It certainly was not to be found among the flood of data Tante Frida had poured over them. Not with what little tangible evidence they had to go on. It was like fishing for sardines with a tuna net. So what was she *really* looking for?

Something, she told herself, that would tighten the mesh and make it so small that, as Tante Frida would say, they would *trip over* the right sardine.

But she would not find it by continuing to stare at the faces of all those unknown women. She abandoned the tablet. It was sapping her energy, not to mention her ability to think clearly.

So she had to backtrack.

Forget about Erika, Horst, Perkman. Drop Gabriel and focus on Mirella. Had they overlooked something? Sibylle slapped herself.

"Mirella . . ."

There *was* something concrete, tangible and objective which neither she nor Tony had considered. Or *somebody*. Someone who might be able to answer a few questions. Not a demon, not an extra in the world of *if*. A witness who would not be at all happy to be disturbed. Sibby Longstocking's specialty.

Why had it not occurred to her sooner? Because, she thought, we've been acting like cocky children. We've obsessed over details and taken our eye off the bigger picture.

Sibylle smiled, ready for one of her tricks. But first she needed to do some shopping. Style, Aunt Helga always said, isn't everything.

But almost.

In a Shanghai shop, she bought a dress that Polianna would have approved of (Sib had noticed her looks, freighted with the same "Do you really have to go around dressed like that?" as Aunt Helga's), then she went online to find out how to get to the region's Hunting and Fisheries Office, changed, took the bus and joined the queue, holding a nice big folder. Naturally, it was full of blank sheets. It was just for show. Like the dress. Style isn't everything, but almost.

When her turn came, she smiled and walked into the office of Mirella's lover.

"Rossini," he said, smiling.

"Buratti," she said in return.

He was startled.

Sib closed the door. "Mirella Buratti." Sibylle sat and crossed her legs. "Tell me about her."

"Please leave."

"Please."

"Get out!"

Sib put the arsehole slasher on the desk. A brand-new arsehole slasher, made in Shanghai, which would not be approved of by either Aunt Helga or Polianna. But definitely by Tante Frida.

2.

"Did you know Collodi was a Freemason?"

"Actually, I didn't."

"Now don't go thinking about conspiracies, UFOs and terrorist attacks. In Collodi's day, it was a kind of club for freethinkers. And that's exactly what Collodi was: a freethinker. Perhaps a little too free, since he was expelled. Because of *Pinocchio*."

"Critics are never kind to geniuses."

Thomas smiled. "What is *Pinocchio* about? The long journey a puppet undertakes in order to become a flesh-and-blood boy. He is assisted by the Fairy with Turquoise Hair. And it's the Fairy with Turquoise Hair who gets him into trouble with the widow's sons. Think about it: until then, nobody had ever used the word 'turquoise' when referring to a female character – if you think—"

"That's right – shades of blue are always for boys."

"As a matter of fact, the Masonic ceremonial apron is turquoise. Collodi's fellow masons saw through it. *Pinocchio* is no more than an allegory for the initiation rite which the aspiring Freemason undertakes in order to achieve ultimate knowledge."

"That's funny."

"Michael See, the forties scholar, stated in one of his essays that Kenneth Grahame had done the same thing with the Von Junzt. He transformed the knowledge contained in the *Unaussprechlichen Kulten* – of which, may I remind you, there were very few copies, fifty in the first edition – into a successful children's story."

Tony thought again about Grahame's book, and could not help laughing. The shy, sweet mole, the water rat who lives down the river, the toad obsessed with automobiles.

"Thomas, I've read the Von Junzt and I loved *The Wind in the Willows* when I was a child, and this is utter madness. Sorry to be so frank."

"Let me finish. According to Michael See, Ignaz Zingerle was the evidence that proved his theory. He's also the reason Edvard Bukreev sends me Christmas cards and never forgets my children's or my wife's birthdays. Zingerle had come across – wait, come and see this."

Thomas showed him a wooden tea chest identical to the one that could be seen weighing heavily on the back of the mule in the photograph of Ignaz and his guide. Tony helped him open it. It contained a strange contraption.

"In Ignaz's day, philology was a very important field. Recovering a sense of the people and their roots was a task very close to the hearts of those who ruled. Which is why Ignaz had almost unlimited funding. And he was a genius. He used this device in his studies. Ignaz didn't just write down the fairy tales and legends he was told. He wanted everything to be transmitted to posterity. He lived at a time of important changes and experienced them very painfully. The railways were levelling the mountains, the airship was conquering the skies. Everything he loved was disappearing. At the same time, however, he valued the novelties technology made possible."

"Is this a recorder?"

Thomas nodded. "Ignaz wanted posterity not only to read the legends but also and above all *hear* them. The tone. The language. The coughing. Everything. Unfortunately, most of the original recordings have been lost. They were destroyed in the 1961 fire. But in 1953, Ignaz's son, my great-grandfather, transferred some onto reels. The famous 'Zingerle reels.'"

He handed him one. It was heavy.

"And Bukreev wants to buy them," Tony said, "even if they're fakes?"

Thomas laughed. "You're right, there were no tape recorders in Ignaz's time. As a matter of fact, he would record on wax. Wax cones, to be exact. These, on the other hand, are tapes from the fifties. That's why few people believe that these reels are an authentic reproduction of Ignaz's wax cones. Actually, to be honest, practically all the scholars deny that the original recordings ever existed."

"But not people like Bukreev."

"Or like me, Signor Carcano."

"Why?"

"Because my father told me he'd seen my great-grandfather transfer the wax cones onto these tapes."

"He could have lied."

Thomas shrugged. "I'm not trying to convince you, Signor Carcano. I'm simply telling you that there are those who believe these tapes contain what Michael See described as a connection between Grahame and the Von Junzt. In other words, the proof that Von Junzt's work was very similar to that undertaken by the Brothers Grimm."

"So the *Unaussprechlichen Kulten* contains some kind of arcane knowledge, which your ancestor recorded on his wax cones, and which Grahame turned into a fairy story in his book?"

Thomas had just finished assembling an old recorder, very different from the one in the box. Not as old, but hardly a latest-generation Sony.

"Exactly."

Thomas inserted the reel into the machine and tightened it. He pushed a couple of switches. The valves crackled and there was some popping. The machine buzzed.

"Allow me to give you the context. Ignaz and Fritz are in Ahrntal. Do you know it?"

"Above the Puster Valley."

"This is 1890, two years before Ignaz's death. It's winter. Harsh conditions. There's a letter from Ignaz's wife that's very explicit about this."

"'Wrap up well, it's cold out there?'"

"More like, 'Where the hell do you think you're going, at your age?' But despite the weather and the season, Ignaz and Fritz take the mule and travel to Ahrntal. Ignaz is over the moon, his letters from that period are full of exclamation marks. After many years and a great deal of research, he had an opportunity to realise the dream of a lifetime." Thomas pushed a switch. The spools started turning. "To interview a witch."

Sixty-Two

1.

"What do you want from me?"

Sib could picture him yelling at Grazia Buratti, Mirella's mother, accusing her of ruining his life and what have you.

The prospect of turning the guy into mincemeat appealed to Sibby Longstocking.

"Tell me about Mirella."

"I should call the police."

Sib toyed with the flick knife. "But you won't."

Rossini looked first at the knife, then at Sibylle's face. He saw determination in both.

"That bloody whore. My wife left me and now I only see my children once a week. By disappearing, in inverted commas, she got me into serious trouble."

"Weren't you in love?"

"I can't speak for her."

"I'm here for your point of view."

Rossini adjusted his tie. He was wearing cheap aftershave. The office was steeped in it.

"I liked her. She was nothing special, a bit clumsy even, but she . . . there was something about her."

"So you screwed her behind your wife's back."

Rossini was startled. "Are you the judgmental kind, signorina?"

"I'm just curious."

"Why these questions?"

"A friend of Mirella's has asked me to do a little investigating into her disappearance."

"Like hell did she disappear. I saw her again. A year later. At a karaoke bar. Did you know Mirella was into that? She always wanted to take me. A real pain. We had to go all the way to Trento, you know, so as not to bump into anyone who might recognise me."

"Why didn't you tell the police?"

"It was late and I was drunk. They wouldn't have believed me."

Despite Rossini's general air of aggression, Sibylle put the arsehole slasher back in her handbag.

"You said you don't like karaoke. That it's a pain."

"So?"

"So I'm wondering how come, a year after Mirella's disappearance, you were at a karaoke bar."

Rossini lowered his head.

The little cockerel's crest has fallen, Sib thought. "Did you miss her?"

Rossini did not reply.

"Be honest, Rossini. You missed her. That's why you were there, isn't it?"

The insensitive arsehole's façade crumbled.

"Yes. I – I missed her. She was awkward, and every time we decided to see each other it was as though we were committing some kind of crime, she was so anxious, but I missed her. At the time I thought she was dead, *murdered*. And I felt responsible. I pictured Mirella, her throat cut, in a ditch or at the bottom of a cliff. Or with a slip-knot round her neck."

"What? Suicide?"

"If there was anybody likely to kill herself, it was Mirella. So introverted, so alone. She had friends, but they were all from school. Always the same ones. Is there anything sadder?"

Yes, Sib thought. The office manager who screws his trainee on the side.

And if Sib pitied him, Sibby Longstocking could not bear the guy. "Which bar?"

"The Tucano. It's near the Trento Sud exit."

"And that's where you saw Mirella?"

"It was her. I'm sure of it. It was dark, from a distance, and I was nowhere near sober. But I'm sure it was her."

Sibylle did not let herself be intimidated. "Are you messing with me, Signor Rossini? What are you hiding?"

"Nothing," he said, sounding weary. "Not anymore. But it was her. I'm sure of it. And you know why? Because she was wearing the coat I had given her. A red coat, very unusual. Sixties style – flower power. There was a conference in Verona. That's where I bought it. She liked it. She said it was her favourite."

"So you saw *somebody*, at night, wearing the same coat. And you want me to believe it was Mirella."

"Let me finish. Mirella said hello to me. Before getting into a car and disappearing. Whenever we saw each other in the office she always made a gesture, 'our secret gesture', she called it . . . because *we* were a secret . . . And the woman in the red coat made the same gesture. Identical. No-one else knew it."

"Then she got in the car and drove away . . .?"

"You know what the oddest thing about it is?"

"Tell me."

"Mirella didn't have a driving licence."

Sixty-Three

1.

... close the window so ...

Sounds.
  Someone clearing his throat.

Here we are. Frau Holle, it's a pleasure to meet you. You have no idea how long ... like you.

Tony looked at Thomas. It was a very poor-quality recording. Rustling, background noise, entire words missing. And the German spoken by Ignaz Zingerle was very hard for Tony to understand, almost incomprehensible. Luckily, Thomas acted as interpreter.
  The woman's laugh startled them both.

I'm not a Frau. I have no ... to rule over me.
  I apologise, Fräulein Holle.
  Not Holle. That's what ... people call me. Stupid people.
  Then ... may I call you?
  Just ... Herr Professor.
  What a beautiful name. Can you come a little closer to this ... that's right, so you can be heard better. Perfect. Can you say your name again?

*

The gravelly voice came out nice and clear through the loudspeakers.

Erika. My name is Erika.

Sixty-Four

1.

It was not a thought but the shadow of a thought that had not yet found the right words to express itself. A sort of itch that became increasingly irritating the longer it went unscratched.

Rossini's words had triggered something in Sibylle's memory, which she could not quite put her finger on. As though she had read something in Tante Frida's papers that her brain had discarded and archived and which was now demanding attention. Sibylle was certain, *certain*, that she had already stumbled upon something useful in the mass of data sent by Tante Frida.

Not in the list of blonde women under thirty. In the other one, the one that catalogued reports filed in error, and solved cases. The largest haystack. People on the run from their debts found curled up in train-station waiting rooms, or individuals with mental health problems who ended up in charity shelters. Kids who had run away from home after being forbidden to go to the cinema, tracked down just a few days later, full of remorse and fear. Lovers who had decided that their new passion was not worth a radical break from their previous lives.

And dead bodies.

Tante Frida's files were full of dead people. Unidentified bodies waiting for an electronic archive to connect their fingerprints with names and faces. Packed in cold storage, waiting for someone to mourn them.

Holding the tablet just a few centimetres from her face, Sibylle muttered to herself as she scrolled, swearing, huffing, hoping that one of those faces, a note or a date would put an end to that damned itch. The shadow of a—

There.

Tony would have described it as Ricky Riccardo stuff, but it was there before her eyes. Black on white.

The dead who returned from their graves.

Sixty-Five

1.

The dead always know where they are. Nothing happens to the . . . They have no masters and they don't . . . pupils. The dead know the world. They're afraid of the world.

Where are the dead? And why are they afraid of the world? Are you afraid of the world, Fräulein Erika?

Underground. At the edge of the wood. I know the world above and the one below. I'm afraid. You're also afraid, Herr Professor.

Me? Why?

Because you have a rifle. Are you afraid of Fräulein Erika, Herr Professor? Do you believe what . . . in town?

Tell me about the dead.

They always know where they are. The wise dead.

Do you mean the cemetery outside the village?

No. No. The dead are beneath the trees, before the clearing.

And what's in the clearing?

Singing and dancing until the sun rises. And many other things.

What things?

You want to know too much, Herr Professor.

A baritone voice came in.

*

Herr Professor has travelled a long way to hear your words. He's an important man. He's—

    Please, Fritz . . .

    I apologise, Herr Professor.

    Does the professor need a teacher?

    Professors always need teachers. I'm a good student.

    Will you speak to the parson? That hateful . . .

The woman's voice grew shriller, she was mumbling her words.

Lies and . . .

    You have my word. That . . . man . . .

Again, the baritone voice.

Mind your language . . .

    Fritz, can you step outside, please?

    Are you sure, Ignaz?

    Fräulein Erika wouldn't hurt a fly. Please . . .

Heavy footsteps.

    A door being closed.

Ass.

    No, Fritz is a friend.

    Every man is an animal. Fritz is an ass. He can't see. He can't hear.

    What about me? What am I?

    A badger.

    An intelligent animal.

    Very important, but not very intelligent.

Ignaz laughing.

*

I'm a man of science, Fräulein Erika. Maybe I'm not . . . you're right. But I can assure you that . . . Everything they say . . .

Lies! Lies! I have never . . . children! Never!

I'd like to . . .

You want to go to the middle of the clearing. It's obvious. You want to meet him. You mustn't. You're not ready.

Who's in the . . .

They know.

. . . children?

A rustle.

Tony had goosebumps. If these tapes were fakes, they were truly well made.

Trembling and joy. Fear and pleasure. In the centre of the clearing. And singing and dancing.

The missing children, are they in the clearing? If I gave you a map, would you be able to show me where it is?

There's no map. The clearing isn't on the map. The children are not on the map. They say that . . .

The voice grew very angry. Ignaz tried to calm the woman down, Fritz's voice came in again, the argument grew more animated and Fritz slammed the door. Calm was restored.

. . . little animals.

The children are little animals?

Mice, frogs, ferrets and sparrows.

Tony held his breath.

He wants children?

Men. Women. Small animals. Everybody has a small animal inside them.

Do you mean the soul?
That's priests' stuff.

The gravelly voice spat.

Animals. Inside. You, the badger. Your friend Fritz, the ass. The country
parson, the pig.
    So then he wants souls.
    They're like honey to his mouth.
    What does he do with the bodies?
    He wears them.
    I'm confused, Fräulein. Despite this . . . horror . . . the little animals
want him. Why should they? Why should they go to someone who wants
to eat their souls? I don't understand.
    The blind mole cries its heart out. Never has it experienced a greater
pleasure. And it never will again.
    Fräulein, are the little animals . . . are they dead?
    Dead? Who can tell? Some have fled while others have turned into
birds and flown away.
    Where to?

Again, that chuckle.

South of heaven.
    I don't think I . . .

A whisper.

The Wanderer. In the centre of the clearing. He sings. You open the door
and he comes. You open the door and you can hear him singing. You're on
your knees, trembling, desperate, on your knees, you'll never experience a
greater pleasure. The Wanderer sings and his song is the wind. The wind
that drives the little animals insane.

Who is the Wanderer? What is the Wanderer?

Silence.

Mumbling, but not a voice.

"What is it?" Tony asked.

"A pan," Thomas replied, looking serious. "Water boiling."

The Wanderer is a stag, a mouse, an ass and a mole. He's a toad, a swallow, an eagle. And he sings.

Have you seen him, Fräulein Erika?

Anyone who sees the Wanderer is no longer a mouse, a mole or a fox. They're the Wanderer.

I'm confused.

A badger. You're a badger, Herr Professor. You can't understand.

Who can understand?

Those who hear the song. Give me your hand, Herr Professor.

I . . .

Are you afraid?

The sound of a chair scraping against the floor.

Eighteen moons, Herr Professor. It's written on your hand. I'm sorry.

Are you saying that . . .

I'm tired, Herr Professor. And I'm hungry. Would you like some of my stew?

One last question, then I'll be glad to try your food.

Take it. It's good.

Bowls. Ladles.

The mumbling grew louder. The sound of a lid being closed.

Excellent.

Sweet as honey. Yes.

One question, Fräulein Erika. Before . . . before it stops working.

It goes round and round, then goes back.

Yes, it's technology. The new world.

The new world will be the same as the old world, Herr Professor. Nothing really changes. So what's your question?

If I'm the badger and Fritz the ass and the parson . . .

The pig.

Which animal are you, Fräulein Erika?

A laugh.

The one who always tells the truth. The f—

The tape cut off.

Sixty-Six

1.

"Eerie, isn't it?"

It was.

Tony was drenched in sweat. "Who was that woman?"

"Poor Ignaz's greatest failure. That's what he wrote in his last letters. Despite a brilliant career and a loving family, Ignaz died an embittered man. He wasn't lured to Ahrntal by scientific curiosity alone. There had been a specific request from Vienna."

"From the Kaiser?"

"Ignaz was very famous and Franz Josef was faced with a delicate matter. A request had arrived from the Brixen bishopric. They wanted to put a witch on trial."

"Fräulein Erika?"

"She had been accused of killing and eating several children in the region."

Tony burst out laughing. "You're joking."

"No, I'm not. The bishop needed the approval of the so-called secular powers to get the trial under way, but Emperor Franz Josef was an enlightened ruler. To be honest, the bishop of Brixen didn't have a mediaeval mind, but . . ."

"*Vox populi, vox dei.*"

As he talked, Thomas began to put the spools carefully back into their cases.

"So the bishop felt obliged to send his request, and the Kaiser, as custom dictated, was unable to refuse his assistance. Tyrol was of strategic importance to the empire. He had to keep the people happy. So he decided to send Ignaz to investigate."

"Having his cake and eating it. On the one hand he was giving the people his undivided attention, but on the other he was sending a man of science who would never buy such nonsense. Right?"

"Exactly. At the end of his investigation, Ignaz wrote a very detailed report about his meeting with the woman, emphasising that he had not seen anything to suggest that she was responsible for the deaths of the children. The Kaiser therefore did not give his consent and the bishop of Brixen no doubt breathed a sigh of relief. Ignaz returned to Innsbruck, where he lived and worked, convinced he had done his duty, and happy with the recordings. But when he arrived home, he found a letter from Fritz Giraldi informing him that the good folk of the town had rebelled against the imperial decree and killed Erika."

"Did they burn her at the stake?"

"That's not how it worked. Witches were thrown into lakes. If, after fifteen minutes, they emerged still alive, which would be impossible unless they had made a pact with the devil, they'd be burned. If, on the other hand, they drowned, then they were proved innocent, and therefore guaranteed a place in heaven."

Tony thought for a few seconds. "Assuming there's any truth to all this . . ." he finally said.

"Michael See and Edvard Bukreev believe that these tapes are the link between the *Unaussprechlichen Kulten*, Kenneth Grahame, and something more ancient. Think about the animals Fräulein Erika lists in the recordings."

"The toad, the mole . . ."

"And even the badger. They're all characters in *The Wind in the Willows*. Look—" Thomas handed him a notebook. "You can keep it, if you like."

Tony leafed through it. It contained a transcript of the tape alongside quotations from the Von Junzt and Grahame's book.

The dead always know where they are. Nothing happens to the dead. That's what the witch had said. In *The Wind in the Willows*, Mole says, "Once well underground, you know exactly where you are. Nothing can happen to you, and nothing can get at you."

The Von Junzt said: "Wherever they might be, they vanish. In peace. They become black food, sweet as honey, for the Friend who lives in the hinges. They are happy."

"And then there's the thing in chapter seven of *The Wind in the Willows*, remember?"

Tony made an effort to recall. "'The Piper at the Gates of Dawn?'"

"Ratty and Mole are looking for Mr Toad, who's gone missing, when they come across an island. They hear the sound of a pipe. Both Ratty and Mole fall to their knees in terror and ecstasy. Grahame describes the creature playing the flute as being like a god in the vein of Pan and calls him 'the Friend and Helper'. The Wanderer in the Von Junzt is also called the Friend. For Von Junzt and for Fräulein Erika, however, the Wanderer doesn't play a musical instrument: he sings. But that doesn't change the concept. Moreover, the ecstatic trance into which the two animals in Grahame's book fall is described very well by Fräulein Erika, don't you think?"

Tony found the page in the notebook. Her exact words were: *You open the door and you can hear him singing. You're on your knees, trembling, desperate, on your knees, you'll never experience a greater pleasure.*

"It's the same in the Von Junzt," Thomas remarked. "Those who find themselves before the Wanderer fall to their knees. And sing with him."

On their knees, just as Gabriel had told Sibylle.

"Assuming it's true," Tony said, "that a fairy tale has been handed down orally about this – this threshold guardian? Demon? God?"

"Creature of the hinge."

"I'm a professional when it comes to embellished stories, Thomas. And this is a classic example. I can't understand how a man like Bukreev can have fallen for it. Not least because, I'm sorry to say it again, these tapes, without the original wax reels . . ."

"Are poppycock."

"Tell me about Ignaz's Von Junzt. He owned two copies, didn't he? A second edition which he gave to the library of the Sabiona monastery, and a first edition that's now in the Perkman collection."

"Horst, not Perkman collection," Thomas said. "Dreadful man."

"Did you ever meet him?"

"The first-edition Von Junzt, the one Bukreev wants to get hold of, was stolen from my family during the fire that destroyed the old Zingerle house. It was most likely arson, to cover up the theft."

"Did Bukreev order it? Or Dr Horst?"

"They were both too young. The Von Junzt went missing in 1961, vanished into thin air for fourteen years, then turned up in Kreuzwirt in 1975."

"How did you find out that it had resurfaced?"

"From a photograph. There was a report in one of the local papers about Perkman and the Krotn Villa, and in the picture accompanying the article Perkman is posing in front of a bookcase. You can see the Von Junzt behind him. My father hit the roof, moved heaven and earth, but how could he prove that *that very book* belonged to our family? Besides, Perkman already knew how to protect his interests. However, my father had already discovered that the theft was most likely ordered by a highly respected man, a Swiss lecturer. His name was August Darleth, and he had been Josef Horst's mentor at the university of Geneva."

"Did Horst get the book from him? Did he steal it from him?"

"Impossible to say. My father couldn't find out any more than that."

"Just one more question. About the death of Grahame's son . . ."

"A sad example of Victorian puritanism," Thomas said. "Or do you, too, believe that a father can kill his own son?"

Sixty-Seven

1.

When Tony returned, he found Sib oddly pale and withdrawn.

"Everything OK?"

"Everything's OK."

Not in the least convinced, Tony showed her the transcript of the recording with Fräulein Erika, then busied himself making a fuss of Freddy.

"Do you think it's a fake?" she asked when she'd read it.

"If it is, then it's a highly elaborate one."

"Perhaps it's some kind of con. Thomas's grandfather wanted to take advantage of Ignaz's fame to scrape a few pennies together."

"And sell the reels to some rich mark like Bukreev? But why use tapes? The story of a copy of a lost original may increase the allure of the legend, but you risk putting off potential customers. Who would pay for something that's ninety-nine per cent certain to be fake?"

Sibylle indicated the Von Junzt stack. "You've read it. Are there really similarities?"

"The language is different, naturally. But yes, there are notions in it that in some ways echo what Gabriel told you. The ecstasy that forces anyone who hears the Wanderer's song to their knees. The Wanderer who wears the skin of whoever has brought him forth from the hinge onto our plane of existence."

"Tommy Raggiodisole."

"Fräulein Erika's description of the way the little animals were terrified and in rapture at the same time closely echoes chapter seven of *The Wind in the Willows*, 'The Piper at the Gates of Dawn'. By the way, there's something I want you to hear."

Sibylle seemed distant. Maybe she's just tired, Tony thought, as he stood up.

He picked a CD from his collection, took it out of its case and put it into the stereo. "Pink Floyd," he said. "*The Piper at the Gates of Dawn*. This is the first song. 'Astronomy Domine'."

White noise followed by guitar chords filled the study. Morse code. The thumping of drums. A gentle, flute-like voice intoned a chant.

Freddy shook his head, grumbled and went to seek refuge on his bed.

Sibylle shared his opinion. "I prefer Led Zeppelin. I've always found Pink Floyd too cerebral."

"To say the least," Tony replied, switching off the stereo. "But Syd Barrett was obsessed with *The Wind in the Willows*. 'The Piper at the Gates of Dawn' is the title of chapter seven. And you know something funny? On my way back here I stopped off to see Chiara at Carnival. I bought a copy of Grahame's book, because I have no idea where mine's gone. I glanced at it as I was leaving, and chapter seven was missing. I discovered that they don't always print it."

"Really?"

Tony opened his arms. "The book is now out of copyright, so anyone can do whatever they please. Someone must have decided that that chapter was too scary for children."

"That's stupid."

Tony sat at Sib's feet, looking serious. He took her hands in his. They were cold. Tony rubbed them to warm them up. A lock of her hair tickled his face. "You're not listening to me, are you, Sib?"

"I went to the Hunting and Fisheries Office. I had a chat with Rossini. The arsehole slasher helped me break the ice."

Tony's eyes opened wide. "Don't tell me you threatened him . . ."

His worried expression made Sibylle smile. At last, there was some life in her eyes. "What, a defenceless maiden like me?"

"You? You're practically an honorary Shanghaian."

The compliment made Sib blush. "Rossini told me he saw Mirella. *After* her disappearance."

"What do you mean, 'after her disappearance'?"

"That, as your new friend Fräulein Erika says –" Sibylle began to read from the transcript Tony had brought with him – "'The Wanderer is a stag, a rat, an ass and a mole. He is a toad, a swallow and an eagle.' In other words, he becomes the little animals that kneel before him."

Sibylle held the tablet up for Tony.

A newspaper article. An interview, in Ladin. There was a translation next to it. Tony read it three times, then looked up at Sib.

"Welcome to the world of Ricky Riccardo, Tony."

Sixty-Eight

1.

Veronika Pohl had a round face and wore glasses with thick frames. She had dimples when she laughed. According to the missing persons report, she worked in the Urtijëi library, even though she was born and lived in Santa Cristina, a stone's throw away, in Val Gardena. On September 3, 2011, Veronika had taken her rucksack and her trekking sticks and vanished into thin air.

She was twenty-seven years old.

Since she had recently broken up with her boyfriend, a certain Udo Trebo, and since Signor Trebo, a mechanic, had a couple of notches on his criminal record (drunk and disorderly, resisting a public official and breach of the peace – the holy trinity of South Tyrolian misdemeanours), the carabinieri had grilled him thoroughly, but they found nothing to incriminate him. Despite searches, appeals and the odd arrested and immediately released suspect, no trace of Veronika Pohl was found until October 13 of the following year, 2012, when, while patrolling on the lookout for poachers in a gorge adjacent to Val Fiscalina, a forest ranger by the name of Marco Kostner came across what, from a distance, looked like the carcass of a stag.

It was Veronika.

This was established through her DNA. The time the body had spent outdoors and the intervention of local animals had left little for a pathologist to examine. As a matter of fact, the cause of death was never confirmed. Maybe a fall, or a sudden illness. The *Usc di Ladins*, the Ladin newspaper that served the Gardena, Badi and neighbouring valleys, had reported the discovery in the same way as *Dolomiten* and *Alto Adige* had covered the hapless Veronika's initial disappearance: just a couple of prudish paragraphs with few details. Out of respect for the family and the community, and also (if one were cynical) to avoid scaring off the tourists. Nobody likes to go on holiday to a place where people go missing, only to be found a year later, eaten by animals.

However, the *Usc di Ladins*, in a separate piece written by a certain Alberto Dapunt, one of its most active journalists, had dedicated space to a theory (branded insane and suspicious by the investigators at the time) put forward by Udo Trebo, Veronika's ex.

This prompted Sibylle and Tony to take a trip to Bruneck.

Sixty-Nine

1.

The man had a wide, pock-marked face and a sparse moustache. He was wearing oil-stained overalls. When he emerged from the darkness of the garage, he only had eyes for Tony's car.

"I hope you kicked his teeth in," he said, pointing at the scratch on the bonnet.

"I've yet to settle that score. But that's not why we're here."

"You're joking!" the man said, outraged. "You can't go driving around like this."

"Let's make a deal, Signor Trebo. If you give me the answers I'm after, I'll entrust my Mustang to you."

"Udo. Just call me Udo. It's written on the sign."

"Alright, Udo," Tony said. "In 2011, you knew a certain Veronika Pohl."

The man stared at him, then at Sibylle. She had a file under her arm, the same kind that Udo had seen piled up on the desks of the carabinieri who had grilled him after Veronika's disappearance.

He grew wary. "Are you from the police? Or the papers?"

"Neither."

"Then how come you've got that file? Who gave it to you?"

"A lawyer. Who – like us – knows how to keep her mouth shut. Relax . . . We're certain you had nothing to do with Veronika's death. She was your girlfriend. Right?"

Udo rubbed his free hand on his canvas trousers. "When Veronika went missing, I spent forty-eight hours in jail. They thought I'd killed her. They questioned my family and my friends. For hours on end. The bastards treated me like a criminal. What else can I say?"

"Was Veronika your girlfriend?" Tony repeated.

"If you have the file then you already know everything."

"Please," Sibylle said. "Try. As you said, the investigation wasn't very thorough. You and Veronika had recently broken up, hadn't you?"

"A couple of months earlier. After ten years. We'd been together since school."

"Your first true love."

Udo shrugged. "So it seemed."

"Sorry to be so blunt," Tony said, "but did Veronika have someone else?"

"Yes. I even told the police. But they didn't believe me."

"Because none of Veronika's friends or relatives had ever seen her with anyone outside the usual circle. And you were unable to provide a name or a description of this person."

Udo gave him a surly look. "I'm well aware of that, Signor Sukks." Veronika's death must still be raw. "I had to move," he said. "My father had a garage in Urtijëi. It was great. There was always a lot of work. Tourists breaking down, the odd collision. Or regular maintenance: changing tyres – stuff like that. But after the business with Veronika, people stopped treating me like ... like one of them. I had to move here. I'm not in touch with anybody in Urtijëi anymore. If you found me, it means someone tipped you off. Was it Dapunt?"

"That's right," Tony said.

"Are you here because of that interview?"

"Dapunt confirmed that you were very convincing back then. That he pretty much believed every word."

"Too bad that's not how the police felt."

Tony weighed up his next words. He didn't want to piss Udo-just-call-me-Udo off. The spanner in his hand did not look friendly.

"Let's recap. Veronika went missing in autumn 2011."

"On September 3."

"Her body was found in 2012, on October 3. It was unrecognisable, but her identity was confirmed through her DNA. She'd been dead for over a year, so it seems likely she died the day she disappeared."

Udo nodded.

At this point, Tony summoned all his tact. Because they were entering Ricky Riccardo territory. "In December 2011, when, as we now know, Veronika had been dead for about two months, you told the police that you'd seen her, alive and well, at an Autogrill."

"That's right."

"The police started interrogating you. This left you angry and frustrated. So, to stir things up, you gave an interview to the *Usc di Ladins*."

Udo put the spanner on a metal shelf.

"It was a mistake."

"May I be frank?"

The mechanic lit a cigarette. "I'd prefer you to be."

"Veronika wasn't exactly skinny."

"Is that a crime?"

"No, but more recently – at least that's what witnesses claim – before going missing . . ."

Udo scratched his eyebrow. "Her famous diet. And the trekking. That was something else new. Veronika and I were the only people born in Santa Cristina who hated mountains. No skiing, no snowshoe walks. I only had eyes for cars and engines, and she wanted to go and live in New York. Then, after we broke up, Veronika suddenly went on a diet and started trekking up and down mountains."

Udo wiped away a tear.

"It was her?" Sibylle said gently. "The woman at the Autogrill was really Veronika, wasn't it?"

"I saw her."

"Please tell us about it."

"What's the point?"

"It's important."

"It was on December 25, the worst Christmas of my life. That morning, I'd been to Mass with my family, and even the priest was giving me nasty looks. We pretended not to notice, but it was hard. Exchanging presents by the tree, taking smiley pictures. In the end, I took the car and went for a drive. To clear my head, you see?"

"Of course," Sib said.

"I stopped at an Autogrill. The one on the A22 outside Brixen. I often go there. I know people who work there – I worked there myself for a while. I needed to get some petrol and empty my bladder. When I came out of that damned toilet, I saw her." Udo smoothed his moustache. "She was standing across the car park. She waved at me."

"What time was it?"

"Nine in the evening."

"Any security footage?"

"If you've read the file then you know that, too. That spot was outside the range of the cameras. The police checked. Nothing. That's why they didn't believe me."

"Was it Veronika?"

"She was wearing a skirt I'd given her for her birthday. Her hair was different: longer and curly, as though she'd had a perm, but it was her. I'm sure of it. And yet . . ."

"And yet that Christmas, her body was lying buried under a metre and a half of snow in Val Fiscalina."

"After I saw her, I went to see her parents. It was such a mess. Screaming, insults. But I ended up persuading them to let me look through Veronika's things."

"The skirt had disappeared," Sib muttered.

"Along with the jacket I'd seen her wearing at the Autogrill."

Udo dropped the cigarette stub on the ground, crushed it angrily with his shoe. Then he picked it up and threw it into a bin.

"You didn't call to her, or go up to her?"

"I tried to, but she was too quick. She had a car, a blue Alfa Romeo. And she whizzed off like the wind."

"How do you explain that?"

"Either I made a mistake or it was Veronika's ghost coming to say goodbye." He kicked the bin. "Now leave," he said. "Please. I need a drink and I don't like drinking with people around. It can be . . . dangerous."

Seventy

1.

It was Sibylle who said it.

"A serial killer."

"A serial killer."

"Do you really believe that?"

A sad smile on Tony's face. "I'm the *avoidive* one, remember?"

Tony and Sibylle were sitting at either ends of the sofa in the Shanghai apartment. They were both holding glasses. Water for Tony, Coca-Cola for Sib.

The ice had melted ages ago.

They were shaken. Exhausted. Scared.

The traffic noise from Via Resia, just like the voices from the café at the bottom of Tony's building, was muffled. The sun was covered by a thick layer of dark cloud. The radio had promised rain but, in the meantime, the closeness in Bolzano was unbearable. Even so, the moment Polianna had left, saying goodbye with a semi-perplexed, semi-concerned look on her face, Tony and Sib had opened the windows.

They needed air. Foul-smelling, scorching, heavy, but air nonetheless.

A melancholy Freddy was lying under the air conditioning, which was turned off. Every now and then, he would lap at his water bowl. Grumbling. In the background, Syd Barrett was singing about some girl called Emily and her tendency to borrow other people's dreams.

"What are the odds of coming across a serial killer?"

Tony shrugged. "The way I see it, one murder is the sum of several pressures that turn a man into a murderer. A serial killer is the sum of many more variables. That's why they're rarer. But I'm no authority on any of this. I've never believed in motives."

"All you have to do is switch on the television or look at a newspaper. People commit all kinds of atrocities for sex or money. You can't tell me you don't believe in motives."

"It's like icebergs. Sex and money are just the tip. The part that allows us to make sense of it."

Sib sat up, legs crossed, and put her now empty glass on the coffee table. "Make sense of it?"

"Have you never noticed how, when the motive for a crime is discovered, people lose interest? The moment the danger is over, they move on to something else. It's stupid, really. Once the murderer ends up handcuffed, there's nothing to be afraid of, right? And yet people feel safe only once they discover the—"

"Motive."

"The motive allows us to say, 'It could never happen to me. Nobody would kill me for the few pennies I have in my current account. I've never had a secret affair, so why should I end up all chopped up in a ditch?' The motive reassures us. But this means that, in our eyes, the victim somehow asked for it. Perpetrator and victim swap roles." Tony took a sip. The water was warm. "That's why," he continued after a grimace, "we're frightened of the serial killer. We discover that Jeffrey Dahmer ate people because he felt lonely and . . . I mean, Jesus, we all feel lonely sometimes, but we don't start abducting people and cutting them to pieces. You know what I mean?"

"An ordinary murder makes us feel safe because it's the victim's fault, really, and since victims have always done something wrong, we'll never be a victim. In the case of a serial killer, however, the victim is always a victim. They were simply in the wrong place at the wrong time, and drew the attention of the worst possible person to impress. And that could happen to anybody."

"That's not all," Tony said, darkly. "A serial killer also makes us afraid that we too, perhaps, with the appropriate variables, if put under the right kind of pressure, could start eating people. Who has never felt like grabbing a machine gun and mowing down the whole damned queue at the post office? Look at Freddy. A sweet lump, right? And yet his ancestors would have had no qualms about tearing us to shreds. The Romans used them as war dogs."

"You're telling me," Sibylle said, "that inside Freddy . . ."

Tony remembered the St Bernard tackling the rabid fox. "There's a bit of Freddie Mercury in him and a bit of Freddy Krueger. The same is true for us humans. The other night, when I saw you brandishing that pickaxe, for a minute there I was sure you were going to split my head open with it. It was a classic Freddy Krueger moment."

Sib started fiddling with a strand of hair again. "Do you think that whoever killed Erika also murdered Mirella, Veronika and heaven knows how many others?"

"It's what Gabriel implied. But what worries me is, it's also what I'm starting to think." Tony rubbed his eyes.

"Both Mirella and Veronika were seen after their deaths," Sibylle said. "And since we don't really believe there's a demon out there who wears the skin of his victims, and since both Rossini and Udo admitted that they only saw Mirella and Veronika briefly and from a distance, it means somebody put on these poor women's clothes in order to be seen. A kind of—"

"A kind of Von Junzt allegory."

Tony stood up. He took their glasses, rinsed them and filled them with fresh water.

"You know what the problem with books like the Von Junzt is?" Tony sat next to Sibylle and handed her the glass. "That everyone can read anything they like into them."

"And what if someone has mistaken the sizzle for the steak?" Sibylle said. "What if there's someone out there who believes that Von Junzt, Kenneth Grahame and even Fräulein Erika talk of concrete things? Someone convinced that the Wanderer is a real entity?"

"That sounds too crazy."

Sib gave him a tap on the shoulder. "Do your job. They pay you to use your imagination, don't they? Do you think it's possible?"

And you've no idea what happens when I go into overdrive . . .

Tony massaged his temples, then started to talk. "Women who go missing. Who alter their habits. The serial killer seduces them, murders them, then parades around in their clothes. He appears before people who loved his victims. Does he enjoy it? Or is it just a way to confirm his power? We don't know. What we do know is that he only lets himself be seen fleetingly, from a distance. That's pretty evident."

"With the exception of Erika. In her case, Gabriel was the ghost, but we know that Gabriel can't be the Wanderer. He was behind bars when Veronika Pohl was killed."

Tony bit his lip. "No, I don't think Erika is an exception."

"Gabriel was the ghost," Sib insisted. "Yvette told us. Or do you think she lied to us?"

"Not necessarily. But maybe Gabriel wasn't the only one who went around Kreuzwirt with a blonde wig on his head."

"Two ghosts?"

"At this stage we can't be certain of anything. I'm just speculating, so let's take a tour inside Gabriel's head. It seems he's always been one step ahead. In the Von Junzt, the Wanderer is also referred to as 'the Friend'. 'Friend' is not a scary word, is it? A friend is someone who gives you advice and encourages you to do your best. A friend is someone who listens to your secrets, cries with you and celebrates your triumphs as if they were their own. You trust a friend. And so, in Grahame's book, the rat, the mole and the animals in the forest are glad to come across the piper. Terror comes later, when they are forced to go down on their knees and adore him."

Tony retrieved the page from the *Unaussprechlichen Kulten*. "'Adoration becomes the Wanderer. Your head up to the stars and a knee on the ground. Penitent and reverent. Where the muscle is strong, it bends. Where the will does not yield, the Wanderer's gaze pierces through. On their knees, the ones chosen by the Friend, who is on the hinge of the world, who is the hinge of the world and who comes from the invisible world, listen to his song.' In other words, when the murderer takes off his mask. But until that moment, whoever meets the Wanderer sees a friend in him."

Sib thought about her nightmare about Erika, dressed in red. "Cut your hair. Lose weight. Drop negative friends. Be happy with me. Only with me. By doing as I say. Men like that give me the creeps. Do you think we should call the police?"

Tony gave his knee a slap. "We have nothing concrete. Just a theory. They'd laugh at us."

"But do you believe it?"

"I'm afraid I do."

"Then we have to find proof."

"But how?"

Sibylle waved the tablet determinedly. "By checking every single case. By talking to the friends, boyfriends and relatives of all the people reported missing in the past twenty years. Including so-called solved cases, like Veronika's. There's people out there who've seen their loved ones after their disappearance but haven't had the courage to tell anyone. Or they have, and they've been branded insane. We mustn't take our eye off Erika, though. The Perkmans. They're the ones keeping Gabriel out of the game. Somehow, they're connected with—"

"Incidentally," Tony said, interrupting her, "do you remember what Zingerle told me? The story about the stolen Von Junzt that showed up again at Toad Villa?"

He rubbed his hands together in satisfaction.

All this cheerfulness made Sibylle smile. "What has Tony Longstocking been up to?"

"Zingerle said that the theft of the first edition of the *Unaussprechlichen Kulten* was orchestrated by a certain August Darleth, who knew Horst very well because he'd been one of his mentors at university. Zingerle used that very word: mentor. I thought it might be interesting to have a little chat. So I called the University of Geneva. I pretended to be a scholar looking for an academic to help me with an article for a PhD. After some toing and froing between the archives and various faculties, I found someone who had worked with Professor Darleth. He was sorry to inform me that poor August Darleth had died many years ago. So I made out I was desperate. I needed a rare and unobtainable publication by that great genius, and so . . ."

"You made them feel sorry for you."

"The guy gave me the contact details of Darleth's son, Samuel, in case he could help me get hold of what I was after. I almost burst into tears, I was so touched."

"And what did this Samuel tell you?"

"I haven't spoken to him, they just gave me his email address. I wrote to him, telling him more or less the same thing I told the administration office at the University of Geneva. His father's publication and so on. So now all we can do is wait and see if the fish takes the bait. But you know the strangest thing of all? Guess what August Darleth taught?"

Sib shrugged. "Medicine, I guess. Horst was a doctor."

"Well, no. Darleth senior taught physics and astrophysics. He was some kind of genius, apparently."

"Then Horst—"

Tony stopped her. "No, no. He didn't just pass himself off as a doctor. Horst was a duly registered member of the medical association, I checked. Strange, though, don't you think? When you're a medical student, you have enough books to swot over, so why suddenly start following a course on astrophysics?"

Sibylle looked at Tony as though he had turned into an alien. "You're joking, right?"

"No. Should I be?"

"You really are an idiot, you know that?"

Tony's confused expression was genuine. How could he be so stupid? "Have you never heard of passion?"

"What's that got to do with—"

"And you write love stories for a living?" she said, exasperated. "When I was fourteen, I asked for my first moped. It was a Testi – older than you – with a two-stroke engine. It took ages to reach thirty kilometres an hour. And I hated that. So I started asking Lucky Willy for advice and he taught me how to tweak the damn thing. I became so good at it that I was tweaking the engines for all the kids in the valley, without," and Sib said it again, so that the concept would have a chance of penetrating Tony's thick skull, "*without* my grades suffering. Otherwise, Aunt Helga would have locked me up at home and thrown away the key. Passion. Do you understand? Like the pen in your hand. That feeling of—"

Tony had finally caught on. "Of something being *right.*"

"Passion is the thing which, at the drop of a hat, makes you someone else. When you realise you've found . . ."

Sib thought she had said something stupid, because Tony was staring at her. That expression she had come to recognise, the one that told her Tony had gone for a stroll *to the other side*. Except that this time all that intensity was focused on her.

"What you were missing," Tony concluded. "To make you feel whole."

"I–It was only to make you understand—" Sib stuttered.

She did not finish her sentence. Tony closed her mouth with a kiss. A light kiss. A caress with his lips.

"Sibby Longstocking," he asked, worried, "and they all fall down?"

"I'm not sure."

Seventy-One

1.

In the middle of the night, Tony was still lying on the sofa. Sibylle was sleeping with her arm around him, her breast pressing against his chest, her lips parted. Freddy was snoring and outside it was raining. The air coming in through the open window was cool.

Tony was tired, frightened and confused, but he did not want to sleep. He wanted to spend the rest of the night looking at the young woman next to him. Right then, all that existed for Tony was the smell of Sibylle's skin, which filled the room like a promise: the world out there was gone.

All was perfect. All was peace. Then Tony noticed his phone light up. An email. Spam, he thought, trying hard to ignore it. Or some misfit who wanted to read his fortune in coffee grounds.

He managed to resist only for a couple of minutes. The light was driving him crazy.

2.

It was not spam, or a message from some self-styled expert in the esoteric, but a reply from Samuel Darleth.

A concise, formal email. Samuel Darleth was pleased to hear that, after many years, his father's studies were still considered worthy of attention. Which of his numerous published papers did Tony require? If he would be so kind as to specify, he would happily do his best to let him have it. The sign-off was brief – just his initials, above a company logo.

When Tony saw it, he thought it was a joke. Then he told himself that, actually, it made sense. As he considered it in greater depth, and his mind began to draw connections between names, places and dates, he felt the same chill he had experienced in the clearing, when the rabid fox had popped out of the bush and, for a moment, the world had turned into a living nightmare.

His heart in turmoil, and careful not to wake Sib, Tony got up from the sofa and shut himself in his study. He sat at his desk, switched on the computer, opened his inbox and went back to studying the logo at the end of Darleth's email.

Unlike the hummingbird smile, which he initially had thought looked like a snake, then a rupestrian arrow, and finally like an alien danger sign, it was an unequivocal symbol, a product of 1970s aesthetics, geometrical, angular and of limited appeal, but very clear. Everyone was familiar with it.

Hands shaking, Tony picked up a biro, put it up to his lips and began to wonder. What if he and Sibylle had fallen into the same trap as Gabriel? What if, with all the chasing after ghosts, they had got lost in the world of Ricky Riccardo? Why had he not insisted on putting weird coincidences, mysterious apparitions and arcane formulae aside, and clung to reason like a proper Shanghaian with his feet on the ground?

Let's start with Grahame and the Von Junzt.

What were *The Wind in the Willows* and the *Unaussprechlichen Kulten*? Paper, books. A children's story and an expensive tome written in pompous prose by a guy who took opium. That's all. And Erika? What was Erika but a lifeless body, lying on a lake shore? A corpse. Betta, too – drowned, her head smashed in. Sometimes, a book is just a book . . .

"And a corpse is just a corpse."

The logo at the bottom of Samuel Darleth's email began to tell Tony such a scary story that it forced him to hammer the computer keys in search of data to prove its inconsistency. A nice "Bye, bye, Tony Carcano" would have been a relief in comparison to the horror taking shape before his eyes.

Tony immersed himself in old newspaper articles, read petitions, deciphered graphs and technical documents. All in the public domain. That was what he found most terrifying about it. The evidence had been in full view. For decades.

The more details that emerged, the more Tony realised, with alarm, that he had uncovered the existence not of just one Wanderer, but of three demonic creatures: August Darleth, Josef Horst and Friedrich Perkman.

When the air coming in through the windows tasted of dawn and the light struck his pupils, Tony emitted an animal sound.

"Krrrka."

Seventy-Two

1.

In her dream, Sibylle was letting herself float on the lake. She was looking at the stars and the stars were smiling at her. The water hugging her body was warm, like a caress.

It did not last long.

The stars above her vanished one by one. Like light bulbs blowing, they sizzled and sank into the darkness. Once the sky had turned into a flat, blinding blackness, the water became cold.

Sib floundered.

Erika emerged next to her. She had long, sharp, red-stained teeth.

Erika clasped at her and said—

Seventy-Three

1.

"Get up!"

Sib looked around, confused. Her clothes were strewn all over the place. It was dawn, and this was not how she had hoped to wake up. She opened her eyes wide when she saw Tony fumbling with a gun.

"What are you doing with *that*?"

Tony inserted the magazine into the .22. "It's time to have a chat with Karin."

Tony concealed the gun between his waistband and his back.

Freddy woke up. He wagged his tail, studying first Tony's face, then Sibylle's. He sniffed the air and crumpled his forehead. He gave up on his morning cuddles and went back to his bed.

"Where did you get that gun?" Sib shouted.

"It was my father's. *Let's go.*"

2.

The Mustang devoured the kilometres with a roar. Sib had stopped asking questions when the speedometer had gone past a hundred and sixty. They left the A22, took the 621 and then route K. The speed limit was forty kilometres an hour, but the Mustang was doing at least twice that.

When they reached Kreuzwirt, Tony did not slow down, but pressed on to the villa. The trees lining the road were whizzing past like demented spots, and the few motorists they passed along the way had no time to sound their horn, and could only swear.

"Tony, slow down . . ."

He finally did, with the front of the Mustang a few centimetres from Krotn Villa's steel gate.

Tony flung open the door but Sibylle stopped him from getting out. "You're not going anywhere with that gun. You're not yourself."

"I've never been so lucid in my life."

Sibylle slapped him. "The gun stays here."

Tony put his hand to his cheek. He hesitated. Sib was not angry. She was not even frightened. Just sad. Her eyes said, *Or there will be no repeat of last night.*

The .22 went from Tony's hand to Sibylle's, and she hid it in the glove compartment.

They got out. A security camera was following their every move. Tony restrained the impulse to pick up a stone and hurl it at it. He found the doorbell and pushed the button.

"What do you want, Signor Carcano?"

Tony looked into the camera and uttered a name: "Darleth."

Seventy-Four

1.

Michl Horst was wearing a tie. He had the face of a man recently awoken from a good sleep, his conscience at peace. He said nothing as they made their way through the house.

The Toad Villa library. That was where Michl took them. Oak furniture, shelves crammed with books all the way up to the ceiling. Some volumes were protected by locked display cabinets: the famous forbidden part of the collection.

An oval table, handmade, finely inlaid. On it, a copy of the *Unaussprechlichen Kulten*, the famous first edition. Dark leather binding with a spiral embossed on the front cover. Michl motioned towards the chairs. Then he sat next to Karin Perkman, who was waiting for them, smiling.

Karin was a shadow of the girl in the Polaroid. Deep worry lines around her thin lips, dark rings under eyes like daggers. She was wearing a long-sleeved blouse and a stern tailored skirt. Unlike Michl, she looked like someone who had to count a lot of sheep to fall asleep. An old grandfather clock was marking the seconds.

"We were wondering," Karin said, "when we would have the pleasure of your company."

Tony ignored her sarcasm, "This is not a courtesy call. I'm here to do my job." He put his tablet on the table. "To tell you a story that begins at the end. Starting from last night, when I received an email from

Samuel Darleth. Samuel Darleth, the son of Professor August Darleth, esteemed physicist, astrophysicist and entrepreneur. August Darleth, who was Josef Horst's mentor at the University of Geneva."

Tony noticed Karin's fingers clench into a fist. He also noticed that she was not wearing rings and that she had cut her fingernails short, as though to stop herself from biting them.

"The same August Darleth who stopped teaching in 1972 to devote himself to his . . . shall we call it his miniature star?"

Tony indicated the logo of the company set up by August Darleth, the logo at the bottom of the email Samuel had sent him that night. A stylised sun.

In the centre of the sun, there was a dot surrounded by three triangles. The symbol of nuclear power. "After all, what's a nuclear power station if not a miniature star?"

"You're mad, Signor Carcano," Karin said coldly.

Tony ignored her. "In August 1972, Darleth left teaching to devote himself to his nuclear power station in Karnach, in Switzerland, the planning of which had started in 1970. In 1972, Darleth leaves his chair, starts up his nice reactor, and shortly afterwards realises there's a problem. He's underestimated the cost of the disposal of fissile materials, so ends up with a load of steaming radioactive shit on his hands and not the faintest idea how to get rid of it." A couple of taps on his tablet: old photographs of demonstrators waving placards; newspaper articles. "There were a lot of protests by environmentalists. Those bloody hippie killjoys start loitering in the proximity of Darleth's plant with a Geiger counter in hand, and they begin to register anomalies in the levels of radioactivity in the air." Tony showed them a document he had found in the online archives of an environmentalist association: "The Karnach power station and its damage to the environment". "Long story short: radioactivity three times higher than the norm. It seemed that the plant's warehouse contained more uranium than was legally permitted. They kicked up quite a fuss, resulting in a formal enquiry."

As he spoke, Tony exhibited a succession of documents, consisting of scanned typewritten pages, a little dark but perfectly legible, and a few Polaroids.

"But when the government inspectors went into the plant, they didn't find anything untoward. Everything was in order. There were further protests, and a war of words broke out between rival experts, with accusations made on both sides of the barricade, and demonstrations that degenerated into violent clashes. And then, at that point, there was a twist in the tale." The screen showed the front page of a local paper: KARNACH PLANT OPENS TO THE PUBLIC. "September 1973, Operation Transparency. August Darleth allowed the hippies to enter the Karnach station, without restrictions. And those fools ended up with egg on their faces. Darleth had performed his magic." Tony crossed his arms. "Interesting man, August Darleth. Physicist, astrophysicist, successful entrepreneur, but also a lover of rare books. Esoteric books. So much so that he was the first and only suspect in the theft of the first edition of the *Unaussprechlichen Kulten*, stolen from its legal owners in 1961. The same volume which, in 1975, appeared in a photograph of this splendid library. Doesn't this sound somewhat . . , odd? August Darleth, a man who goes as far as commissioning the theft of a rare book, suddenly gives it away for no reason? Out of the goodness of his heart?"

"Has it never crossed your mind," Karin said, "that my father may have simply bought it?"

Tony allowed himself a snigger. "I'm a writer – I don't believe in fairy tales. In 2006, Edvard Bukreev made an offer of seven million euros for that book. Even if we factor in a Black Friday-style discount, your father did not have this kind of sum in 1975. And if he had, he would certainly not have spent it on a book, because Friedrich had his own little miracle to nurture. It was Horst who was obsessed with that bullshit, not him. And Horst could only have owned fifty per cent of Friedrich's business at most, and I doubt even that much, frankly." Tony brushed the embossed spiral on the cover of the *Unaussprechlichen Kulten* with his fingers. His impulse was to wipe them on his T-shirt afterwards.

"And now," he continued, "we come to Josef Horst. A doctor, and the father of a little boy called Michl. Josef Horst arrives in Kreuzwirt in 1973, without a penny to his name, just like Friedrich back when he was being bankrupted by a failing sawmill. And yet as soon as he starts doing business with Perkman, all his problems are solved. But what about the Von Junzt?"

He waited.

Neither Karin nor Michl replied.

Tony clenched his fists, put them on the table and leaned forward. "Do you know what a mutual friend with a bizarre Russian accent told me? That books – certain books – are worth a great deal of money. They're *investments*. So what could Friedrich have, which was so valuable that he could offer it to August Darleth in exchange for his treasure?"

Sibylle let out a moan. A stifled cry that filled Tony with pain.

Sib had understood.

"A safe place," she said. "The Perkman property. The land. The lake in the middle of the peat bog, deep, remote and rarely visited. Horst acted as intermediary between Friedrich and Darleth, didn't he?"

"Yes," Tony replied.

"Horst proposed that Friedrich sign a pact with the devil," Sibylle went on, her voice colder than the blade of the arsehole slasher. "A little like Kreuzwirt as a whole. A quiet life, geraniums at the windows and the occasional tumour. And everyone knew. Because this toing and froing of radioactive containers couldn't be kept concealed, and yet nobody ever asked any questions. Until Erika. Spooky Erika . . ."

Sib's voice faded away in a rattle.

She stared into space.

"Erika," Tony continued on her behalf, pointing a finger at Karin and Michl, "commits suicide in your family dumping ground. So Erika's body needs to disappear, because it's evidence. She has to be cremated. For the same reason Betta has to be. After all, she died in the same water as Erika. Water from the lake. Perhaps the two corpses hadn't absorbed much radiation, but why take the risk? Another problem: that idiot

Gabriel keeps asking questions. He's crazy, of course, but . . . he nearly worked it out. In truth, there isn't just one Wanderer, but three."

Karin's lips had shrunk to two thin, bloodless strips.

Despite his ostensibly confident expression, Michl was breathless.

"August Darleth, Josef Horst and Friedrich Perkman. Now tell us," Tony concluded, "how many radioactive drums will we fish out of that lake?"

"Zero," Karin replied.

"Don't make fun of me."

"The trafficking," Karin said, "barely lasted two years – 1973 and 1974. In '74, Darleth's plant adopted new systems and there was no need for it. However, after all the bribing of civil servants, experts, customs officers, and so on, Darleth went bust that year. In order to settle his debt he had to give Friedrich and Josef the Von Junzt. In any case, they would never have agreed to continue trafficking that stuff."

"Is this what you tell yourself," Sibylle said, "so you can sleep at night?"

"No. It's the truth. Friedrich wanted to protect Kreuawii t from the effects of the sawmill closing down, and Horst was eager to start something new. They weren't greedy, just ambitious. The lake is clean now. If you were to dive into its waters, you wouldn't find a single drum of uranium. They made them disappear in 1998."

"1998?" Sibylle said. "When Erika ran away from home? Did she see something she wasn't supposed to see? Did they kill her because she'd worked out what they were doing?"

Karin's reply took Sibylle's breath away.

"Erika," she said almost gently, "was murdered, yes. But not by my father. And not by Michl's father, either."

Seventy-Five

1.

Betta always wore the same jacket all winter, and her skirts were covered in patches. Betta never had a penny in her pocket and she was ashamed of her parents, who smelled of dung and looked so much older than their years, hunched over as they were from the hard work of *maso* life.

Karin, on the other hand, had wardrobes full of clothes she had only worn once and a roomful of shoes, not to mention the necklaces and jewels her mother had bequeathed her, and yet she would have traded everything for an hour, a solitary hour, of the freedom Betta did not know what to do with.

And Betta was beautiful. As she was growing up, Karin became increasingly aware of it. She could wear make-up and dress according to the latest fashion, but Betta ... Betta had it within her. Whenever she entered a room, it was as though somebody switched the light on.

Above all, Betta was not forced to carry the burden of the Perkman surname on her shoulders.

Sometimes, Karin also envied Spooky Erika. When they were younger, she found Erika a little scary. The tarots. The mysterious phrases. Then, as she grew up, she realised it was all an act. Finally, in 1998, while secretly drinking beer with Betta on the school roof, she found out that Spooky Erika was actually Slutty Erika.

"Aren't you happy you're an aunt?" Betta had said. "Auntie Karin. It sounds nice."

"What are you talking about?"

"Erika and Martin."

"You're not serious."

"I'm totally serious. Slutty Erika's found a way to get money. Your money."

"But—"

"Martin the maniac would never have given in?" Betta said, sneering. "Do you want me to show you the scar? Do I need to remind you of all the times he came out of nowhere to hug me and touch me up?"

There was no need to say it. Betta would dart away from Martin's embraces at the speed of light, while Erika just laughed and laughed . . . and rubbed herself against him?

"You're stuffed now. You'll have to feed her for the rest of your life. When your father finds out—"

"Martin never leaves the villa."

"Don't lie. You know he sometimes does."

"Alright, but he does it on his own. How could he have arranged a meeting with Erika?"

Betta clicked her fingers. *Snap. Snap.* Then faster. Like a volley. *Snap-snapsnapsnap.*

"Are you drunk?"

"I've just said 'See you later'. In Erika and Martin's language."

That gave Karin the giggles. "You're mad."

"I've seen them," Betta said, a serious look on her face. "Erika climbs onto the wall and Martin stands at the window. And they talk. They have their secret language. Like this."

She clicked her fingers. *Snap.*

"You're—"

"The monster can't talk, can he?"

"He can't talk, but . . ."

Snap. Snap. Had she not heard these sounds? In the middle of the night?

Betta changed the subject, but the seed of doubt had been sown. Karin needed evidence, though.

From the observatory turret, you could see the entire east side of the villa. Including the window of Martin's room and a section of the boundary wall near the peat bog that was obscured by tall trees. From this position, Karin took to spying on her twin and discovered that Betta had been telling the truth. Martin stood at the window and Erika hid among the trees, sitting astride the wall, and they would communicate in that strange secret language. Karin was furious. She began plotting her revenge.

If there was one thing she had inherited from her father, it was willpower: Erika would pay. By Martin's hand. And Karin knew how to bring it about. She started neglecting her duties: no longer checking that Martin's door was locked, that his wrists were securely tied. She stopped reading *The Wind in the Willows* to him (God, did she hate that book!), to put him on edge. Make him more aggressive.

The opportunity to put her revenge into practice fell into her lap. By spying on their secret conversations, Karin discovered that Erika and Martin had arranged to meet by the lake on the night of the Maturaball. That evening, the door to Martin's room would remain open. Martin would be able to go on his date. Very, very on edge. And when the monster was on edge . . . Betta knew all too well what happened whenever Martin lost his head. He got angry. Very angry. Soon Erika would know, too.

Seventy-Six

1.

"Am I Martin's daughter? Am, I . . . your niece?"

Karin did not reply. She turned to Michl. "Will you do the honours?"

He nodded, stood up and went to an oak cabinet, unlocked a display case and removed a few books from the shelf, revealing a safe from which he produced an orange envelope. He handed it to Karin, who slid out a sheet of paper folded in four and showed it to Sibylle.

Michl explained. "It's a DNA test. Your DNA. One of the many tests arranged by my father. There is no Perkman blood in your veins."

"That's what you claim," Tony said.

"Why would we lie?"

"Because your little story is very convenient," Sibylle said icily. "Martin killed Erika, drew the symbol in the mud and went back home. Horst noticed something was wrong and retraced Martin's steps as far as the lake, where he found the body. We know the rest. It's perfect. Too perfect. And you two come out of it as white as snow."

Karin opened the Von Junzt. It contained the impossible photographs. Photographs two to six. Erika lying on the lake shore, beside the hummingbird smile.

"Nothing's perfect. The truth never is."

"The photos," Sib said, "why keep them?"

Karin grimaced. "To punish myself."

"Like Martin?"

"Martin . . . yes, of course. Poor little Martin. Martin the little mole. Martin the *victim*." Karin stood up and leaned towards Sibylle, her fist raised. "And what about me? I'm shut up here with him. I had to look after that idiot. I had to protect him from Erika. I have to keep the secret. I have to protect Kreuzwirt. *I have to—*"

"Darling . . ." Michl gently touched her.

His gesture seemed to calm her down.

"I keep the photos to remind me of the consequences of my actions. And to teach me not to do anything so stupid again."

"And possibly," Tony said, "to stop Martin from killing again?"

"Do you mean Betta? That was an accident. Betta was not the good girl everybody said she was. She never was. But she died in that damned stream, so—"

"She, too, was cremated," Tony said. "The picture. Number one. Who gave it to Sib?"

"We think it was Martin," Karin replied. "He took advantage of the confusion at my father's funeral to steal it and make us pay. Like a good Perkman."

Tony felt his blood curdle. "Is he not sedated? Tied down?"

"Not always."

"So he can go out. If he wants to."

Michl sneered. "Are you thinking of the Wanderer?"

"How much does Gabriel know?" Sib asked.

"Nothing. But the problem with lunatics like Gabriel is that they shout so much that people start paying attention. Even though the drums are long gone, there are still traces of radioactivity in the water, which a lab could discover. So when he started asking questions we tried to bribe him, send him far away. The kid gloves didn't work. He was madly in love with your mother. He didn't have the courage to tell her outright, but it was obvious. And it was equally evident that Erika didn't even know he existed. When Erika died it was a severe blow to his mental health. It was Gabriel who started the business with the ghost, you know? It was his way of—"

"Of making Kreuzwirt pay. Why not kill him? As a matter of fact, why not kill them both? Gabriel and Martin. Get them out of the way, and you won't have any more problems."

"We're not murderers," Michl said. "And I think it's time we returned to reality. We all know that they'll never be able to charge Martin with Erika's murder. There's no evidence. Not anymore."

"That's true," Tony replied, "but we can take a glass of water from the lake, have it analysed and ruin you for ever."

"Unless you wish to accept the identity of Sibylle's father in exchange for your silence. And we know for certain. We know where he lives. And we know for a fact that he is her father. We have a DNA test that confirms it."

"And what's stopping us from accepting, shaking hands and then ruining you anyway?"

"Never strike a dying animal," Karin said. "They have no qualms about biting you. *Truly* biting."

The paper remained suspended in mid-air.

Sib stood up, flung the door open and shouted, "You're finished! Finished – is that clear?"

She left.

Karin handed Tony a business card.

"Make her see reason, Signor Carcano. We'll give you until tomorrow. Or—"

"You'll take countermeasures."

3.

Outside, it was raining. A warm, disgusting, light rain. Rudi was waiting by the door, and when Tony walked past him Rudi pointed to the Mustang beyond the gates.

"Nice car. They don't make them like that anymore."

The fist took off by itself.

Rudi staggered back. He tripped. Fell.

"Now we're even," Rudi said, massaging his sore jaw. "But I'm sorry you took it personally, Signor Carcano. It was an act, you see? That's all. I do what Karin and Michl ask me to. I carried on doing what my father used to do for Friedrich: giving people a fright, injecting foxes with rabies . . ."

"So that people wouldn't get close to the lake. Fuck you and fuck those fucking foxes."

Rudi got to his feet and brushed off his trousers. "I hope, Signor Carcano, I really hope—"

"You hope you won't have to kill me? Is that what you're trying to say?"

Rudi shook his head. He seemed sad.

"I hope you and Signorina Knapp will be happy. We'll always be trapped here, but you can be free."

Seventy-Seven

1.

Tony was driving. Sibylle was huddled in the seat next to his. It was not hard to imagine what she was feeling. Pain. Anger. Despair.

"We need to talk, Sib."

"No."

"It's not up to me to decide."

Sib turned towards him, furious. "And I've made up my mind. We're setting off the bomb."

"Not like this. You can't take this kind of decision in—"

Sib slapped the dashboard, switched on the stereo and turned the volume up full. Elvis. "Hound Dog". This song had been waiting there in ambush for twelve years.

When they reached Eisacktal, Tony turned down the volume. "The Carcanos have always worked their fingers to the bone. My father worked in a factory. My grandfather was a labourer. So was my great-grandfather. It's no different on my mother's side. Folks who broke their backs in the sun ploughing other people's land. The Carcanos lived in a shitty world and they were OK with that. Angry, of course, but it was the Carcanos' very own anger. It gave them the strength to get ahead, one centimetre a day, until they dug their graves." Tony opened the window. The warm air slapped his face. "When my father was diagnosed with a tumour, the oncologist gave him six months to live. My father hung on for two years. A Carcano end: forced to fight until the last breath.

But cry at home? Impossible. The Carcanos don't cry. So I'd take my mother to the cinema and we'd cry there. Remember when I told you about *Two*? The young man and the girl who held hands in the cinema? They never existed. That was my mother and me."

Sib had her back to him.

Tony continued. "When *Two* made it onto the bestseller list, my father was in hospital, dying, but he refused to let my mother read him the reviews. For him, my success was a system error, and when the system realised that it would destroy me. The Carcanos work their fingers to the bone, but they have no success. That's why I ordered the Mustang. My father loved that film, *Bullitt*. I added the CD player because he liked Elvis. That's right, Giuseppe Carcano listened to Elvis Presley. Every night, I'd pray that my father would hang on for one more day, so I could show him the Mustang. I wanted him to understand that I'd made it. It was a slap in the face, not a present. It arrived when my father was nearing the end. He was unrecognisable, even though his eyes were still those of Giuseppe Carcano. A man who believed that getting into fights with his own son would help the boy grow up. When I announced that I was leaving home, that I'd never work at the steel factory, there was quite a bout. I left home covered in bruises, with nothing in my pockets. That night, I slept under Resia bridge. I've never slept better, I can assure you. I fell asleep swearing I'd show that bastard. That Tony would not end up like all the other Carcanos." Tony smiled. "You know what my mother said to me at the funeral? That they were the same words my father had thrown at his own father before taking his suitcase and emigrating to Bolzano."

Elvis started singing "Love Me Tender".

"My father always judged people by the money they had in their pockets. Those who do are better than those who don't. The Mustang spoke his language: it cost what he earned in four years. I parked outside the hospital room where my father was dying. I wanted him to see my poisoned gift. Then I went up, lifted him out of the bed, dragged him to the window and showed it to him. He mumbled that he wouldn't believe me until I proved it was really mine. I carried him to the car park in my arms. I opened the door. 'See?' I said, 'it's really mine.' And the bastard replied that, yes, maybe it was mine, but the engine probably wasn't really a 428 like Steve McQueen's. I opened the bonnet and showed him the 428, then got him to sit where you're sitting now, turned on the engine and let him experience the roar of this beast. 'Who's the loser, Papà?' I asked. 'Who's the loser now, you stupid son of a bitch?'" Tony shook his head. "And you know what he did? He said . . ."

Seventy-Eight

1.

Giuseppe Carcano proffered a hand, a hook devastated by his illness, and said, "Give me a cigarette and let's go for a spin, Tonino."

"You know I don't smoke anymore."

"But you can drive a car, can't you?"

Tony drove into Via Vittorio Veneto. He turned on the stereo. "Elvis," his father said.

"A tough guy like you, right, Papà? Because he had the courage to sing like a black man in front of all those white fucking racists."

Tony was echoing one of his father's refrains, but Giuseppe Carcano gestured with his hand, as if to say, *Don't talk nonsense.*

"You really believed that? Elvis reminds me of the first time I made love to your mother. The rest is bullshit for stupid little boys like you. In Elvis's day, people listened to the radio, and on the radio skin colour didn't matter, smart arse."

"Is that what I am to you, Papà? A stupid little boy?"

"A stupid little boy who knows nothing. Nothing."

The traffic lights turned from red to green.

Tony took off, making the Firestones screech. Giuseppe's laugh was the death rattle in his lungs.

"That's the way," he said. "Put some fire up this lady's arse, Tonino."

"I hate it when you call me that."

That laugh again.

Tony sped up.

"You know nothing," he said. "Nothing about me. Nothing about yourself. You don't know that I'd take Mamma to the cinema so she could cry in peace, since you – stupid idiot! – won't let her cry in front of you. Because you're afraid. You're afraid of all the love you have for us. Tough guy, right? The Steve McQueen of Via Resia."

He overtook an Alfa Romeo. Then a Ducato. The driver hurled a volley of insults at him. Tony did not have the courage to look at his father.

So he pressed down on the accelerator again.

"And I have to say this, Papà. You got yourself a tumour to piss me off. Because it would have been lovely to see you grow old, it would have been lovely to see you buying one of my books – fuck, to see you happy, *happy* about what I'm building. Because I am building something. A happy ending for the Giuseppe Carcanos of this world. I cast out ghosts, I erase hatred. But you're a man of integrity, you don't accept that stories can have a happy ending. You're the guy who leaves before your son finds the strength to tell you what you, you coward, should have told me years and years ago . . ." He jumped a red light. A grey Toyota had to break hard. Tony just managed to avoid it. "That I love you, you stupid bastard."

The Mustang went from a roar to a rumble. It slowed down.

"I love you, Papà."

Tony was dripping with sweat. At the first junction, he reversed. He finally found the courage to look at his father. He was asleep. Tony burst out laughing.

You win! One–nil, Papà.

When they arrived back at the hospital, he woke him up. Confused, Giuseppe asked him for a cigarette. Tony dragged him out of the passenger seat. A male nurse rushed towards them, pushing a wheelchair, showering him with insults.

Once he had been carefully placed in the wheelchair, his father opened his eyes. He moved his lips.

"I don't smoke, Papà."

Giuseppe motioned to him to come closer. Tony had to bend down and inhale the smell of illness.

"I told you I don't—"

Giuseppe squeezed his arm. Hard.

2.

"It's over," his father said, panting. "The time when the Carcanos bent their heads down, right, boy?"

Seventy-Nine

1.

Shanghai.

Sib wiped away a tear.

"People like the Perkmans always fall on their feet," Tony said. "They'll never go to jail. There'll be a scandal, some member of staff will be fired from the company, but Karin and Michl? They'll stay there, at Toad Villa. Kreuzwirt will forget. It's good at forgetting, you know that better than I do. I was able to argue with my father. I was able to understand how much of him there is in me. And even though I wanted to hurt him, I understood how to make him happy. At the eleventh hour, yes, but I had that chance."

2.

The call came at three in the afternoon. Karin was pacing up and down, slightly tipsy.

Michl picked up. "What conditions?" he said, frowning. His face tightened into a grimace. "The first one is possible. But the second one . . ."

Silence.

"Alright. This evening." He hung up.

Karin took another sip of Martini.

"So?"

"They agree."

"I knew it," Karin said, glowing.

"But Sibylle wants to speak to Martin. And Carcano has asked . . ."

Eighty

1.

Tony was the third news item, after the escape of some pigs from a *maso* in Val di Maces and the statement of a councillor about the viability of fixing a landslide in Val Gardena. The television camera was focusing on a woman dressed in black who would have been very beautiful were it not for her stern expression.

Polianna extinguished her cigarette. If Tony discovered that, in the evening, after dinner and a small glass of cordial, she indulged in one of those killers, he would hit the roof. But true ladies must always have their secrets. It's part of their charm. Polianna rubbed her hands, looking forward to the performance.

The woman in black took centre stage.

The caption read, GIOVANNA INNOCENZI, JOURNALIST.

"It was just a mistake," the woman said. "A source who deliberately tried to push a negative image of *Giò's Pearls* by discrediting it with fake news and skilful editing that painted a false picture."

"It was at the expense of the well-known writer Tony Carcano."

"Of course, him, too."

"So we can say that the pictures of the writer that showed him . . ."

Annoyed, the woman shook her head. "The source was playing a practical joke on our editorial staff. So . . ."

Lying on the sofa, Polianna ground her teeth. She turned up the sound.

"So, we apologise to our readers, and above all we apologise to the party concerned."

"You mean Tony Carcano?"

"Yes, that's who I mean."

The director lingered on Giò's face for a few seconds. She looked as though she had just swallowed two kilos of lemons. Polianna burst into a resounding laugh. "Bloody bitch!" she sneered. "Take that, you bloody bitch, because that's what you are!"

The insults went on for a long time. But, just as with the cigarette, Polianna did not feel guilty even for a moment. She was born and bred in Shanghai, after all.

Eighty-One

1.

Tante Frida stopped brushing Severino's coat as soon as Giovanna Innocenzi's face appeared on the fifty-inch screen in her living room. Sensing tension in the air, Severino curled his tail and rubbed his head against her wrist. No sooner had the black-clad journalist started to speak than Tante Frida leaped to her feet, and Severino promptly got out of her way. The time for caresses was over. He did not take it personally. He was a cat, and cats do not hold grudges. At least not until the next time Tante Frida came near him. He nimbly jumped onto the bookcase, curled up on a copy of *Moby Dick* and closed his eyes. There was no better place for a nap.

The news report faded out.

Tante Frida grabbed her phone. *What are you up to, Tony? What's going on? Why aren't you answering?*

Eighty-Two

1.

The smell of the peat bog swept his tiredness away. Scents. Smells. A delight.

The sounds of this place, on the other hand, scared him. Not as much as thunder, because there was nothing worse than thunder, but that creaking, that rustling, reminded him of the drooling Thing that had come out of the forest. The drooling Thing that screamed "*Krrrka!*", and which Freddy had dreamed of more than once.

Except that in his dreams, instead of disappearing, the Thing would attack him. Worse: the Thing would sink its fangs into Tony's flesh. Tony would scream, beg for his help, but Freddy could never stop it. Freddy grumbled.

They were just dreams. He was awake now and nothing bad would happen because Tony was with him and Tony was not like other humans. Tony could sing that magic song, the one that chased fear away.

The very song Tony was humming at that moment without even realising it.

2.

Michl escorted her into the villa. Together, they went up to the first floor where they followed a corridor to a steep, winding staircase that led to the observatory turret. Karin was expecting her. She seemed pleased to see her. When Sib sat opposite her, though, she realised that she was just drunk.

"This is for you," she said, sliding an envelope across the table. Sibylle didn't even glance at it.

"Where's Martin?"

"Martin isn't—"

"Martin, or the deal is off."

Karin tidied her hair. There was malicious joy in her eyes. "I just wanted to spare you the pain."

She left her alone. Sib grabbed the envelope and turned it over in her hands. It did not contain the name of her father but the name of a ghost. Tony would never understand. Just as he wouldn't understand what she was about to do. That was why she had told him a lie. *I need to say goodbye to Erika and I need to do it alone.* Tony had not protested.

Ghosts can be very fierce and instructive, he had once said to her. Sib agreed. Erika had been cruel to her. Even though she knew her mother was murdered, that she had not abandoned her, the anger she had harboured for all those years would be with her for a long time to come. Perhaps for ever.

That was why Sib had lied to Tony. She had not agreed to the pact with the Perkmans in order to discover her father's identity. Her father was a ghost and she did not want any more of those in her life. Sibylle had done it so that she could meet Martin, experience through his words the events of the night of March 21, 1999, say goodbye to Erika's ghost and stick the arsehole slasher into the heart of her killer.

3.

Ghosts can be very fierce and instructive, Tony thought, as Sibylle was swallowed up by Krotn Villa, with those ivy-covered walls, the mausoleum and the observatory turret that looked like a finger pointing to the sky.

To indicate God?

Maybe. Or the dark space between the stars. The obscure hinge between worlds, as Von Junzt would have called it. It was to escape from such thoughts that Tony ventured into the thicket as far as the lake.

Looking out over it, calm under the full moon, he was surprised. He had expected to pick up on something, evidence of the blood shed on its shore, or else the echo of death nestling in its depths. But of the horror that had played out there, of Erika's death and the destruction of her body, there was no trace.

Even Freddy was wagging his tail, as though this was just any ordinary place. Perhaps the St Bernard was right, Tony thought. Hell was like any ordinary place.

He crouched and gave Freddy a couple of pats as the dog licked his face in return. "Good boy, good boy."

Polianna had called to tell him that Giò had apologised on the news. It was the first condition Sib had set for the Perkmans. "You should have seen that smug bitch's face," Polianna had said. Tony had never heard Polianna use such language. Then she had asked him to be careful. *I don't know what you're up to, but I like that girl. And like the fact that she likes you. Keep an eye on her. Do it for me, will you?*

Tante Frida had also bombarded him with calls, but Tony had not picked up. A conversation with Tante Frida might complicate things. All in good time.

The lights from the villa attracted his attention. He had not realised how close the lake was. He figured eight hundred metres, as the crow flies. In the darkness surrounding the peat bog, the observatory turret was glowing like a lighthouse.

313

A monster was what Karin had called him. That was nasty. Nevertheless, it was exactly what Sibylle thought for a moment when Martin was ushered into the room by Michl. His face seemed to have been chiselled by a cruel, idiotic god.

One half had been ravaged by the fire, while the other, free of burns, was practically identical to that of the radiant Friedrich Perkman – noble and proud – in the wedding photographs Aunt Helga had shown her.

Michl helped him sit down. Martin's blind eye stared at Sib as he put his hands on the table. He had long, powerful fingers. He was wearing a dark suit, with a black tie, to which a small pin shaped like a bird was fastened. A tiny hummingbird spreading its wings.

"If you need . . ." Michl did not finish his sentence. He walked out and closed the door behind him.

"You killed my mother."

No reply.

"Was it you who put her picture into my letterbox?"

Martin adjusted his tie.

"Why did you do it?"

A shudder.

"Why did you kill my mother?"

Martin clicked his fingers. *Snap. Snap.* In quick succession. Then a melodious whistle.

"'The Wild Wood is pretty well populated by now,'" he recited in a raucous, tentative voice, "'with all the usual lot, good, bad, and indifferent – I name no names. It takes all sorts to make a world. But I fancy you know something about them yourself by this time.'"

"*The Wind in the Willows*?"

Martin nodded. *Snap. Snap.*

"Lehrerin Rosa said you're not an idiot. Don't pretend. I want answers." The arsehole slasher made its appearance. "At all costs."

"Sometimes," Martin's awkward voice said, "I confuse dreams with reality. And the other way round. Sometimes, like this evening, I think there's no difference between what I dream and what I see. Can you swear this is reality? Can you prove to me that I'm not dreaming? Or that you're not dreaming? Or that the two of us are no more than the dream of a young woman dying by the lake?" Martin gently touched the ravaged part of his face. "Erika was the only one who wasn't afraid of me. She never pointed a knife like that at me."

"And if she had she'd still be alive. And you'd be dead."

"How can you be sure I'm not?"

Sibylle clenched her teeth. "Stop these games."

"Did you agree to the deal? Like my father did? Like everybody in Kreuzwirt?"

Sibylle did not bother replying. She grabbed the envelope and tore it in half. Then tore the halves into quarters, reducing her father's identity to a heap of paper and ink. "I agreed so that I could speak to you. Alone."

"And kill me."

Sibylle looked at him for a long time before responding.

Sibby Longstocking said goodbye to Tony. There's no future for murderers, she thought. "And kill you."

Eighty-Three

1.

A shadow emerged from the villa.

The shadow was smiling. It looked forward to the death the night would bring.

2.

"Erika would sing for me. For the mole. The mole is underground. Like the dead. The dead are at peace. The dead know everything. I was not at peace, but I knew everything. I knew what my father and Horst had hidden in the lake. I heard them talking."

A cackle.

"Mice. Like mice in the walls. They never found me out. No-one sees the mole. The mole is quiet. The mole is invisible. Only Erika could see the mole. And she'd sing. Sing for me. She was the only one who wasn't afraid of this face. Of my—"

"Madness?"

Martin nodded. Then he shook his head. "It's not madness. The mole hates. Just hates."

"Who?"

"Everybody." Martin uttered it with odd, youthful glee, as though universal hatred were the most natural thing in the world. Sibylle gasped, and clutched the flick knife even tighter.

Martin rubbed his nails together. *Tick-tick-tick.* Like an insect.

"Karin used to say that the fire had killed the good part of me and spared the bad. That's why I am the way I am, she said. The mole. That's why the flames attacked me and not her. That's why I'm alone and she's found love."

"Michl."

"The man whose scars are on the inside."

"He—"

"Like his father. Horst and his books. If you're here, then you've read the Von Junzt. And you know about Grahame."

"Did Grahame kill his son?'

"Maybe. Maybe not." Martin looked around the room. "But he had him locked up."

A giggle. A double click. *Snap. Snap.* Martin stood up. So did Sibylle, abruptly, knife ready to strike. Martin didn't seem to notice.

He went to the window, turning his back on her.

"I want you to tell me about Erika," Sib said. "How did you kill her?'

"Erika predicted this moment. With her tarots. She said a very beautiful, very angry woman would come and see me. That she would bring cruel words that would turn the mole into a prince. Erika always had hope. Always. That's why she died. Because she trusted everybody."

"She trusted you. And you killed her. You'd arranged to meet. She wanted to take you to the Maturaball . . ."

"Yes, the Maturaball. Singing, dancing and laughter. So much laughter. Erika wanted to show me to the world. Erika said that people would be frightened, some disgusted, but that many, many would understand. That the little mole wouldn't have to be dead anymore, didn't have to stay underground. The mole, Erika said, could see the sunlight."

"She loved you."

"Yes."

"And you killed her anyway."

"Karin found out. She listened to our private conversations. She deciphered our language. She tormented me for days before the Maturaball. She wanted to make me angry. Like with Betta. She left the door open. Then she went to the Maturaball with Michl. But I didn't go out. I never left the villa that night. I was afraid. Of all those eyes. Of all those people who would stare at me. Who would see the monster." Martin turned away from the window, his ravaged face streaked with tears. "It wasn't me who killed Erika."

3.

"I've always loved this place," the voice said from the darkness.

"Michl."

"Did I startle you? I'm sorry."

Michl bent down and stroked Freddy's muzzle. The St Bernard gave a grunt of pleasure.

"Have you been following me?"

"I thought I'd find you here. As I said, it's a beautiful place. I've always loved it. It has the power to calm ugly thoughts."

"You don't look like an insomniac."

"I'm not. Karin has trouble sleeping, but I wouldn't call her an insomniac, either. At least not in the technical sense of the word."

"What about Martin?"

"Martin is a simple soul," Michl replied. "He needs little."

"Someone to read him *The Wind in the Willows* and cover up his murders?"

"You used the plural. Murders. Do you think Martin is the Wanderer?"

"Actually, I was wondering where *you* were on March 21, 1999."

Michl burst out laughing. His laughter echoed for a long time. The darkness of the peat bog fed on it.

"I took Karin to the Maturaball," Michl said. "She was wearing a stunning dress. Everybody kept looking at her. There was a lot of gossip that evening, if you see what I mean."

"In other words, a lot of witnesses. All good Kreuzwirt folk, I imagine. Heavily indebted to the Perkman family. Everybody who knew about her father's trafficking."

The smile vanished from Michl's face. "Best not joke about certain things."

"Is it that easy to buy a human being?"

"Are you interrogating me, Signor Carcano? Or is it just that your writer's soul feels inspired by this landscape?"

"I'm an inquisitive person."

Horst gave Freddy a pat, then pointed a Beretta at Tony.

Freddy tensed up.

"Throw the .22 down, please," Michl said.

"What .22?"

"The one you're hiding behind your back."

Tony obeyed. The .22 disappeared into the peat bog bushes.

Freddy was growing agitated. Michl pointed the gun at him. "Keep him still, I hate the idea of hurting a dog."

Tony crouched and began to stroke the St Bernard, trying to calm him down. "There was no pact, right, Horst?" he said, as Freddy slowly calmed down. "Was the plan to make the bodies disappear in the lake?"

"The bodies will be found horribly burnt. Dear friends of ours at the hospital will identify them as the remains of Michl Horst and Karin and Martin Perkman. In the case of the latter, they won't even need to lie. A real tragedy, don't you think?"

Tony got up. Michl's gun was pointed at him again. Freddy whimpered, but nothing more. His muzzle was shifting from Tony's face to Michl's.

Tony gave him one last pat on the head. "You underestimate Polianna," he said.

"Your housekeeper?" Michl sneered. "Now why doesn't that worry me?"

"It should. If Polianna doesn't find me at home tomorrow, she'll hit the roof, then she'll start to worry and try to contact me. If she doesn't succeed, she'll call my agent, who'll be seriously pissed off, because I'm due to deliver a novel for which I have already cashed a handsome cheque, from which he has already deducted his sacrosanct commission. This would trigger a chain of events that would lead a lot of angry people to start looking for yours truly. Trust me, never get between a publisher and his book."

Michl burst out laughing. "Good try. Really. This way, please. After you. And keep that nice big dog on the lead. There are a lot of rabid foxes around."

Eighty-Four

1.

Karin was drenched in sweat. Michl had flown into a rage when he had found her drunk and forced her to gulp down coffee until she felt nauseous. She had sobered up just enough to be able to do what she had to do. Burn down the prison. Krotn Villa. Destroy it.

When her father died, she and Michl had breathed a sigh of relief. Their captivity was over. A mishap on the stairs would eliminate the monster, and they would be free. But Martin had ruined everything. He had given Sibylle the photograph, and when Karin and Michl had realised that, when Sibylle had started asking questions ... all their dreams of freedom had gone up in smoke.

So they had to prepare a new escape plan that would ensure not only Martin's disappearance, but also that of Sibylle and Tony.

"But the monster must die first."

Her words echoed through the villa. That damned villa was full of ghosts. But, Karin thought, they too would die in the fire.

Carrying the canister of petrol, she headed to the observatory turret.

2.

Martin's face contracted into a pained grimace.

"If I had gone out, maybe Erika would still be alive. But I didn't. I stayed by the window, listening to the music coming from the Black

Hat. I told my father, I told Dr Horst, but they didn't believe me. I was just the mole, the monster, why should they? The only one who took me seriously was Gabriel. I told him what had happened and he—"

"He lost his mind."

"No, Gabriel was always the most lucid little animal in the Wild Forest. The only one who understood that Tommy Raggiodisole is among us."

Sibylle gasped. "The Wanderer?"

"The Wanderer exists. The Wanderer kills. And all the little animals in the forest sing for him."

That was when the smell reached them. Petrol. Then the noise. Like an explosion. Then the smoke. Acrid. It filtered through under the door in thick, black spirals.

Sibylle tried the handle. It was locked. "Sh—"

Martin was over her.

The arsehole slasher flew far away.

3.

Michl was shielding his face with a handkerchief. The wind was blowing the smoke towards them, and the smell was nauseating.

Ahead of him, Tony kept coughing. Freddy was looking around, frightened, trembling, but he wasn't pulling on the lead. Freddy would go with him all the way to hell – he would never abandon him. And this made Tony angry. He clung to this anger. It was better than despair. Despair was the image of Sib writhing in the flames that were coming from the villa's turret. Tony dismissed it. Sib was alright, she was not dead, and if he wanted to help her he had to keep a clear head, or else he would be unable to grab any chance Michl might give him.

Michl pushed Tony towards the door of what was once Signora Perkman's conservatory, which had been turned into a kind of tool shed after her death.

"Go on. It's unlocked."

Tony kicked it open. "Fuck you."

"Theatrical but liberating," he heard Michl say behind him. "There's a handrail on your left. Hold on to it and follow it."

A window exploded above their heads. The fire was spreading fast. Freddy yelped.

4.

Karin had expected flames, not an explosion. But no sooner had the match landed on the patch of petrol than a hard, invisible hand pushed her down to the ground.

She got back up, groped for the stairs and staggered up to the second floor of the villa. She sped along the corridor to the library. The floor was covered with rugs, and Michl had left a canister of petrol for her, exactly as planned. Karin was about to pour out the contents, but something held her back – a detail out of place: the Von Junzt was missing from the oval table, where they had left it the day before.

Michl, Karin thought. Michl did not want that book to burn with the others. He had protested when she had told him that the *Unaussprechlichen Kulten* would meet the same end as all the other books in the collection.

Karin hated that book. The book which Dr Horst had forced her and his son to spend hours hunched over, straining their eyes and filling their heads with bullshit. She hated it almost as much as she hated her own twin, who was always eavesdropping. And her father, who had allowed this torture.

No, the Von Junzt must be reduced to ashes. Michl had given in. It was just a silly book, he had said, kissing her on the forehead. A Judas kiss. Michl had lied to her. And he would pay for it, Karin decided, leaving the room.

When she was halfway down the corridor, a voice called out her name: Martin.

Karin clenched her fists.

Michl had assured her that the door to the observatory could not be forced, that it was solid. That idiot had said that Martin and Sibylle would die from the smoke before the flames. But instead . . .

"Karin!"

There was accusation in that call. There was anger. There was *rage*. Karin turned to him and smiled. "Darling brother."

Martin froze, taken aback.

"I love you, my darling brother. I've always taken care of you. Remember? *The Wind in the Willows*. Who's been reading it to you all these years? Who fed you? Who sheltered you from the cold? Who let you out into the woods, as far as the lake?"

Martin swayed.

And not because of the weight of Sibylle's lifeless body hanging over his large shoulder.

Karin opened her arms, "Come here, darling brother. Leave that woman. She's dead. There's nothing more we can do for her. She died a long time ago."

"No, Sibylle—"

Karin laughed and her laughter dominated the crackling of the flames. "That's not Sibylle, silly. Sibylle's just a baby. It's Erika you've killed, it's her body you've been dragging around for far too long. Come here, let's go away. Together. I'll take care of—"

The world was devoured by a roar that seemed to shake Krotn Villa to its foundations. The flames had reached the canister in the library. Thick smoke followed the deafening sound.

Karin tried to save herself by heading for the stairs leading down to the ground floor, but she was stopped by an excruciating, blinding pain that struck at her ankles and made her cry out. Her legs gave way, her knees buckled, and when she sank to the floor her head was whipped back by some unseen force.

That was when Karin saw it. She realised she had been blind and deaf her whole life. Just as Von Junzt had written, the Wanderer existed. And just as the *Unaussprechlichen Kulten* instructed, she was on her knees before him.

Eighty-Five

1.

When they reached the main lounge of Krotn Villa, passing before the eyes of the portraits of Friedrich Perkman, his wife and Dr Horst, Michl instructed Tony to turn around. He obeyed. The muzzle of the Beretta seemed huge. "Kneel down."

"Like for the Wanderer?"

"Don't be ridiculous."

Tony shook his head. "Sorry, the days of the Carcanos going down on their knees are long gone, Horst. If you want to kill me, you'll have to do it looking me in the—" Tony leaped forward. He clearly saw Michl's finger pull the trigger. The Beretta boomed. Tony closed his eyes. The bullet whistled a few centimetres past his neck.

Frightened, Freddy barked, but he did not run. A second bullet thudded into the floor between his paws, but he did not run away even then.

At this point, Tony headbutted Michl square in the face and felt the texture of the nose cartilage give way under the impact.

Michl swayed and raised his hands to his face. Tony struck him a second time, aiming at his liver, and Michl doubled over. A blow from Tony's knee made him collapse to the floor.

Tony did not give him time to catch his breath, but hurled himself at him, pinning his arms with the strength and weight of his legs. Then, sitting astride Michl's chest, he began punching him methodically until his knuckles spurted blood. Michl whimpered one last time, then his eyes rolled back and he lost consciousness.

Tony grabbed the Beretta and pointed it at Michl's forehead. It would be easy. It would be right. Maybe. The "maybe" was enough: Tony did not pull the trigger.

He let out an animal cry, got up, gave Michl one final kick, but did not shoot him. Instead, he bent over Freddy, who was trembling, trying to avoid the sparks that were raining down from the ceiling like a hellish snowfall.

"Let's find Sib," Tony said to him, "then get out of here. OK, Freddy?"

A wheezing voice called out his name. "Carc— Carcano!"

Rudi.

His face was a mask of suffering. His lips had split, and his left eye was so swollen that he could barely keep it open. He was struggling to breathe, holding his side in a way that made Tony suspect he had more than one broken rib. Despite all that, Rudi was dragging himself down the stairs, groping for Martin, who had reached the bottom step by now, and who was also smeared with blood, carrying Sibylle's lifeless body in his arms. Freddy yelped.

"Erika's dead," Martin said, showing him Sibylle. "Erika's dead."

There was no pain. There was no anger or even despair. Tony felt nothing.

Only cold.

He pointed the gun. "Her name is not Erika. Her name is Sibylle."

"Sibylle is the little girl. Sibylle can't sing."

"You," was the only word that came out of Tony's mouth.

He curled his index finger around the trigger.

"The world is the centre of the clearing," Martin said. "We are the little animals. I am the mole. Erika was the fox. Erika is dead now. Sibylle is . . ."

Sibylle stirred.

The Beretta remained silent.

From the corner of his eye, Tony saw that Rudi had almost caught up with Martin. He was clutching a knife with a sharp, narrow blade which reflected the light of the fire. Tony watched as he reached for the banister with the hand that held the knife, clutching his chest with the other as he tried to stand.

Hurry up, you stupid bastard, and I swear I'll forget the engraving on the Mustang.

He had to stall for time.

"It was you who killed those women, wasn't it?" he said to Martin. "How many? How many did you kill?"

There was no reply.

"It was Erika you were killing each time, wasn't it?" Tony continued. "It was her you were killing over and over again. Then you went around wearing their clothes. Like the Wanderer."

There were flames everywhere. The air was unbreathable. Soot swirled in black eddies. The heat was unbearable. Tony prayed that the sweat would not drip into his eyes.

He prayed that Rudi would hurry.

That this nightmare would end.

Rudi got to his feet with difficulty and hunched over, the knife still in his right hand.

Do it, Tony thought.

Rudi caught his breath and arched his back, gathering the necessary torque for the blow by flinging his arm back, the edge of the blade facing out, as though he were about to strike Martin with a whip rather than a knife. The steel flickered in the light of the flames. Rudi put his full weight into the strike, bending his legs and curving his upper body like a child bouncing pebbles on the water.

The blade sketched a glowing arc, sliced through the smoke and slashed Martin's flesh just above his ankles in a single, efficient, practised and almost elegant gesture. Blood spurted from the wounds and Martin's legs abruptly gave way.

With a stifled cry, he came crashing down on his knees the very moment Rudi was staggering back up, and Tony realised that he wasn't clutching his chest but clutching something *against* his chest.

A black-bound book, with an embossed spiral on the cover. The *Unaussprechlichen Kulten*.

Martin's eyes opened wide, and he let go of Sibylle's body. A voice in Tony's head told him he should step forward and catch her, but he could do nothing but stare at the cover of the Von Junzt and the way in which, despite the fire and the surrounding chaos, before tucking the book into his trousers, Rudi first wiped the splashes of Martin's blood from its cover. Martin, who was on his knees, whimpering something. On his knees, Tony thought. Like . . .

3.

"Rat!" he found breath to whisper, shaking. "Are you afraid?"

"Afraid?" murmured the Rat, his eyes shining with unutterable love. "Afraid! Of HIM? O, never, never! And yet – and yet – O, Mole, I am afraid!"

Then the two animals, crouching to the earth, bowed their heads and did worship.

4.

"Adoration becomes the Wanderer. Your head up to the stars and a knee on the ground. Penitent and reverent. Where the muscle is strong, it bends. Where the will does not yield, the Wanderer's gaze pierces through."

5.

. . like before the Wanderer.

Tony shifted the Beretta from Martin to Rudi, who, in the meantime, had reached Sibylle and lifted her off the floor, and was now holding her up by the waist. He no longer resembled the living dead as he had just moments before.

"Don't do it," Tony said.

Rudi seemed taken aback.

"Down!" Tony shouted. "Throw that thing on the floor. And let Sibylle go."

On his knees, Martin gurgled something. "*Erika.*"

To Tony's ears, it sounded like *Kkkraka*!

Rudi pointed the blade at Sibylle's throat. "Do you want to hear her sing?"

For the first time, Tony saw the thousand-faced Rudi as he truly was. The local boor, the Perkmans' henchman, the friend who takes you fishing, the guy you can have a pleasant chat with. The man who knows how to watch, study, calculate. The predator. The one who suggests new hobbies, new friendships, new hairdos. Had the smile that hovered on his now swollen lips, so sincere, so *harmless*, seduced Mirella? Perhaps, but behind all those masks Tony saw the face of the Wanderer.

"Do you want to hear her sing?"

"No."

Rudi came closer, using Sibylle's body as a shield, holding the blade to her throat.

"Throw that gun down."

Tony lowered it and the Wanderer approached.

"Throw it down."

Tony hurled it into the flames. Rudi smiled. "I am the Friend who comes from afar," he said.

Tony recognised the quotation from the Von Junzt.

"I've travelled a long way to come to you, Tony. I have crossed worlds. The hinges are my home, the worlds my hunting ground. I bring you ecstasy, glory and—"

"Blood," Tony said.

Rudi nodded. "That's what is written."

Tony went down on his knees. "As it's written in the Von Junzt. You are the Wanderer. I can see that now. You have the power to show worlds. I beg you, show me the worlds."

Rudi was keeping out of Tony's reach. "Is this a trick, Carcano? Are you insulting the Wanderer?"

"Show me the worlds."

Tony bowed his head, put his hands between his thighs and his calves, and pinned them with his own weight. In this position, there was nothing he could do to protect himself from Rudi's knife. The Wanderer came up behind him and dropped Sibylle. She moaned and raised a hand to grab Tony but Rudi kicked it away. Tony did not move.

The Wanderer came up close behind him. Tony held still. The Wanderer felt the back of Tony's neck and his hands travelled down, along his spine. Tony could sense Rudi's fingers counting the vertebrae.

The Wanderer found the spot, grabbed Tony by the hair and forced him to bend his head back, exposing his throat, then raised the knife like a bullfighter ready to deal the death blow. A drop of Martin's blood fell on Tony's face. He felt it run down his cheek. Warm And only now did Tony speak.

Never," he said, a glint of madness in his eyes, the eyes of a rabid fox, "never threaten the owner of a hundred-and-ten-kilo St Bernard."

That frightening growl wasn't coming from the fire. Rudi threw himself back, his arms protecting his face.

Too late.

Six months later

Eighty-Six

1.

A harsh tramontana had whitened the peaks of the surrounding mountains. When the radio crackled, Zanone, the warden, ordered the gates to be opened. Quickly.

The Mustang drove through, with Tony behind the wheel. The word "Sukks" could be seen on the bonnet, sprayed to perfection by a graffiti artist from Shanghai. The best, Tony insisted. He liked it. It added class.

Same old show-off, Tante Frida had commented, never one to mince her words. The Prostate Boys agreed with her. But nobody said it to Tony's face. He silently greeted Tante Frida.

Sibylle also emerged from the Mustang. Dark skirt suit, hair in a ponytail. Sunglasses. Tante Frida walked up to her for one last attempt. "You don't have to do this."

"I know."

The prosecutor's voice interrupted their thoughts. "We can go in."

2.

There wasn't even a window. Just a metal chair bolted to the floor.

Rudi was sitting on it.

Ever since he had been handcuffed, the little animals in the forest had been quaking. They quaked when he was carried into the ambulance.

They quaked while they patched up the injuries caused by the dog. Ninety stitches, one for every chapter in the Von Junzt.

They quaked while he dictated his terms. A full confession, details about every murder, even those with which he had not been charged, but which the police would never have discovered by themselves. But only if Sibylle would go and see him. Otherwise, they could try deciphering the Wanderer's work on their own.

They had the bodies he had dumped in the Kreuzwirt lake, the safest place in the world, but those were not the only ones. There were those Rudi had not managed to take to the lake. Sometimes because he had been unlucky. Some had been killed before he realised that the Kreuzwirt lake, with all its secrets, was the perfect hiding place for his prey. If they wanted those bodies, they had to call Sibylle.

He wanted to talk to her. To tell her about Erika. They had quaked. They had obeyed. Better still, Sibylle had obeyed. And why should she not have?

Nobody in this world could oppose the Wanderer.

3.

Tony watched Sibylle enter the interview room. There were no two-way mirrors like in American television series, just a camera that was linked to the screens in the room where Tony sat with the lawyers, judges, carabinieri and police.

He saw Sib sit on a second chair a warden had brought in for her. He wished he could be there with her, Freddy at his side. There was only one reason Tony had stopped the St Bernard from killing Rudi, dislocating his shoulder to restrain the dog's rage. If Freddy had completed his task, he would have been put down.

Tony could not allow the St Bernard to become the Wanderer's final victim. So he had stopped him and led him outside, taking Sibylle with him.

He'd done the same with Rudi, Martin and Michl. Not Karin. Too many flames, too much smoke. They told him it would have been too late in any case. While Tony was dragging Sibylle and the others out of a Krotn Villa ablaze, Karin was already dead, devoured by the fire she herself had started.

Michl, too, was dead. He had committed suicide in his cell. The day he hanged himself using his bedsheets, he and Gabriel had bumped into each other in the prison yard. Witnesses said that at the end of the conversation Gabriel hugged Michl. What they said to each other was still a mystery.

The following day, Gabriel was transferred to a psychiatric hospital but, despite all attempts to wring the details out of him, he hadn't said a word about Michl. He had, however, sent a note to Sibylle through Tante Frida. It said *Thank you.* In lieu of a signature, Gabriel had drawn the hummingbird smile. Sib had thrown the message in the bin.

Tante Frida placed a hand on Tony's shoulder. "She'll be alright."

4.

Sibylle's first words were, "Do you really think you're the Wanderer?"

"One of his vessels. Like Grahame."

"Was Grahame the Wanderer?"

"He used the Von Junzt to summon him. His son was the door through which he could enter. That's why Grahame killed him. To complete the work."

"There's no evidence that Grahame killed his son, let alone that he had a diseased mind like you. And Von Junzt was just a drug-addict and a compulsive scribbler. You were taken in by a book full of bullshit which is now nothing but ashes."

Rudi gave her a smile full of pity. "The Von Junzt is not ashes."

"Oh, really?" Sibylle said mockingly. "Then where is it?"

"The *Unaussprechlichen Kulten* has a life of its own. It has been written in a thousand languages by a thousand different hands. It travels between worlds, changes shape, cares nothing about time. How should I know?"

Sibylle made a sound of disgust. "Did Horst make you read the Von Junzt? Was it he who screwed up your brain?"

"Horst was an idiot. Like everyone else at Toad Villa. Karin, who was jealous of her brother without even realising it. Betta, who was envious of the Perkmans' power, of their money. Did you know that she did everything she could to seduce Friedrich?"

"No. And I'm not interested in gossip, frankly."

"That was why old Perkman decided not to have kids at the villa anymore. Betta tried to kiss him. I saw everything. I heard everything. I know all Kreuzwirt's secrets."

"Rudi the peeping Tom."

"That was before I became the Wanderer."

"What about Betta? Was it an accident?"

"Both."

It took Sib a while to decipher Rudi's cryptic response. "The attack in '88 and the one in 2005?"

"In '88, Betta had found a nest. A small bird's nest. And she was killing the chicks. One by one. Such a little bitch, right? So Martin hit her. Can you blame him?"

"Did Martin kill Betta?'

"It was chance. Fate. Many things had changed in me since . . . since Erika's death. Many things. But I still didn't understand. It was Betta who made me realise what I'd become."

Eighty-Seven

1.

She was drunk. She was stoned. And she still could not get over it. The bank had refused her a loan. Fifty thousand euros. A trifle. But with that money she could have increased her turnover. Hired a couple of new guides, improved the online profile of her work. Attracted new clients. Idiots to fleece.

She drained what was left of the bottle of vodka and hurled it into the distance. That was when she saw Rudi. Or rather, she saw his shape in the bushes. But she knew it was Rudi. Rudi the peeping Tom. He was no longer the skinny little boy who had always clung to her gang of friends. *Friends* – right . . .

Gabriel the idiot, Karin the daddy's girl and Spooky Erika. A nice bunch of losers.

Betta sighed. If the vodka and weed weren't working, there was only one thing to do to get over it. She took off her T-shirt. She wasn't wearing a bra. She removed her trousers, then her pants. In the starlight, her body was like a fairy's.

"Come here."

Rudi approached out of the darkness.

Betta kissed him. She rubbed against him and felt his erection. It occurred to her that this would perhaps be his first time, since she had never seen Rudi the pervert with a woman. She took him by the hand and led him towards the stream. "Do you want me?" she said.

2.

"I struck her with a stone. She fell into the water and drowned. That's how I realised that the Wanderer had gone through Erika to get inside me, to become me. Thanks to Erika."

Eighty-Eight

1.

The Maturaball was his favourite time of year. The air sizzled. Like electricity. Rudi could sense it. A current that penetrated his skin, went through his belly and rose into his brain. He had spent all day fantasising about the moment when the entire town would pour into the Black Hat's car park, leaving their houses, bedrooms and wardrobes unattended.

Rudi couldn't describe the feeling that entering people's houses gave him, he only knew that he could not do without it. Studying the pillows on which his fellow townsfolk rested their heads before falling asleep. Smelling their fragrance. Touching their belongings, their jewellery boxes, their scrapbooks. Bottles, glasses in the sinks still marked by the lips that had drunk from them. Toothbrushes, perfumes. Wearing their clothes. When he put them on, he was altered. No longer himself. He became them. He became Signora Trina, who hid porn magazines under the kitchen sink, in the only cupboard her husband never rummaged through. And he became Hans, Trina's husband, who kept SS badges in his bedside table drawer, with his socks and pants. He became all the young women in Kreuzwirt.

It excited him to the point of ecstasy.

He had started with Karin. The first woman Rudi ever saw naked. He was helping his father carry wood for the fireplace in the villa when he saw her. Karin had left her bedroom door open. She was combing her hair in front of the mirror. Naked. She had done it deliberately. She didn't consider Rudi and Peter, but that was natural, since Rudi and his father were just .... extras at Krotn Villa, and no-one paid attention to them. But Karin knew that Michl might see her.

She had put on the show for his benefit. But it was Rudi, not Michl, who saw her. And dreamed about her. And, two days later, entered that room.

He had narrowly escaped being seen by Michl. Rudi liked Dr Horst's son. Once, when Rudi was five years old, Michl had removed a thorn stuck under his thumbnail without hurting him. Michl would encourage him to read and study. *Just because your father is a boor*, he would say, *doesn't mean you have to follow in his footsteps. You can choose. Do you want to be like your father?*

Michl had given him access to the library. A copy of the keys. Rudi liked books. His father hated them, and if he ever found him with a book, he beat him. But Rudi persevered. He read, learned. Listened. It was nice to eavesdrop while Lehrerin Rosa read Martin's book, *The Wind in the Willows*. There was magic in these words. That was what his father could not understand. Words were magic.

They could lay open worlds.

And that was not all.

Words could persuade people. Words helped you not to be just Peter the boor's son. Words were like his father's hunting rifle: you could point them at something and, if you were a good shot, that something would fall down.

Michl was a master of this art. Rudi could see it. Karin was head over heels in love with him. Rudi did not mind. He wasn't jealous. He wasn't interested in people. Rudi was interested in the sensation. The alteration. In any case, he had almost immediately forgotten about Karin. He liked Erika. And Betta.

He adored Betta. She was his favourite. But he had a devil of a job getting into her bedroom. Up there in that *maso*. He had managed it only once. Becoming Betta had triggered such a powerful sensation in him that he'd had to run out of the *maso*, down the mountain and throw himself into the cold water of the lake to calm himself down.

Erika, on the other hand . . .

Erika talked to animals. Erika foresaw the future. Erika had a magic that Betta and Karin could only dream about. Of all the men and women in Kreuzwirt, Erika *glowed*. She was just as that book said, the book in the forbidden section, the one with the hummingbird smile. Erika was halfway between two worlds.

She was *ethereal*.

That was why, on that March 21, 1999, Rudi was hiding, waiting. He wanted to get into her room, put on her clothes, brush his tousled hair with her comb. Become her. To glow the way she glowed. Rudi would wait for Helga to switch off the light and fall asleep. Then he would seize his chance.

However, Erika had not headed to the Black Hat, and that had intrigued him. Kreuzwirt had more secrets than residents, and Erika was the best-kept secret of all.

Rudi followed her.

The peat bog was his home. He and his father would spend days there, setting traps for the foxes. They would catch them alive, then his father would infect them with rabies and set them free. His father had taught him how to do it. All you had to do was keep bats (special infected bats) in Signora Perkman's mausoleum.

Rudi followed Erika to the lake. He watched her look around, sit down and check the time. Then, just as the young woman was standing up to turn back, as the wind carried the blaring music from the Maturaball to his ears, Rudi heard the sound. Something falling into the water. A fox had slipped into the lake.

Foxes can't swim. He knew that. Erika knew that.

She didn't think twice. She waded into the lake. One shoe was left behind at the edge of the water, caught in the mud. The sky was clear. Erika sang to the fox to calm it down. Her wet dress clung to her body. A flush of pleasure, verging on pain, enveloped Rudi, and he came out into the open, drawing closer.

Erika didn't notice him. She was too intent on catching the fox, which was panting and biting the air. Rudi fell to the ground. He grabbed the mud with both hands, more excited than ever. He was watching Erika, up to her knees in the water. He was watching her glow. Rudi drew the hummingbird smile in the mud. "Erika!" he called out.

Then he began to throw stones.

Eighty-Nine

1.

In the interview room, Rudi's chained figure looked huge. With every word, Sibylle felt the walls closing in on her, suffocating her.

"Stones . . ." she murmured.

"I didn't know what I was doing but the Wanderer did. It was he who guided my hand. To begin with Erika thought it was a joke. She told me to stop. I didn't. Every stone I hurled was a step closer to the middle of the clearing. I could see it through Erika's body and I could hear the Wanderer saying to me, 'Go on, go on.'"

"And you obeyed."

Rudi nodded, jangling the handcuffs that kept his wrists shackled behind his back. "I kept hurling stones until I forced her beyond the ledge, to the point where the lake gets deep. The water's much colder there, and the cold numbs your muscles. At first, Erika was angry, then she started to beg. The fox drowned first. Erika stopped struggling, her head began bobbing up and down, up and down. Swallowed by the blackness. The door was open. The worlds were aligned. And Erika sang. It was the Wanderer singing through her. He was calling me. So I dived in and carried her to the shore. I felt no effort. I felt no cold."

Rudi looked up.

"Erika," he continued, "was already on the shore when Horst found her. He lied about that, too. Erika was dying when I dragged her out of the water, but she was taking too long over it. So I sat on her. I wasn't much older than a child and I hardly weighed anything, but it was enough to choke her. When she stopped breathing, we were a single thing. There was an explosion. Like in Grahame's book, when the rat and the mole hear the piper and they're scared because they've never heard anything so beautiful. That's how Erika made me feel. That's how I became the Wanderer. Then . . ." Rudi gave a deep sigh. "Then I stole Erika's shoe. The one she'd left on the shore. I wanted to keep it. But on the way back I realised how pathetic a gesture it was, so I abandoned it in the peat bog. After that, I never went back into the homes of Kreuzwirt residents. I continued to spy on them, just to extract their secrets and perhaps someday take advantage of them, but everything else seemed stupid to me. Insipid. Erika changed me, even though it took me some time to work out how to hear her song again."

"Erika wasn't singing," Sibylle said, gasping and wiping sweat from her forehead. "She was drowning."

Rudi ran his tongue over his lips. "I found Horst's medical books in the villa library. I studied them for a long time to understand how it's done. First, you have to make them kneel. The Von Junzt says so. That's easy, you just have to cut their Achilles tendon. Then you count the vertebrae and find the right spot. C6. That's where you have to stick the blade. A thin blade. It slices through the carotid artery and the trachea. You have to plug the wound immediately and keep holding it because the blood needs to stay inside. In the lungs. That's when you can hear blood breathing, and they—"

"Drown," Sibylle said. "Like Erika."

"They sing. Do you want to hear their song?"

"No."

"Don't you want to see the worlds?"

Sib got up. "You think you're a god, don't you, Rudi? You're nothing but a parasite. Feeding on all those young women, on the villa's residents, on Kreuzwirt. On its secrets. Its sins. I've come to get rid of Erika's ghost, not to listen to the ravings of a parasite."

"Where are you going?" Rudi shouted.

"You wouldn't understand."

Rudi burst out laughing. Sibylle reached the door to the cell, her fist ready to hammer it to get herself out of there. Rudi's laugh died away. "Don't you want to know about your father? Don't you want me to reveal the mystery of your conception?"

"You know who it is?"

"I know all Kreuzwirt's secrets," Rudi murmured. "But you'll never know if you leave this cell."

"So much the better."

Sib struck the steel. Once was enough. The door opened. Tony was on the other side, waiting for her. She smiled at him, and it was as if he started breathing again.

"I don't need any more ghosts," Sibylle said to the man who had believed himself to be a god, and who would spend the rest of his life tormented by the doubt that he was nothing more than a parasite. "I only came here to say goodbye to my mother."

Ninety

1.

Karin woke up.

Disorientated. Her eyes shifted from side to side. A bedroom. Shadows. A monitor. Tubes everywhere, coming out of her. She could not speak. She could not manage it.

It all came back to her. The fire, Rudi coming out of nowhere with that knife, Martin attacking him to defend her and then, thinking she was dead, carrying Sibylle to safety. Rudi running after him with the Von Junzt against his chest. The floor under her feet giving way. The pain. Then only flashes. Lights, very bright lights.

Her throat was dry. Her lips were sore. Everything hurt. She tried to get up, but found that her ankles and wrists were tied to the edge of the bed. She struggled, but could not break free. She was too weak. A figure came into her field of vision.

Edvard Bukreev adjusted his glasses and smiled at her. "Signorina Perkman."

Karin cursed him.

No sound came out of her mouth.

"Your health is not great, but it will improve. You have burns on ninety per cent of your body. I'm afraid you'll never go back to the way you were. But you're not dead, contrary to what everyone thinks. You will be my guest for as long as it takes to build up your strength. Naturally, we're not in Kreuzwirt, but this is an equally pleasant location.

When it's light, a nurse will show you the view. It will take your breath away."

Karin tried to speak. She wanted to know, to understand. All she managed to do was cause herself pain.

Bukreev gently touched her hand. "Don't strain yourself, your vocal cords are damaged. Irreversibly, I'm afraid. But I think I know what's going through your mind. I've reached an agreement with your brother. A gentleman's agreement. They said he was mad, a useless wretch, but instead I've been dealing with a young man who is wilful and capable. Even more admirable than the legendary Friedrich Perkman, if I may say so. Martin knows exactly what he wants and how to obtain it. He had the presence of mind to save the Von Junzt from the fire, swiping it from the lout who wanted to steal it, and the intelligence to understand that if he wanted to take care of himself and his beloved sister he would have to sell it to me. Don't worry, I'll look after it. It's in good hands."

The man disappeared from her field of vision.

"I'll leave you two alone."

He closed the door.

Martin emerged from the shadows. He was in a wheelchair. He was wearing a blonde, curly wig. Karin tried to scream, but only a gurgle came out of her mouth. Martin stroked her head. Then he checked that the straps were firmly tied.

He kissed her on her forehead.

Acknowledgements

The list of people who have shown patience, faith and love for this book can only start with Alessandra, who knows how to tame ghosts. My gratitude then goes to Maurizio, Michele, Piergiorgio, Luca, Francesco, Herman, Paolo, the entire Einaudi family and Seve, who I know is reading these words out loud. Thanks also to the three generations of Shanghaians who decided to mix their memories with mine. Whether these were reality, invention or trickery is of no importance. We bad boys from Via Resia, Via Parma and Via Piacenza know very well that the best way to tell the truth is to do it Shanghai-style: by cheating.

Acknowledgements

LUCA D'ANDREA was born in 1979 in Bolzano, Italy. *The Mountain,* his first novel, was translated into thirty-five languages and was a bestseller across Europe. His second novel, *Sanctuary,* was the winner of the 2017 Scerbanenco Award. Overall, his books have sold more than 400,000 copies worldwide.

KATHERINE GREGOR is a literary translator from Italian and French who has also worked as an EFL teacher, a theatrical agent, a press agent and a theatre director. Recent translations include works by Marion Brunet, Alberto Angela, Donato Carrisi and Stefania Auci. She writes a monthly column about Italian books for the European Literature Network.